Omar the Perfume Seller
and other fantastical tales

Rob Stuart

Omar the Perfume Seller and other fantastical tales

Published by The Conrad Press Ltd. in the United Kingdom 2023

Tel: +44(0)1227 472 874
www.theconradpress.com
info@theconradpress.com

ISBN 978-1-915494-44-3

Copyright © Rob Stuart, 2023

All rights reserved.

Typesetting and Cover Design by:
Charlotte Mouncey, www.bookstyle.co.uk

The Conrad Press logo was designed by Maria Priestley.

Printed and bound in Great Britain by Clays Ltd, Elcograf S.p.A.

For Malcolm Stuart,
a big brother who watched over me

Contents

Preface	7
Omar the Perfume Seller	9
Say it with Flowers	47
The Kidnap Kaper	87
The Fabulous and Wonderful Frowla	145
Stag	327
Gossip	329
Acknowledgements	331
Also by the same Author	332

Preface

These short stories were written between 1983 and 2022 but all of them have been redrafted (hopefully for the better) during Lockdown when we all had a lot of time on our hands. The stories are fantastical – that is to say set in unreal worlds that make no pretence of bearing any relation at all to the world as it exists.

Omar the Perfume Seller came about in 1983 when my little family were living in Cyprus and I was eking out a living as a teacher of English as a Foreign Language. Books for children were hard to come by and so I began writing stories to entertain my own children. Over the years they have forgotten most of what I wrote but have kept a soft spot for *Omar*. I offer it up here in its slightly more adult incarnation but it still serves as a suitably cautionary tale for bedtime reading!

Say it with flowers is the most recent of the stories and was inspired by the heaps of flowers piled up against buildings and purchased by people who had never met the deceased person the tributes are intended for. Witness the floral mountains at Balmoral and London for her late Majesty Queen Elizabeth II.

The Kidnap Kaper is my tribute to the 'hard-boiled' detectives created by the likes of Raymond Chandler and Dashiell Hammett and was written in the 1990s when I was working at the University of the United Arab Emirates. I thought the Brothers Grimm should have delved a little deeper into the effect on the economy that a hobgoblin who could mass produce gold might have.

The Fabulous and Wonderful Frowla is a tale of obsession and the way one person might cynically exploit another. It was written during my time as an EFL teacher to, firstly, an oil company based in Kuwait, and, secondly, the Kuwaiti military. Those who know Kuwait will know that it is mainly flat and empty. It was my first experience of Arabia and I fell in love with the desert. This is my tribute to that part of the world. Sort of!

A *frowla,* by the way. is the Greek word for *strawberry*. It is something similar in Arabic but I forget exactly what.

I hope you enjoy them and take them in the spirit in which they were written.

Rob Stuart

February 2023

Omar the Perfume Seller

A cautionary tale

1

Omar the Perfume Seller lived in Cairo at the time when the great Saladin and his brothers were rulers of all the lands of the Faithful, which lay along the rivers Nile and Tigris and Euphrates. It was a long time after Haroun Al-Rashid held magnificent court in Baghdad and heroes like Sinbad and Ali Baba walked the Earth and rivalled Caliphs and Emirs with their wealth and adventures. Yet the people of Cairo had long memories and spoke of those long-ago times as if they were but yesterday.

Omar lived over his shop in the Street of the Perfume Sellers which was just one of the myriad streets that made up the labyrinth that was the Grand Bazaar of Cairo. Of all of the wonderful places in the whole world at that time, the Grand Bazaar was surely the *most* wonderful. It was a place of magic and enchantment; within its narrow, twisting streets you could haggle for anything your heart desired from the far reaches of the world. Here, in the palace-like caravansaries, the caravans trudged in at the end of their long overland journeys from India and far Cathey. Feluccas sailed up the Nile bearing treasure of gold and ivory from Africa; dhows and galleys plied the Mediterranean trading with the lands of the Maghreb and Al-Andalucía.

Each trade or craft had its own street or quarter in the Grand Bazaar. There was the Street of the Goldsmith in the Metalworkers Quarter where the men sat outside their tiny shops tap-tapping away with their hammers, beating sheets and ingots of gold into beautiful objects that blazed like fire in the bright sunlight; the wares of the Silversmiths shone like the moon; the Coppersmiths made more modest wares for use in the kitchen or on the table but were no less noisy in their industry.

And there were fruit sellers with cherries and pomegranates piled high and butchers swatting the flies away from the meat that hung on hooks over their counters and bakers with piles of flat loaves hot from the charcoal ovens and carvers of wood and weavers, rich merchants with silks and fine stuffs from the East, carpet dealers with their carpets from Persia and Afghanistan laid out in the dust of the narrow passageways, blazing with designs of beautiful gardens. And there was the Fish Market where none but the brave ventured after the heat of the sun had been beating down for hours.

Through the twisting alleyways and thoroughfares, a river of humanity flowed, shouting, laughing, remonstrating, wailing, haggling, whispering secrets, offering tempting and illicit pleasures. Beggars rubbed filthy shoulders with richly-dressed and haughty Captains of the Guard; donkeys and camels plodded wearily along under their loads while men sweated and called out their wares, pulling handcarts laden with vegetables from the black-earth fields outside the great city. Fakirs and snake-charmers performed tricks and shows for a handful of coins. Doctors and apothecaries sold cures; muezzins chanted the call to prayer from the tall minarets. Here a water-seller shouted his prices, there a cooked-meat man yelled tempting offers at passers-by and wafted mouth-watering sticks of kebab, sizzling with herbs, succulent and juicy under the noses of potential customers. Visitors, newly arrived in the city, came just to gape and marvel at the size of the city, lost amid the hustle and tumult of its streets. And the pickpockets flitted in and out amongst them, their nimble fingers darting everywhere a coin might lurk. All was noise and dust and heat.

Of all the maze of streets and ginnels in the Grand Bazaar, Omar loved his own street best of all – and not just because he lived there himself. Other streets had their own smell – leather, meat, spices – but his street smelt of Paradise. Here the hot air was heavy with the scent of attar of roses, night-blooming jasmine, of frankincense and myrrh, of cardamom and cinnamon and all the sweet essential oils and distillations and blends that went to make the fragrances that perfumed the bodies of the fine ladies who lived behind the barred windows in the fine houses of the city that lined the banks of the river. Here, in this street were made the perfumes that were paid for with heavy bags of yellow gold by the slaves of the Vizier but also the tiny vials purchased for a copper quarter dinar coin by the young, shy, black-eyed girls from the poorer parts of the city who hid their faces and giggled behind their hands. For the one there might be a distillation of musk oil from the far-off Himalayan Mountains of Hindustan and for the other, a little jasmine water made from flowers picked from the bush in Omar's own back garden. Rich and poor alike mingled in the Street of the Perfume Sellers and the Perfume Sellers waxed rich and prosperous.

The trade of perfume making had been in Omar's family for many generations. Now Omar and his younger sister, Yasmine, were all that was left of the proud line. Their parents, brothers and elder sister had died in the Plague two years ago, when

Omar was still only fifteen years old and Yasmine twelve. Like every other long-established perfume making business, Omar's family had its own signature fragrance, unique to the family. Omar's father had initiated Omar into the secret of the formula before he died. The manufacture was a delicate business, relying on a keen sense of smell rather than a written formula. The family was, understandingly, loath to commit its secrets to paper lest the formula fall into the wrong hands. It was only Omar's knowledge of this secret that had saved both Omar and Yasmine during the lean time after their parents and siblings died and many of his father's clients drifted away. Now, at seventeen years old, Omar could hold his head up proud in the company of the best perfume sellers in the whole guild in Cairo, because Omar was a Nose. He could detect and correctly identify the tiny, teeniest component of a fragrance and reproduce it *exactly* in the correct proportions so that even the original parfumier could not tell which was his own and which was Omar's copy. In matters olfactory, Omar was a giant.

But the hard times had left their mark on Omar. He was mean. He made Yasmine scrimp and save and hoard every copper they earned. If he had been able to have his way, they would have lived solely on stale flat-bread and raw onions had not Yasmine pointed out that his breath would be a poor advertisement for their wares.

Their years of hardship had had the opposite effect on Yasmine. She was compassionate and open-handed where her brother was tight-fisted. She would sneak out of the house when Omar was occupied and give gifts of bread and vegetables to the poor and on occasion she even managed to secrete a few small coins to give to the mullahs to distribute to the needy after

Friday Prayers. This deception was not easy as Omar always counted the day's takings each night by the light of a single oil lamp before locking them away in a stout money-chest. Yasmine scrimped the money from the meagre house-keeping allowance that Omar grudged her.

The friends of their childhood no longer came to visit because Omar offered water instead of sherbet, dry bread instead of Turkish Delight, beans instead of roast lamb. Yasmine too was treated like a precious possession. Omar's plan was to marry her off to a rich merchant but as he hardly let her leave the house and he was too stingy to entertain a potential suitor, it was unlikely that any rich merchants were aware of her existence.

But despite everything, Yasmine kept herself happy, preferring to remember the good times rather than dwell on the bad.

Our story starts one afternoon just before Omar was going to shut up shop for his afternoon rest. Given the choice, Omar would have stayed open all hours but in the heat of the afternoon there were no customers and all the other shops on the street were closed. Omar was putting away the morning's takings in his strong-box and muttering to himself that it could have been more, although he had, in fact, done very well.

When he looked up he saw a little old woman dressed in a worn and shabby mantel standing in the doorway. Her face was hidden behind a burqa that had seen better days. She gazed about her at the glass jars full of shining liquids, at the bubbling cauldrons, at the distillation dripping from alembics into tiny bottles. Lastly, she gazed at Omar, who stared back, his face drawn into a frown, for he was hot and tired and had been looking forward to a nice lie-down on a pile of comfy cushions in the cool of his inner chambers.

Had the old woman been a great lord, or even a great lord's factotum, his reaction would have been completely different. Then he would have bowed and scraped and offered a seat after carefully dusting it with his sleeve. After all, grovelling servility cost nothing and there was a good chance of profit at the end of it. This old woman, however, was obviously poor and not worth wasting time and effort on so Omar saw no reason at all to be civil.

'Well, old woman, what do you want? Be quick!'

'Master, she said in a voice that trembled with age, 'I have heard of your wondrous perfume called *The Flowers of Gold*. I wish to have the very smallest bottle you have for sale.'

Now, *The Flowers of Gold* was the signature perfume of Omar's family and it was the possession of this secret that had helped Omar and Yasmine through the hard times after the death of their parents. And because it was a unique scent among all the perfumes of Cairo it was much sought after and very, very expensive.

'Old woman, *The Flowers of Gold* are not for the likes of you. Such rare essences are for the gilded lilies in the Harem of our lord Saladin – long may he reign and prosper,' he added judiciously – who never knew who might be listening. 'Bugger off back to whatever midden you crawled out of.'

The old woman looked dismayed but she held her ground and repeated her request in the same quavering voice.

'What part of "bugger off" do you not understand?' Omar demanded. '*The Flowers of Gold* is not for the riff-raff off the streets. Take yourself off before I take a stick to you, you withered old bat!' Omar could turn quite nasty with people he could bully with impunity.

'Why do you speak so harshly to an old woman, my son? I come to you as an honest customer,' replied the woman in a gentle tone.

'You dare to address me, *me*, as "my son", you harridan! And then persist in your demands for...' His voice trailed off. A sudden thought had occurred to him. What if she *did* have money? Looks could be deceptive. Did not the fabled Haroun al-Rashid sneak around the streets of Baghdad in disguise at all hours of the day and night, poking his nose into things that were none of his business? This old woman might be the latest in a long line of rich eccentric loonies.

A cunning expression stole over Omar's face and his next words dripped honey.

'Ah, Mother, forgive a hasty word. Most certainly you shall have your heart's desire. A small bottle was it? Or something a little larger?'

The old woman crinkled her eyes at him. He assumed it was a smile but her face was hidden by her burqa so he wasn't sure. 'A tiny bottle, please. The smallest you have.'

Omar felt a twinge of doubt about his theory. Still, even a tiny-weeny bottle of *The Flowers of Gold* fetched quite a tidy sum. He fished one out from beneath his counter like a conjurer producing a bewildered rabbit from a hat.

The woman came forward eagerly to take it, her hand outstretched. Omar clutched the bottle protectively to his chest.

'Ah, the price is twenty-eight dinars,' he said, prepared to settle for twenty-one after a respectable bout of haggling.

'Alas, my son...' said the old woman.

'What is it with the "my son" business,' Omar thought.

'...the perfume is for my only daughter. A peach of a girl who is to be married in four days to a man of distinction. She will wear the perfume in his honour on her wedding day.

'Get on with it,' Omar said.

'I will pay you whatever is a fair price *after* the groom has paid the marriage settlement. Today, alas, I have no money. You must give me the perfume on trust.' She crinkled her eyes at him again and held out her empty hands to him.

'*What!*' shrieked Omar, clutching a hand to his chest to still the alarmed beating of his heart and almost dropping the bottle of perfume. This really was *too* much. This miserable creature from the gutter actually expected credit as if she were one of the noblest in the land who settled their bills each quarter without quibbling. It was akin to robbery. She had shamelessly played on his good nature and led him on.

With an angry shout he stashed the bottle under the counter again and reached for one of the wooden rods he used to stir the vats of perfume, thinking to drive the woman out of his shop with a hail of blows.

He had not moved more than half a step towards her when there was a flash of light so bright that he was halted in mid-stride, dazzled and confused, his senses spinning. When he could focus his eyes again the old woman was gone. In her place stood an Ifrit, terrible to look upon. The creature stood eight feet tall, resplendent in emerald-green silk pantaloons, its torso gleaming like polished obsidian, its eyes red fire. It was a demon out of the old tales, sent to punish and plague men for their sins. Omar fell to his knees, covering his head with his arms, shaking in terror, moaning in fear.

In a voice that sounded like a great stone door grinding open in some dark underground cavern, the Ifrit spoke.

'Know that you are amongst the most miserable and accursed of men, Omar the Perfume Seller. You who have no pity. You who love money more than you love your fellow humans. You who would beat an old woman for the crime of being poor. You who have no friends will be punished for your wickedness.'

There was a second blinding flash and Omar was all alone in the shop. For a moment he was stunned, speechless, his head in a whirl. Then he began to wail and curse. He tore his turban off his head and threw it to the ground, stamping and jumping on it and wishing he had a cat to kick.

The door in the back of the shop burst open and Yasmine came running in to see what all the row was about. Getting no sense out of her brother, who was shrieking about old women going around in disguise and tricking honest traders, she swiftly shut up the shop before the neighbour came to see what was going on and caught her brother in some kind of a fit. If word got around that Omar was less than stable, the business would suffer.

Slowly, slowly she extracted the story from him – or, at least, his version of events that cast him in the role of a hapless victim of a vicious and unprovoked assault by a legion of nasty supernatural Beings intent on doing him harm for no reason whatsoever.

Carefully, he felt himself all over. Everything that should be there was in place and in the right proportion. Nothing appeared to be added, like a hunch or an extra limb; Yasmine recognized him, so he didn't have the head of some animal, or worse, an insect like the scarab-headed god of the ancient people of Egypt. In a small and pathetic voice, he asked Yasmine if he still looked like the Omar of an hour ago when she had brought him a cup of water to slake his thirst. She laughed and reassured him that he did, more's the pity. She was not at all sure that she believed his fantastic story, wondering if the heat had finally got to him. She suggested that a nice lie-down might be in order.

Quickly he re-counted the money he had been counting when the old woman came into the shop. It was all there; nothing had changed. The Ifrit had done nothing to him. He decided that he must have imagined the whole thing and started to blame Yasmine for keeping him working long after the other shopkeepers had packed up. He must be faint with hunger: that was it! The Ifrit was an hallucination brought on by over-work. Blaming someone else for what happened immediately made him feel a lot better.

Yasmine, who had heard it all before and took no notice, shrugged and turned to go back into their rooms behind the shop to make something for their lunch. Suddenly Omar gave a great sneeze. And then another. His nose began to drip and his head felt heavy and hot. He was *definitely* feeling poorly.

It must be remembered that in Egypt in that day and age disease was rife. Amongst the illnesses that could, and did, carry people off were: bubonic plague (always a favourite), typhoid, cholera, malaria (seasonal), beriberi, rabies and scabies, yellow fever, scarlet fever, green monkey fever, swamp fever, dysentery and the old favourite – leprosy. A cold in the nose was, however, rare. Thus, Omar had no idea what ailed him but made up his mind there and then that he was not long for this world and there was nothing anyone could do about it. Along with all his other unpleasant character traits, Omar was a hypochondriac of the first order, but in view of all the nasty things you could catch (see above), that was not altogether surprising.

Yasmine, getting alarmed when her brother collapsed to the floor and lay there moaning and wailing, half carried, half dragged him off to his bed. Then she went off to make him a nice hot cup of mint tea to see what good it might do him. It did nothing.

That afternoon, against all Omar's protests (admittedly half-hearted) about the cost, Yasmine went out to find a doctor who promised he would come as soon as possible and advised keeping the patient warm and supplied with mint tea in the meantime.

When the doctor finally arrived, it was early evening and the call for the twilight prayer was ringing out all over the city. Omar was in a foul temper. He had sneezed until he thought his head was coming off; his nose ran and dripped; his sleeve was soaked through where he had used it to wipe his nose.

The doctor poked his stomach, took his pulse, collected a sample from his runny nose and a sample of urine, prodded him with little sticks, tickled the soles of his feet, tut-tut-tutted, spoke of an imbalance of the humours and muttered about leeches and drawing blood. With a flash of inspiration, he asked if Omar had had any dealings with the heathen Franks who were said to suffer constantly from this kind of malaise, especially those led by Richard the Terrible (or Lionheart – it depended which side you were on).

When Omar denied any such contact, the doctor shook his head, pursed his lips, said there was nothing he could do and asked for ten dinars in gold for his professional services. Yasmine quietly paid him while Omar screamed down curses on the man's head for a robber and a bandit. Thoroughly alarmed, the doctor fled from the house, resolving to spread the word about the ungrateful wretch of a perfume seller throughout the medical fraternity of Cairo.

Omar's temper grew even worse.

After two days Omar decided to get up. He was no better but the thought of all his customers going elsewhere and spending the money that should rightfully be his was more than he could bear and he didn't trust Yasmine to be as ruthless in business as he was himself. It was fine for her to run the shop for a couple of days while he waited to see if he was going to die or not, but enough was enough! It was back to work, runny nose or no.

Stocks were beginning to run low so his first task was to make up a new batch of perfumes. Normally he worked by his sense of smell alone, only referring to the rough and ready notes of the formulae for the actual essences that made up the fragrances. Today, however, to his horror, he found that he was unable to distinguish one essence from another by smell. He was forced to make up the mixtures by guesswork and experience. His existing stock sold out after a few days – much to his satisfaction – and then he was left with the new stock he had prepared after the unfortunate unpleasantness with the Ifrit.

As luck would have it, the first customer for the new batch was a High Official from the Palace buying perfumes for the Sultan's ladies. With his customary abject servility, Omar bowed and scraped and fawned and ended up well pleased when he pocketed a bagful of gold dinars. He considered the embarrassment of having to wipe his streaming nose on the sleeve of his djellaba every few minutes was a small price to pay and the High Official was gracious enough not to comment upon it.

2

That afternoon, as Omar lay stretched out on his divan taking his afternoon nap under a light coverlet of finest silk from far away Cathay (Omar was a miser but allowed *himself* the odd luxury – Yasmine slept under a cover of cotton!), there came a fearful beating and banging on the door of his shop. This was immediately followed by the sound of wood splintering and a crashing as the door was forced off its hinges. Suddenly his house was full of very large soldiers with very sharp scimitars and very fierce expressions. The sort of expression that said: *Here it is, mid-afternoon and so far today I haven't killed anyone! Oh dear, I do hope the day won't be wasted.* Omar, in a total panic, tried to leap out of bed but was stopped by the point of a sword pressing into his Adam's Apple.

The High Official, who had earlier bought the perfume, stormed into the room, his face black as thunder, his eyebrows bristling most alarmingly. Omar grovelled down amongst the cushions, the soldier standing over him, the blade of his scimitar gleaming in the gloom of the room, his teeth shining in a very credible imitation of a hungry shark and thinking that perhaps the day wasn't going to be wasted after all.

'Miserable son of a mangy she-camel!' roared the High Official. Omar quaked in terror, quite at a loss to know what he had done to upset this powerful man and bring this rain of wrath down on his head. He tried to hide under the coverlet but that was never going to work.

'M…m…master,' he stammered. The soldier glared and ground his teeth.

'Know, O worm, that you have aroused the displeasure of the Sultan himself,' the High Official hissed.

Oh bugger! Omar thought and racked his brains thinking what he might have done and when he might have done it. The Sultan was famous for the inventive ways he had those who displeased him dispatched.

'I, Master? How can a humble creature like myself offend His Most Sublimest?'

'That *abomination*, that *filth*, that *effluent* you concocted in that sewer-water you sold me this morning. It has made several ladies of the Harem *most* unwell and the Sultan had a nice orgy planned for tonight. And *you've* gone and spoiled it! His Mightiness is *not* happy! Not *at all* happy. In fact, he's mightily pissed off. At you!' he added, in case Omar was unaware of just who the object of the Sultan's displeasure was.

Omar's heart sank as he heard these words and his head spun. The High Official's words made no sense. 'Effluent...filth? But I use only the very best...'

'Smell this, you maggot,' replied the High Official as he uncorked the bottle Omar had sold him just that morning. Omar obliged and took a deep sniff, but could, of course, smell nothing. He wiped his nose on his sleeve (which by now was quite snot encrusted and rather disgusting) and had another long sniff but still nothing came. His olfactory sense was well and truly shot.

The two soldiers who were standing over him both turned a peculiar shade of green and he thought he heard them say something like 'yurk' but wasn't sure as they were gagging so much. The High Official turned his head away and held his nose tightly. Even Yasmine, hiding behind a curtain in the background, felt her lunch threatening to return.

'But, my Lord, that is *The Flowers of Gold*, the finest perfume in all of Egypt,' explained a mystified Omar.

'*Flowers of Shite*, more like,' muttered one of the soldiers through clenched teeth and glaring nastily at Omar, testing the edge of his scimitar with his thumb.

'Forgive me, Lord,' cried the other soldier as he ran from the room with his hand clamped firmly over his mouth. Seconds late the sound of retching was heard from outside the shop.

'You see? O speck of vileness,' said the High Official, hastily ramming the cork back into the neck of the bottle.

Omar did not see. Quite obviously something had gone terribly wrong with this latest batch of perfume, with a preparation he had concocted a hundred times. But what?

Suddenly, the answer dawned on him.

'Lord, forgive me. I am ill. Under a curse. An Ifirt.' Omar spread his hands in supplication and made puppy-dog eyes at the High Official.

To no avail.

'I'll say you are ill. And you are going to get much worse,' the High Official answered with a ominous rasp to his voice. 'How do you fancy being boiled in oil. That would make you *very* ill indeed. *Very!*'

'Ohhhhhh,' wailed Omar and looked around for somewhere to hide whilst the soldiers were still feeling indisposed and might not notice his escape.

As a last resort, he thought, I'll have to give the gold back and this caused him as much misery as the prospect of being boiled in oil.

'Or being buried upside down, alive, in the burning sands

of the desert? Or being thrown to the crocodiles,' the High Official mused, a wistful little smile playing about his lips. 'or something very, very, nasty indeed that the Royal Executioner and the whole of the Privy Council will think up especially for you.'

Omar could not, offhand, think anything nastier than the suggestions already on the table and hoped that the Sultan, the Privy Council and the Royal Executioner would be likewise stumped. Being boiled in oil was *quite* nasty enough for anyone, thank you very much!

The High Official's wistful smile was replaced by a distressingly unpleasant expression and he rubbed his hands together in anticipation of Omar's eventual fate.

'My Lord,' said Yasmine, coming forward from behind the curtain where she had been lurking and listening, 'if I might explain?' She was not wearing her veil and her beauty made the High Official pause in mid-gloat. She carried a cup of foaming sherbet and wore her sweetest smile.

She gave the sherbet to the High Official and while he sipped at it she explained gently all the things that had brought Omar to this sorry pass as far as she had been able to prise the truth out of him. As the sherbet drained from the cup, so the High Official's anger ebbed. In actual fact, he wanted *absolutely* no truck with anyone who had had dealings with the supernatural world. Who knew what could rub off by association?

While Yasmine was beguiling the High Official with Omar's sad tale, Omar saw his chance and tried to hide himself under the large rug that covered the floor. Somewhat unconvincingly.

'I see,' said the High Official at the conclusion of Yasmine's tale. He looked around for Omar and spotted his arse sticking out of the rug. A swift, well-aimed kick brought Omar out and kneeling, trembling, at the feet of the High Official.

'Well,' said the High Official, 'I will not add to the punishment of an Ifrit. That is not a task for a mortal man. The ways of the Supernatural are not for Man to meddle in.' Having covered himself to any of the said supernatural beings who might be invisibly eavesdropping, the High Official passed a mortal judgement: 'You cannot stay here in Cairo. You are accursed. You may take with you only what you can carry on your back and a small purse of money for your immediate needs. The rest of your property is forfeit to the state' (*after I've had a good rummage and taken what I fancy*) the High Official thought to himself. 'You must leave the city within one hour. At that time, I shall return and if I find you are still here things will go very badly for you. *Very badly!*'

So saying, he turned on his heel, clapped his hands for his soldiers, stepped over the ruins of the door his men had kicked in and was gone.

*

Omar spent the next half an hour blaming the world for his misfortune, including poor, innocent Yasmine. He wailed. He tugged at his wispy little beard. He struck his chest (not particularly hard, it must be said) and gave his teeth a good gnashing.

Yasmine, on the other hand, calmly set about packing. Although she had not been specifically included in the sentence of exile, she had determined to share her brother's fate. She had no wish to stay behind in the city without her only living relative, the brother she loved despite all his faults and petty acts of selfishness. She reasoned that he was going to need help as he was about as much practical use as a chocolate teapot.

Omar only stopped bewailing his fate when he saw Yasmine pick up the strongbox that contained his savings. He snatched it from her hands and shooed her out of the room while he crammed as much gold as he could into the small purse the High Official had allowed him. The rest he stuffed down his underpants.

Just within the appointed hour, the two of them left the city though the South Gate. Omar clutched his purse tightly to his chest and tried hard to walk without the coins in his underpants chinking and arousing the interest of the guardians of the gate. Yasmine carried everything else wrapped up in a bundle tied to a pole that she carried over her shoulder.

The wide-open spaces of the countryside presented a strange and forbidding aspect to these two children of the Cairo streets who had never before seen a reason to venture outside the city walls. Why would you, when everything you could possibly want or need was at hand in the twisting streets and souks of the city?

Omar cast one last look back at the city where he had spent his entire life, gave a sigh followed by a great sneeze.

They were exiles without a friend in the world

3

A year had passed since their exile from Cairo, a year of Omar sneezing and being chased from village to village as a bringer of ill-fortune. It was while they squatted in the shadows of a flickering Bedouin campfire, trying to make themselves as unobtrusive as possible, that Omar heard a whisper about the Region of Magic, said to be located far away in the Delta to the North. Before dawn the next day Omar was striding away with Yasmine in tow, heading North as fast as his legs would carry him. In a small farming hamlet near the coast they rented a tiny one-room shack with a miserable strip of sandy soil that the landlord called a garden. Somehow Yasmine managed to coax beans and onions to grow, the main crop of the area, working the land just like all the women of the district; Omar went out every day hunting for Djinns.

This may sound like a strange occupation and serve only to garner a reputation for barking lunacy but it wasn't. All the men were employed in the same quest while their women tended to the needs of the family. This was why this part of the great Nile Delta was called the Region of Magic.

The Men of the Delta, by nature an idle, shiftless gang of ner'-do-wells, leapt out of bed at first light, grabbed their fishing nets and headed for the Nile to start work. So far, so good, so normal. But there was a twist. The men were fishing for ancient bottles, oil lamps, magic rings and suchlike that they were convinced contained powerful Djinn imprisoned by the great king Solomon during the war he waged against the Djinn many centuries ago when the world was still young and Men and Spirits walked the Earth side by side.

Other men, who were not prosperous enough to own fishing nets, spent all day shouting things like 'Open millet seed!' or 'Open Cauliflower!' at likely-looking rocks and boulders in the hope of finding secret caverns stuffed to the roof with bandits' treasure there for the taking. The less stable members of the community scoured rubbish tips for stray bits of old rug to sit on while muttering strange incantations of their own invention, fully expecting the carpets to whisk them away into the sky and the palaces of Chinese princesses, who would immediately beg their flying suitors to marry them and inherit their fathers' kingdoms.

Being a professional, full-time Djinn-seeker was by no means not all sherbet and skittles. There was always the danger that your net would become clogged up with fish and waste precious time while the luckless fisher sorted through the slippery catch for a bottle engraved with magical signs and words of power and chucking the useless fish back into the river before casting the net back into the water in the hope of a *real* catch.

And even when such a bottle *was* found (which no-one could actually remember happening – but that did not mean that it *couldn't*) your troubles were by no means over. Djinn, it was well known, were tricky creatures and were not always in the best of tempers after being confined in a small bottle or lamp for thousands of years and did not always express their gratitude to the finder of their prison upon their release. Often, they had raging headaches or harboured an undeserved grudge against all of humankind that had had time to fester. You couldn't guarantee your three wishes and a life of wealth and luxury in return for undoing the stopper on a bottle or giving some old lamp a bit of a polish. Oh dear, no. Magic circles had to be meticulously drawn before you got down to any willy-nilly net casting; incantations incanted; words of power remembered and intoned forwards, backwards and in a variety of ancient languages that had long gone extinct.

All in all, it was hard graft and the hours were long. It took real dedication and devotion and was not for the faint-hearted.

Or women.

The fact that no supernatural inmate of a drinking vessel had been found in living memory served in any way to dampen the enthusiasm of the Djinn-hunter.

While it was true that a fisherman's wife *had* found a pot of gold coins, she was digging up her garden to plant lettuces and just *found* it and, all the professionals agreed, that didn't count. Her husband, a die-hard traditionalist, refused to have anything to do with such a mundane find and so his wife very quickly became his ex-wife and moved post-haste to Alexandria where she invested in the slave-trade and eked out her days in considerable comfort.

Some of the Djinn-seekers, it must be admitted, were getting a bit down-hearted at their spectacular lack of success and there was much talk of re-locating to Baghdad and the area of the two great rivers when half a dozen or so men with unintelligible accents turned up in the Region of Magic. When they managed to make themselves understood, it turned out they were *dis*-enchanted Djinn-hunters from the Realm of Enchantment (Baghdad, to the uninitiated) seeking to try their luck in Egypt. This proved rather a set-back to plans to emigrate until it was remembered that a young man reputed to be called al-Adeen was said to have done well for himself in far-away China, a mere two-year's journey away.

The most optimistic started their packing.

Omar had been wrestling with the decision whether or not to join the exodus to the East. He enjoyed an almost superstar amount of celebrity and respect in the Region of Magic. The Curse of the Ifit was still upon him; his nose dripped with monotonous regularity and his sneezes could be heard in the next village.

But he was *Living Proof* that Djinn and Ifits and magic carpets and winged horses and fabulous beasts and magic caves stuffed with the loot of bands of forgetful robbers and enchanted princesses *did* exist. He stood as a symbol of hope in the face of patent futility. He was held up as exhibit A when wives nagged their husbands into seeking out real jobs that actually paid real money that might be used to buy food, pay the rent and clothe the children.

Never mind that his dealings with the other world had not been what might be described as a triumph, that the encounter, far from making him rich beyond the dreams of avarice, had cost him his home and his livelihood and thrust him and his sister into poverty. He was a tangible link between the mortal world and the world of the supernatural and Omar was very loath to turn his back on the sort of awe and respect in the community that he had never enjoyed in Cairo. Men many years his senior would humbly seek out his opinion on knotty questions on the most esoteric points of magical lore and seemed to be quite happy to accept whatever old tosh he sprouted back at them. For, truth to tell, Omar had not the slightest idea what any of them were talking about.

As for Yasmine, she took in washing to try and make ends

meet, like most of the village women, so competition was fierce and the market glutted with profits meagre at best. Omar and Yasmine often went hungry and only desperation forced Omar to keep the odd fish caught in his Djinn-net.

They had reached a very low ebb; respect and celebrity didn't fill an empty stomach. They were poorer than they had ever imagined was possible. At least in the hard times after their parents had died Omar had a trade and a pleasant, comfortable home-cum-shop in which to practice it. Now their prospects were zilch.

His year of poverty, coupled with the ongoing Curse of the Ifrit, had changed Omar: he was now twice as mean and grasping as he had ever been in his Cairo days. Yasmine, though, was still as sweet-tempered and generous as she had ever been – although she had precious little to be generous with nowadays.

4

One morning, after Omar had given both the oil lamps a good rub to see if their luck had changed overnight (it hadn't), and then set off despondently with his net over his shoulder and another day's casting for trapped Djinn, Yasmine was sitting outside their hovel and mending the sleeves of Omar's second-to-last shirt. Something made her look up from her sewing to see a man driving a camel along the track that ran past their front (and only) door. The camel was truly a sorry sight, old, knock-kneed and moth-eaten. Its fur was scraggy and liberally spotted with bald patches that shrieked 'mange!'. Long ropes of foam hung from its slack-lipped mouth and it was uttering a noise that reminded Yasmine of water running out of a bath (and, oh, how she missed the simple joy of a warm, scented bath). Interspersed with these loud gurgles were loud groans of discontent. As far as it is possible to tell, the camel appeared to be cross-eyed and swayed from side to side in a manner most erratic.

The man driving it cut a figure hardly more prepossessing. His turban could best be described as a strip of rag, his djellaba was torn and utterly filthy. On his feet, instead of proper sandals, he wore flimsy affairs made out of palm fronds stitched together with thread. From the look of his long, black fingernails and the bits of his bony body that peeked through the holes in his djellaba, he had not been in contact with soap and water for many a year and Yasmine realised that it was the combined stench emanating from the two travellers that had first attracted her attention.

'Greetings, sister,' he called in a high, cracked voice.

'And peace be with you,' she replied. Telling him to wait, she went into the house and came back with a rough clay pitcher of sweet water and an old cracked clay cup, the best they had in the way of crockery. She gave the cup to the ragged man who drained it in a single swallow, smacking his lips.

'Blessing upon you, sister,' he said and made a bow in her direction.

'Where are you bound, sir?' she asked him.

'To the knacker's yard. With this great lump of useless meat.' He pointed at the camel with his thumb. Did she imagine it or did she see a look of alarm flicker across the camel's face?

'Oh,' said Yasmine in alarm. Although she had happily eaten meat in the days of their prosperity, the thought of actually killing helpless animals always upset her. It was a facet of her kind nature to want the best for all beings.

She looked at the decrepit old camel with a look of sadness and compassion: she was that kind of girl. The camel shuffled its feet and assumed a worried expression, for all the world as if it understood that its ultimate fate was the subject of discussion.

The beast's unsavoury owner noted Yasmine's look. A crafty expression crept over his face. His lips slid back to reveal two black and broken teeth in what he imagined was a smile.

'Would the little sister be interested in purchasing this fine animal for herself? He's a much better beast than he looks. Appearances can be deceptive. He's strong. A hard worker. It is only my own poverty that forces me to sell him. He's like a brother to me.' Somehow, the dirty old man managed to force a tear to fall from his eye.

Yes, Yasmine thought to herself, I can see the family

resemblance. Out loud she just said: 'Oh, I...'

'No, no,' said the man, 'I cannot sell him.' He paused, as if giving the matter serious thought. 'And yet...'

'How much?' Yasmine asked before she could stop herself. She had been a city girl and a member of a retail family: trade was in her blood.

'His father was a racer. A champion.' He pretended to regard the camel carefully. 'You may not think so with just a cursory glance but I promise you his appearance is deceptive.' The man shuffled closer to Yasmine, crowding her. His last meal had heavily featured garlic and onions and his breath could stun flies on the wing. This was one time when Omar's Curse might be a blessing she thought as she tried, discreetly, to edge away.

As if aware of what was being said about its fate, the camel seemed to make an effort to stand up straight and look noble. The attempt failed. The man threw it a withering look and made slashing gestures across his throat with his hand.

'Maybe it *is* for the best if he goes to the butcher's,' he said.

The camel shuffled about on the end of its tether nervously.

'Your price, sir?' Yasmine asked, caught up in the thrill of negotiation.

'Five dinars.'

'Impossible. The butcher would only take the animal from you as a favour. He would probably charge you a slaughter fee!' Yasmine could not be sure but she thought she heard the camel gulp. 'I will give you half a dinar out of charity.'

'I would rather drown myself in the Nile,' replied the smelly old man, settling happily into the routine. 'Four!'

'Four dinars!' Yasmine snorted and gathered up the pitcher and cup as if to go back indoors. She paused. 'One dinar.'

'You seek to rob me, sister!'

'On the contrary. I give alms for the love of charity.'

'Three.'

'One and a half,' Yasmine answered firmly, putting down the pitcher and cup and folding her arms.

'Two and a half. And that is my final offer.'

'Two.'

'Done!'

'Agreed!' cried Yasmine, caught up in her own enthusiasm. She had not had a good bargaining session for a long time. It was just like the good old days back in the city. She felt a glow of satisfaction as she went back into the hovel to rummage around for the money box. Omar hid it in a different place every night before going to bed as a precaution against being robbed or Yasmine frittering away the contents on luxuries like food.

The house was a tiny shack and not overflowing with potential hiding places so she soon found the box. She picked the lock, lifted the lid and found to her horror that the box only contained three solitary dinars, their whole wealth in the world. But she had struck a bargain with the raggedy man and she could not possibly go back on her word.

With a heavy heart she took two dinars and gave them to the unsavoury old man. He pressed each coin between a tooth and his gum, juggled them once in the air, slipped them into a wallet that he wore around his neck on a frayed bit of string and skipped away with a sprightliness Yasmine had not suspected he possessed.

His cackle hung in the air long after he was gone

The full folly of her action struck her like a blow from a fist.

She had squandered almost the last of their meagre savings on the scabbiest camel she had ever seen. She had been right when she said even a butcher would not take it out of charity. The beast was too old and stringy to eat, even if you stewed it for a full day. Its mangy hide was not worth having and as to it carrying a load, the proverbial straw alone would prove too much of a burden.

What would Omar say? He would go ape.

What was she to do?

For the moment she gave the wretched animal a drink and its sour expression mellowed into something approaching pleasantness – but it must be remembered that a happy countenance is something quite alien to a camel – and it lay down in a patch of shade beside the house by Yasmine's little veg patch. While her back was turned, it made short work of her bean plants and when she turned back it was to see the last of her onions churning in the creature's jaws. The odd leaf or two was plastered to its cheeks by gobs of saliva. It looked very pleased with itself.

'What have I done?' she shrieked, tearing at her hair and beating her breast. The thought occurred to her that the old man was another Ifrit in disguise sent to turn another notch on their punishment.

There was only one thing for it. Taking the camel by its halter and screwing up her courage she set off to find her brother and confess to her stupidity.

5

She found Omar turning over rocks looking for crocks of gold or the odd hidden ruby dropped by a passing band of bandits. He had not had any luck and was in a more than usual foul temper. When he saw her leading the camel he rubbed his eyes in disbelief but when she had recounted the whole sorry tale he was incandescent with rage. He stamped his feet and spun around in circles. He gnashed his teeth. He spluttered. At last he gave a great sneeze which seemed to do little to clear his blocked-up nose.

'By dunny!' he said. 'You've spent by dunny on a knocked up, raddled, old camel.'

'It seemed a bargain at the time, brother,' she said as sweetly as she knew how.

Her words did nothing to mollify Omar's tantrum. He tore at his hair (not too hard) and had a bit of a go at rending his robe. As the sleeves were permanently wet with snot he didn't have much success. He gave vent to a loud burst of sneezes and his eyes rolled and watered alarmingly. He even threw a handful or two of sand over his head. His face turned the gamut of shades from pale pink to deepest purple. For good measure he moaned loudly that his sister had ruined his life.

His virtuoso performance soon drew a crowd of admiring bystanders who only scant minutes before had been kicking palm trees to see if they contained secret doors to underground chambers packed with treasure.

He finally managed to control himself long enough to gasp out the story of his sister's madness and the men all made sympathetic noises and clicked their tongues in disapproval. Women were notorious for their folly and here was yet another example to prove the point. All were in agreement that Omar had no choice in the matter and that Yasmine and her camel (the instrument of her act of madness) must be banished from his household lest she cause more damage. Not even allowed to pack her few bits and pieces Yasmine was to be sent off into the desert to fend for herself as best she could.

Omar tried to point out that having paid good money for the camel, he should at least be allowed to keep it to try and recoup his loss but was overruled by his peers who pointed out that the vendor was obviously a Supernatural Entity and that he, Omar, of all people, must recognise the sign. It was, opined the crowd, a symbol of malign bad luck and he was far better off well shot of it and, they added in case he was wavering, his crazy sister with it.

And so it was. With tears streaming down her face Yasmine set off into the unknown, leading her millstone by its halter into the unknown.

When Omar returned home that night there was no meal waiting for him. The hovel was dark and cheerless. There was no smiling face waiting to ask him how the day's labours had gone. There were no words of comfort and commiseration at his lack of success.

The utter meanness of his actions came flooding home to him as he realised that for the first time in his life he was utterly alone.

He loved it.

Yasmine's cheery character had only served to depress him. She was so *happy* in the face of adversity instead of giving way to a good old bout of misery and short temper like any normal person (ie, him).

And she was always spending money.

He was well rid of her!

Savagely, he threw the fish that he had stuffed into his shirt much earlier that day in the direction of a nest of ants.

The ants gave it a wide berth.

6

For three days Yasmine and the camel, whom she had named Mustapha (because every few minutes it must have a drink, a rest, something to eat), wandered south towards the capital. It was slow going. She once attempted to get Mustapha to kneel down so she could mount on his back but once she was perched astride its hump it made such a piteous groaning noise that Yasmine jumped off in alarm, fearing the animal was going to die there and then and she never again attempted to ride him.

They begged food where they could and ate wild dates where they couldn't. The dates were not yet ripe but the camel didn't seem to mind and Yasmine had no choice (but the unripe fruit did give her the runs, further slowing their passage). It was that or starve. To drink they had the waters of the Nile and that was free and plentiful.

Yasmine bitterly resented her impulsive purchase and she spent much of her time in tears, her sunny disposition a thing of the past.

After several more days of wandering they came to a tiny oasis, half a dozen date palm trees and a puddle of muddy water. It would do for the night. Yasmine picked them both a scanty meal of dates and as the sun dipped below the horizon in a great orange ball they lay down to sleep. The night was chilly and so, ignoring as best she could, Mustapha's pungent odour, Yasmine huddled up close to the camel for warmth.

It was then that she noticed a tiny glint of light shining from the camel's right fore-hoof like a star far off in the night sky. She looked closer. Stuck into the hoof was a silver pin, partly obscured by fur. The moonlight was reflecting off it and making it shine. She bent closer to examine it. The head of the pin appeared to be covered in intricate engravings. How long, she wondered, had the poor creature had that stuck in its foot. No wonder it looked miserable all the time.

She started to work the pin out. It was stuck fast. She tugged at it harder and harder. With a final wrench the pin shot out and she tumbled over backwards.

There was the customary terrifying flash of light that, for an instant, turned night into day. Where the sorry-looking camel had been laying stood a sorry-looking Djinn. He was well over ten feet tall and wearing grubby red silk pantaloons with an embroidered green brocade waistcoat. On his head was a badly tied turban with a droopy feather stuck in it at an angle.

Yasmine fainted.

She came round to see the Djinn splashing muddy water over her face and muttering about the frailty of mortals in general and this one in particular. She noticed he had made a bit of an effort to tidy himself up and then the shock hit her again and she gave a sort of a moan and almost fainted for a second time. The Djinn made to throw more water over her so she made a great effort to pull herself together. The Djinn lifted her gently and propped her up against a palm tree and then with great difficulty sat itself down opposite her on the ground, its legs crossed tailor fashion.

'I suppose you want to hear my story,' said the Djinn in a mournful, booming voice.

'Well, if you like,' replied Yasmine with a shiver, water dripping down her face. She felt she ought to show some enthusiasm but was not at all sure what the correct protocol was in these situations.

'It's part of being released,' the Djinn assured her, as if reading her thoughts (which, in fact, it was). 'You are supposed to explain your backstory. How you became enchanted.'

'Oh, is that so? Go on then,' she sighed.

'It's the usual story,' began the Djinn. 'I was conjured up by Solomon and then managed to do something to upset him. To be honest, it was so long ago I've forgotten what it was. Doesn't matter. We Djinns were forever getting on the wrong side of the old bastard. We must have been more trouble than we were worth. There was probably some kind of demonic war.'

Yasmine yawned. She couldn't help it. It had been a long day and the Djinn was threatening to make it a long night. *Getonwithit*, she thought.

'Anyway, long story short,' he *could* read her mind! 'he imprisoned me in the shape of a camel. That pin you pulled out and no-one else noticed for the best part of two thousand years, was the seal. You see, Solomon got cunning. Or maybe he just got bored. He realised that bottles and lamps and what-have-you would get found and the Djinn released. That's why you hardly ever find one nowadays. Your brother and the other losers are wasting their time, I can tell you. But who would suspect that an old camel with a tiny pin in its foot could be a powerful Djinn. Well, pretty powerful. Maybe not in the first rank of Djinns, but still...'

'Imagine,' said Yasmine, her eyes beginning to glaze over.

'Two thousand years I've been a mangy camel. Two thousand rotten years. Can you begin to comprehend what that must be like? Of course, you can't. Which mortal could? Three score and ten and you're shuffling off the mortal coil. Blink of an eye!

But that sadistic swine Solomon could. I've lived in fear and trepidation of the knacker's yard as long as I can remember. But my owner has always managed to offload me before it got that far. Come to think of it, that might have been a part of Solomon's plan. Evil old git! I've had some close calls, I can tell you.'

'I believe you,' Yasmine said, getting bored and hoping there was not much more to tell.

'Anyway, said the Djinn, reading her thoughts again, 'let's get down to business. What do you want? Three quickies. Revenge on your brother? That's always a popular one and good for a laugh. Loads of dosh? Marry a handsome prince? Your own palace with swimming pool and hot tub and a fully equipped and staffed spa?'

'A what?'

'Aha, said the Djinn, 'you're a smart one. No rash decisions. I like that and I like you. You were good to me, as camel owner go and you don't strike me as the vindictive type. Trust me and I'll set you up proper. We are not supposed to but I'm going to make an exception in your case. So, what's it to be with the brother? Boils? Impotence? Flatulence?'

'No! No. It's not his fault that he bitter and twisted. He's happy that way. It gives him an interest in life.'

'He's the one that got you kicked out of Cairo. He's the one that threw you out when you saved me from the glue factory. It's payback time!'

'He's my brother. I don't want anything bad to happen to him.'

'You're sure?' The Djinn was incredulous.

'Can you cure his cold?'

'No way. No way,' said the Djinn hastily, spreading out its hands. 'He's been cursed by another member of the Guild. There are strict rules about interfering with the workings of a fellow Guild member. No can do.'

'Then let him find *something*.'

'You don't give up, do you? Tell you what I'll do. Next time he casts his net in the river I'll fix it that he finds a small crock of gold. Just enough for him to live on if he is sensible. Which I somehow doubt.'

'Oh, thank you, thank you,' Yasmine gushed, tears of gratitude in her eyes.

'You *are* a kind body,' said the Djinn, smiling at her. 'Tell you what I'll do, I'll get you out of here.'

'Out of this oasis? Where will we go?'

'No, out of this time. How would you like to be famous?'

7

And that, Ladies and Gentlemen, Boys and Girls is the true story about the mysterious past of Princess Yaz, the billionaire fashion, cosmetics and lifestyle influencer with millions of followers on TikTok, Twitter and Whatsapp.

'No way. No way,' said the Djinn hastily, spreading out its hands. 'He's been cursed by another member of the Guild. There are strict rules about interfering with the workings of a fellow Guild member. No can do.'

'Then let him find *something*.'

'You don't give up, do you? Tell you what I'll do. Next time he casts his net in the river I'll fix it that he finds a small crock of gold. Just enough for him to live on if he is sensible. Which I somehow doubt.'

'Oh, thank you, thank you,' Yasmine gushed, tears of gratitude in her eyes.

'You *are* a kind body,' said the Djinn, smiling at her. 'Tell you what I'll do, I'll get you out of here.'

'Out of this oasis? Where will we go?'

'No, out of this time. How would you like to be famous?'

7

And that, Ladies and Gentlemen, Boys and Girls is the true story about the mysterious past of Princess Yaz, the billionaire fashion, cosmetics and lifestyle influencer with millions of followers on TikTok, Twitter and Whatsapp.

Say it with Flowers

A kind of detective story

1

The city of Southwark stretched along the south bank of the Thames opposite its more sedate cousins of London and Westminster. Where London was geared up to make money and Westminster projected a serious face of responsibility for the government of the realm, Southwark was Sin City. It was where the sober citizens from the North Bank went to dabble with sin. Theatres, cinemas, night clubs, concert halls, cock pits, pachinko machine arcades, bingo halls, bookie shops all rubbed shoulders with strip clubs, clip joints, massage parlours, S and M dungeons and brothels catering to every taste and need. Southwark never slept. Night-time was illuminated by a blaze of neon light and a cacophony of music made sleep impossible. But no-one went to Southwark to sleep.

Winchester Mews, named after the Bishops of Winchester who established the first knocking-shops in the area, was a small street of semi-detached houses tucked just off the river. Number 11 displayed a red light twenty-four hours a day in the bay window and catered to a discerning stream of gentlemen callers; number 15/17 was a sports bar with a 72-inch television on which punters could follow the fortunes of football, rugby, baseball, basketball, cricket and American Football teams as the sun moved across the globe and they drank themselves insensible. It was said that the bar-staff were not averse to taking the odd bet, unhindered by any gambling legislation that might apply north of the river.

Number 13 carried a flashing neon sign with the message:

BAZ SEABUB INVESTIGATIONS

in a reassuring bright yellow that matched the yellow curtains, permanently drawn over the ground floor windows.

The woman walked cautiously in the middle of the street, avoiding the flocks of painted trollops staggering along the pavement in micro-skirts shorter than their heels and T-shirts with the slogan: Traceys' Hen Night Fancy a Shag? blazoned across the front and I'm Tracey on the back. The woman was wearing jeans and a loose cotton top that had something of the Far East about it. On her feet she wore open-toed, wedge-heeled sandals. Her dark hair was pulled back from her forehead into a ponytail held in place by a red scrunchie. Judging from the expression of alarm on her face, she was feeling anything but comfortable in her surroundings.

Spotting Seabub's sign she darted to the doorway and raised her hand to knock. Before her knuckles could connect the door was flung open by a young woman wearing a pair of shorts cut down (probably with garden shears) from a pair of jeans. Her blue polka-dot shirt was tied in a bow under her breasts. Her long blond hair hung in two bunches either side of her head and her face was sprinkled with freckles that gave her a winsome look. Her bare feet were thrust into flip-flops, what she would call thongs. She was the fresh-faced, unsophisticated, Antipodean type of girl that lacked the charisma for bar-work.

'G'day,' she greeted the visitor in a strong south Queensland accent. 'Baz is expecting you. Come in.' She stood back from the door to let the visitor enter.

'How did he know I was coming?' she asked.

'You'd be surprised what Baz knows. I can tell you.' It was

a long-established business practice at Seabub Investigations for his receptionist/secretary/filing-clerk/tea lady and occasional lover to lurk behind the curtains spying for punters and pretending to them that they were expected. Truth to tell, business wasn't that great.

They stood in a narrow hallway papered in a fading floral pattern wallpaper. A light cable hung from the ceiling with a bulb nestling inside a globe of paper that had once been white but was now yellow and dusty, casting a dim light into the hall.

'I'm Ninette but everyone calls me Sheila,' the girl bubbled at the visitor. 'Baz is through here.' She knocked on a door leading off the hallway and opened it without waiting for an answer. 'In you go.'

The woman entered the room. With the curtains drawn, the room gave the impression of sunlight seen through smog. A desk filled the apse of a bay window. A man sat at the desk, facing into the room, seeming to be oblivious to the world passing by on the street.

It was hard to judge his height from his seated position but she got the impression that he was tall rather than short. His glossy, obsidian-black hair was swept back from his forehead in a widow's peak and tied back in a pony-tail much like her own. His eyes were partially hidden behind yellow-tinted John Lennon glasses that perched on a strong Roman nose. His lips were thin and tight over a firm chin. A prickle of day-old dark stubble covered his cheeks. His hands, resting on the desk, were long and narrow, a musician's hands and his skin had the perma-tanned tone associated with someone who spent a lot of time on the beach. He wore a pair of knee-length Bermuda shorts of a pattern that even the most hardened cruise passenger would not be seen dead in and a short-sleeved Hawaiian shirt that was open at the front showing an impressive six-pack. His bare feet rested on the desk.

'Why don't you sit down and tell me what can I do you for, Miz…?'

'My name is Jane Stamford' she said as she sat down obediently in the chair in front of the desk like a good dog. 'It's my sister.'

'What is?'

'The reason I'm here to see you.'

'Missing, is she?'

'No.'

'Looking for a divorce?'

'No. It's nothing like that. She's dead.'

'Ah,' said Seabub, losing some of his bounce. He swung his feet off the desk and assumed his 'serious and concerned' face. 'There's probably not a lot I can do about that. I'm good,' delivered with a modest smile, 'but I can't bring the dead back to life. I'm working on it.' He saw Jane Stamford was not smiling and abruptly cut out the banter like turning off a tap. 'I'm sorry. Why don't you tell me how I can help?'

'She was killed when the car she was travelling in ran off the road and hit a tree.'

'OK,' said Seabub cautiously.

'I don't think it was an accident.'

'I take it there was an investigation, Miz Stamford. What did the police say?'

'They said it was an accident.'

'But you don't accept that?' It was not the first time a distressed would-be client had turned up in Seabub's office refusing to believe a loved one had died of natural causes. Usually they had. Seabub had *almost* felt guilty taking a client's money to investigate the deaths but, hey, rents in Southwark didn't come cheap.

'No. She died in a car crash driving the lanes around her home. She *knew* the area. She'd lived there all her life. No way she could have misjudged her driving.'

'Any other vehicle involved?'

'No one has come forward to date. Apparently, she hit a tree and was killed instantly. At least, that is what the police told me.'

'But you don't believe it?' Seabub allowed a palpable tone of scepticism to creep into his voice.

'No. I think someone killed her.'

'Why? Did she have enemies? Had she fallen foul of someone? What reason might there be for a murder?'

'Oh, she had enemies alright.' Jane said bitterly. Seabub narrowed his eyes.

'We all have enemies but mostly they don't go around killing us. What was special about your sister?'

'She was called Sally. Sally Stamford. Ess in the family. But you might of heard of her as Sally Effingham? Or Maggie Barfield?'

Baz Seabub was a Sidneysider born and bred in the Cross but in certain situations he liked to affect the fruity language of a bush stockman of the 1950s. He thought it gave his image a naïve, rustic charm. This, he thought, was one of those situations.

'Bugger me with a dead dingo's todger!' he said.

2

Sally Effingham. Queen of the Soaps. She played the character of Maggie Barfield, the lovable matriarch of a family of villains in *Treloyhan Close* which aired three nights a week to audiences of over eight million viewers. Her death in a car crash near her Wiltshire home had led to a national outpouring of grief akin to that following the death of Diana, Princess of Wales or Her Majesty Queen Elizabeth and thousands lined the streets to pay their respects as the hearse carried her coffin through the streets of Salisbury to the crematorium. A vast carpet of flowers, mostly still in their plastic wrapping, flooded the fields and roads around her modest house in the country bearing heartfelt messages of grief from people who had never met her but felt they knew her. At the age of 42 Sally Effingham had joined the ranks of celebrities who had died before their time and at the height of their fame. An icon never to become tarnished.

And here was Sally Effingham's sister siting in Baz Seabub's office claiming that she was murdered.

Would he take the case? Just try and stop him! He doubted that anything would come of it – hadn't the police looked into it and concluded it was a simple RTA – but the publicity for Baz Seabub Investigations he could drum up was incalculable.

Like many thousands of his countrymen, Baz had immigrated to the UK after the Big Burn had destroyed vast tracts of Sydney's suburbia and threatened the city itself. Global warming was rapidly turning the southern Australian littoral into a desert like most of the interior of the continent. Baz had been a Probationary Constable in his first year in the NSW Police when he decided to chuck it in and move to London. He'd tried to join the Met but the Met was downsizing and there was a freeze on recruiting so he'd set himself up as an investigator. So far, he had scrapped a living doing divorce work, security surveillance for companies who suspected their employees of ripping them off and the odd bit of very discrete bodyguarding for wealthy visitors to London who preferred to keep their activities private. A case involving a high-profile celeb was as good as money in the bank.

'Did your sister, Sally, have any enemies? I suppose a successful woman like her must have done. But enemies who might want to *kill* her?'

'I was down staying with her the weekend before she died. We sat up talking on the Saturday. Got through a couple of bottles of white Rioja.' She paused, playing the memory back in her mind, a slight smile on her lips, savouring the moment. 'We talked about everything. Her life. My life. Where we were going. What plans we had. A real sister-to-sister catch-up. We'd not seen each other for a while. She'd been busy working and I'd been living abroad with my boyfriend and had only just returned to the UK. As the evening got later, her mood got darker and she started to cry. I asked her what was wrong and she said that people in her life "hated and feared her". Her exact words. I thought she was being a touch melodramatic. She always liked the melodramatic. That's what pushed her in the direction of acting, I suppose.' She paused again. 'I'm sorry, have you got anything to drink?'

Baz wondered if she meant alcohol, she had been talking about glugging down wine, after all. If she was an alcoholic, that put a different complexion on things.

'Tea? Or coffee? Coke?' she clarified. He wondered if she could read his thoughts.

'I'll see what we can do. Sheila!' he shouted. A moment later Sheila appeared in the doorway, bright-eyed and bushy-tailed, eager to please, irrepressibly bouncy.

'You called, boss?'

'Can you rustle us up a billy of tea? We're as parched as a stockman's throat.'

'I'll see what I can do. Milk? Sugar?' she asked Jane.

'Milk. No sugar, thank you.'

'Coming up!'

'You were saying,' Baz prompted.

'We were on our second bottle...' Jane started to say.

'Yeah, alcoholic,' Baz confirmed to himself.

'...when she started to cry. Little, snuffly sobs really. I put my arm around her. Asked her what was wrong. She said that nothing was wrong. But there obviously was, so I pressed her. She was my sister and I hated to see her so upset.'

'You said something about hating and fearing?'

'She'd broken up with Joe Bembridge who she'd been with for years.'

'That's Joe Bembridge as of Joe Bembridge, lead guitar of *Septic Tank*?' asked Baz, as if there might be a different Joe Bembridge dating Sally Effingham.

'Sally told me his drug habit was getting out of hand. He'd always taken something or other. Said it helped the creative process, but Sally said he was zoned out all of the time. It was like living with a zombie, she said. *She* loved to party but Joe was curtailing her social life and she certainly couldn't invite her friends home, with Joe in a vegetative state most of the time.'

'Bummer!' Baz agreed.

'She'd given him the elbow,' Jane said. 'He didn't take it very well. Bad for the Rock God image to be dumped. Made all sort of threats – when he was lucid, that is. But what was not generally known was that she had recently taken up with Peter Ward. You know, the Junior Minister for the Environment.'

'Yeah, I've heard of him. Something of a media whore. Always on-line or on the box. Getting to be some kind of a saint, like David Attenborough. See me kiss a koala!'

'That's him. But, apparently, he's not as squeaky clean as he likes to pretend. Sally told me he let slip once when they were smoking a post-sex joint in bed that he had some dodgy dealings with a mining company that was going to make him a shed-load of money. He didn't say what and she didn't push it but a few days later he asked her if she remembered what they'd talked about. Pretended he was too stoned to remember and had *she* told him anything important that *he* had to remember. She said no and he changed the subject but it left her thinking. If it came out all his eco-warrior credentials were just a front for a business-as-usual money-grubbing politico, bang would go the public image and he could wave goodbye to his political career.'

'Now that is a motive, too true.' Baz felt his body tingle with goose-bumps. Headlines were flashing through his mind: *Aussie private eye unmasks star's killer; Police baffled – case solved by Aussie super-sleuth; A grateful nation thanks brave Aussie hero!* No, perhaps that last one was a bit much. But a boy can dream, can't he?

Sheila chose this moment to come back bearing two tin

mugs of tea that looked strong enough to tar a road with. She placed them on the desk, warned that the mugs were hot and hung around the doorway hoping to hear what was going on. A bit of showbiz goss was worth its weight in gold (if, indeed, the spoken words had any weight – which it hadn't). Sheila was not a girl to worry about metaphors. Baz made sideways nodding motions at her, indicating that she should leave; she ignored him. He widened his eyes at her; she ignored him. Finally, he was forced to say: 'Haven't you got any typing to finish?'

'Nah, Baz. We haven't had a sniff of a client for ages. You know that as well as I do.'

Jane takes a sip of her tea. 'Gah,' she says, her face scrunching up, 'that's disgusting.'

Sheila assumes the look of a persecuted possum. First her employer and now his client. Everyone a critic! She storms out of the room, her head thrust back.

'Sorry about the tea. She used to work in an Army canteen back in the old country. Reckon it was part of the training programme. If you could stomach Sheila's brew you could live for weeks drinking your own piss and really appreciate it. Must be an Australian thing.'

Jane says nothing.

'Where were we?'

'I was telling you about people who might have a motive for wanting Sally dead.'

'Yeah,' says Baz, holding up his hand and counting off on his fingers. 'One, Joe Bembridge, dumped zombie ex-boyfriend. Two, Peter Ward. Current squeeze. Minister of State for all things Great and Good. Why him?

'Maybe he had been a bit careless with his pillow-talk. Let

something slip. I don't know. I'm speculating. And then there is Myra.

'Myra?'

'Peter's wife. A woman scorned.'

'Ahh. So, the philandering Minister was not quite footloose and fancy-free?'

'Sadly not. Apparently, he's always had an eye for the ladies but she seems to have had enough.'

'Why wouldn't she kill *him*? Rather than the opposition?'

'How should I know? I'm just going on what Sally told me. I don't know where she got the idea from.'

'That's three,' says Baz, counting off on his fingers, 'any more?'

'There is always Elizabeth Downing, of course.'

'She is in the same show, isn't she?'

'*Treloyhan Close*. Yes, she was the bar maid. Sally said there was speculation on set that she might be about to be written out. But Sally's death would have saved her part. The producers couldn't afford to lose two cast characters in quick succession.'

'Four,' Baz counted. This was adding up nicely. Plenty of suspects equalled plenty of investigations at a *per diem* and expenses.

'Then there is Donald Antrobus, Sally's agent. Sally was convinced he had been ripping her off for years. She was about to sack him and set the accountants on him, dig out the dirt.'

'So that's five, then. Any more?'

'Isn't that enough?'

'It'll do to be going on with,' Baz admitted. 'Keep me busy. Who was the SIO on Sally's death?'

'The what?'

'The SIO. Senior Investigating Officer. The copper in charge of the investigation.'

'That was a Detective Inspector. A woman called Ellie St John. Pronounced *Syngen* for some reason.'

'Local?'

'Sorry?'

'Where was it again where your sister died?'

'Wiltshire.'

'Right, so is DI St John local plod?'

'Yes.'

'So that is where I'll start my investigation. I assume you want me to take the case?' *Oh please. Oh please. I need the work,*

'Of course. That's why I'm here.'

'Sheila! Sheila!' Baz yelled at the closed door.

Sheila waited just long enough to register her disapproval at her earlier dismissal before she deigned to answer. She came in, bottom lip pouting in petulance.

'Yes?'

'Ah, Sheila. Print out a client contract for Miz Stamford, if you'd be so kind.'

'No kidding?' Sheila asked in surprise. 'We've actually got a client?'

'Thank you, Sheila. If you would just do it, please,' Baz growled through gritted teeth, all the while maintaining a tight smile for Jane's benefit. Just office banter. Take no notice. And also speculating where he would find a replacement for Sheila who would come cheap and occasionally let him sleep with her.

'So,' he said a few moments later after Jane Stamford had safely signed the contract, 'I'll get right on it.'

'I expect you'd like a down payment?'

'Er, yes. That is our standard practice.'

'Jane peeled a roll of bills out of her bag and detached a satisfying number.

Bonzer! The wrist will be raised in homage to the amber nectar tonight!

3

'I followed her to Southwark. She went to see an investigator called Baz Seabub,' the man said into his burner mobile.

'Did she see you?' the woman asked.

He didn't dignify the stupid question with an answer, just a snort of derision; he was a consummate professional, one of the best. NOBODY saw him if he didn't *want* to be seen.

'Know anything about Seabub?' she asked.

'He's an expatriate Australian. Came over here after the Big Burn. Was a trainee probationer in the New South Wales police. Looks like somekinda Bondi Beach surf bum. God knows how she found him. Doesn't look like punters are beating a path to his door. Which, by the way, is right in the middle of Sleazetown. Nothing for you to worry about, I'd say.'

'But it doesn't seem like she's prepared to let it go?'

'As I said, don't worry, I'll keep an eye on things. Nothing's going to get back to you.'

'Good. That's what I pay you for.'

He broke the connection, took out the SIM card for destruction later and dropped the burner into a rubbish bin after wiping it carefully.

4

The voice that spoke to Baz Seabub on the telephone was pure Estuary. Baz guessed she had come up through the Met and moved to the sticks to take up a promotion.

'DI St John. CID.'

'Oh, hi. My name's Baz Seabub. I'm an investigator. Based in Southwark.'

'And I'm sure that is very lovely for you.' Oh, good, a copper moonlighting as a comedian. Baz decided to play it straight.

'I'm investigating the death of Sally Effingham.'

'That's easy,' said St John. 'Soft object in metal box meets hard, immovable object at terminal velocity. Soft object ends up with engine on their lap. Chest crushed by steering column. Demise of soft object.' The sharing, caring face of the modern constabulary.

'So, you're saying it was a routine RTA.'

'Did you not hear me?' Whoa, Baz thought, this one has anger issues.

And indeed, she had. Effie St John was unmarried in her late thirties and had been passed over for promotion more than her fair share of times. It was only by being willing to accept a post in the wilds of Wiltshire that she had finally made the rank of Detective Inspector. And apart from the odd attempted assassination of Russian defectors, Wiltshire was a far cry from the action she craved and had enjoyed in the Met. And like many in the Met, she had a low opinion of private investigators (unless they were ex-Job and supplementing their pensions), seeing them as little more than peeping-toms poking their noses into other people's affairs. And here was another one, milking the family's grief, making money out of tragedy. Oh, she hated them.

'I'm sorry,' said Baz, pouring on the Aussie charm in his voice, 'we seem to have got off on the wrong foot.'

'And what foot is that?' she sneered. Probably the left foot like all those bastards who got promoted ahead of her. Bloody trouser-rolling, funny handshaking mafia.

'I've been hired by Miz Effingham's sister to look into the circumstances of her death. I just needed to confirm with you whether you were satisfied that it was all kosher. The sister reckoned that Sally Effingham had a number of people who might have a reason to wish her dead.'

'Haven't we all got a list of people we'd like to see dead?' Ellie snarled, before she could stop herself.

Whoa again.

'I'm sorry to hear that, Inspector.'

Shit! Ellie thought. Did I say that out loud? Whoopsie. Keep it tight, girl. 'Look,' she said, modulating her voice, 'Sally Effingham ran her car into a tree. The autopsy failed to reveal any excess level of alcohol or traces of drugs, recreational or prescription in her blood. Road conditions were good. We think she was speeding and misjudged a bend in the lane. The road went one way and she went another. Into a tree. A large oak, as it happens. Been there hundreds of years, apparently. The locals probably dance around it at the full moon, stark bollock naked and waving bunches of mistletoe.' Oh, even when she was trying to play nice that little shot of bile *had* to sneak in.

Baz was beginning to warm to her. He liked a woman with

attitude; reminded him of his dear old mother who had run a gentleman's entertainment venue back in the old days when King's Cross was in its hay day and not overrun by bloody tourists. Dorothy Seabub had a reputation akin to an eastern brown snake – fast and deadly with a cut-throat razor or a broken bottle. Sydney's protection racketeers paid *her*. It was at her insistence that young Baz had applied to join the Force. She reasoned that it never hurt to have someone she could trust on the inside of whatever side there was.

'Did you check out the car?'

'Not me personally. I'm a detective, not a car mechanic.'

'Give me a break, Inspector. Please.'

'OK,' said Effie, relenting a little. '*Of course* the car was checked out. Mechanically sound. No cut break lines or loose wheel nuts. Just a bloody great dent in the bonnet where it ploughed into the tree. The Fire Service had to cut the roof off to get her out. So, instant convertible job.'

'Did you interview any of her friends or people she had professional dealings with?'

Who let *him* off the boat? Effie thought. Doesn't he get the message. '*It was an accident. She was killed in her car. I'm not Miss Fucking Marple!*'

"I'll take that as a No, then, shall I? None of the people who stood to benefit from Sally Effingham's death? Her agent? The long-time lover she had just dumped? The actress who was about to be written out of her soap?'

'What did you say your name was again?'

'Baz Seabub.'

"Well then, listen very carefully, Mr Seabub. Sally Effingham died in a Road Traffic Accident. She was driving too fast along one of our quaint little country lanes and drove into a tree. Just like the late lamented Marc Bolan and God knows how many others. So, no, I did not waste taxpayers money in chasing up and investigating everyone she knew or had any kind of dealings with on the off chance that she had been murdered by person or persons unknown. Now, is there anything else, *Mr Seabub* or can I get back to my job chasing sheep rustlers and people driving their tractors in a reckless fashion.'

You are one bitter and twisted woman Baz thought as she put the phone down on him.

But I like you.

5

'Y'see, the trick is: who stands to gain? Find that out and you find your killer.'

'I thought you said that lady Inspector told you it was an accident,' Sheila replied, shifting her gum from one side of her mouth to the other. She was fiddling around with the clutter littering her desk in the hope that Baz would get the hint and leave her alone to go back to watching her favourite influencer on line.

'I've got a feeling in my water about this one.'

Sheila had had a feeling in her water once about the possible love of her life but that had turned out to be nothing more exciting than cystitis and the love of her life had decamped with her best mate. She had got on the plane to London shortly after.

'According to Jane Stamford, Sally Effingham had enemies. I've checked out her will and the bulk of her estate goes to her sister. But Jane Stamford would hardly hire us to find out who had killed her sister if she had done it herself, now would she?'

'Double bluff,' Sheila offered, to show she was paying attention. 'But can you be sure it really *was* murder?' She wished Baz would stop pacing around her small office; it was making her nervous.

'Jane Stamford swears that her sister was a rally-class driver who knew the back lanes around her house like a dingo knows its own smell. There was no way she could have crashed her car into that tree. I'm going to have to talk to the suspects.' He came to a halt and assumed a resolute expression on his face to impress Sheila.

It failed. 'You'd better get on with it, then,' she said.

6

Baz tracked Joe Bembridge down to a sprawling top-floor apartment in a mansion block in Kensington. The estate agent had described it as 'a highly desirable penthouse in the heart of London' and Joe had bought it for cash out of his share of *Septic Tank*'s first album *Hernia*. Subsequent albums and world tours of sold-out stadia gigs had resulted in more property acquisitions: - a place in the country; a beach-side villa in Grenada; an apartment in Bangkok that Joe had forgotten about and was now occupied by a tribe of street kids; a small chateau in France, converted into a recording studio; an apartment in the Dakota Building in New York. Joe Bembridge was very, very wealthy and very, very spoilt with a floating entourage there to cater to his every whim and shield him from the reality of day-to-day life.

Baz rode the ancient cage lift rattling and banging up to the top floor of the building, yanked the gate open and stepped out onto the landing. There was only one doorway with no indication who might dwell within. Loud music spilled through but Baz, undaunted, rang the bell anyway. Much to his surprise, the door was opened a few moments later by an elderly man wearing a striped waistcoat. 'Can I help you, sir?' he said.

'My name's Baz Seabub. I have an appointment to see Mr Bembridge.'

A woman in her late thirties, expensively dressed in a formal business suit of austere black, materialised at the butler's shoulder and looked Baz up and down. From the expression on her face she seemed to have reached the conclusion that Baz was something nasty that the cat had dragged in. 'You are..?'

Baz resisted the urge to reply: 'Pretty hacked off at being kept out here on the landing,' and said, instead: 'Baz Seabub. I made an appointment to see Joe with his agent, Frank Green.' His intonation rose at the end of the sentence, making it sound like a question.

The Woman in Black gave Baz another scowl, told him to wait and then stalked off into the apartment. The butler gave Baz a look of sympathy and then shut the door on him.

They kept Baz waiting for ten minutes. When the door opened again, the butler at least, had the grace to look shame-faced, unlike the woman, who announced that he would be admitted to the Presence.

The apartment was obviously the work of an interior decorator with a penchant for the Gothic Revival look, all dark purple drapes and deep crimson flock wallpaper; the preferred mode of lighting seemed to be tall candles in candelabras artfully festooned with stalactites of melted wax – a fire hazard waiting to happen. The floors were covered in thick carpets overlaid with rugs. A strong smell of some kind of sweet perfume hung in the air. Baz guessed that the decor had not had a makeover since that late 1960s. Or, indeed, much of a clean.

He was ushered into a darkened room that stank of opium. Joe Bembridge lay on a chaise sucking on an ornate brass shisha pipe for all the world like the caterpillar in *Alice*. Music thrummed from speakers situated at strategic points around the room and a huge television screen hung on a wall. An assortment of guitars on stands lined the walls. Cutting through the smell of poppy was a strong odour of unwashed body emanating from Bembridge.

'Mr Seabub, sir' said the Woman in Black.

Bembridge showed no response.

'You agreed to see him. Just now. Remember?'

Bembridge took a long toke at his pipe and let the smoke dribble out of his nose. His eyes were glazed. Baz understood why Sally Effingham had dumped him. He also understood why *Septic Tank* had not been touring for the past few years.

'I'd like to talk to you about the death of Sally Effingham.' Baz told him.

Bembridge made an effort to sit up, failed, and slumped back on the chaise.

'Sally Effingham,' Baz said again, raising his voice.

'Sally, man,' Bembridge croaked. 'Yeah.'

The Woman in Black shot a triumphant glance at Baz, as if to say 'waste of time.'

Baz persevered. 'She ended your relationship.'

'I've not seen her, man.'

'No. That's because she's dead.'

'Who is?'

'Sally Effingham.'

'Bummer.'

'You didn't know?'

'Know what, man?' Bembridge asked, taking another mighty toke and filling the room with smoke. Baz tried to avoid breathing. At least one of them needed a clear head but he was fast coming to the conclusion that Bembridge was not his man.

'When did you last see her? Sally Effingham?'

'Is Sally here? Wow. Cool.'

The Woman in Black shook her head almost imperceptibly at Baz, who thought he detected a tear in the corner of her eye.

He got the message. Joe Bembridge had checked out of Planet Earth for the duration. Who knew if he would ever re-visit. Baz thanked him for his time and turned to go. The Woman in Black followed him to the door.

'How long has he been like that?'

'A couple of years now but he's been much worse since Sally dumped him. We have suggested rehab but he is not interested. As long as he's got the money the staff here will look after him. He's got everything he needs.' Her voice betrayed a quaver.

And a woman who loves him, Baz thought.

'Please don't tell the world what you found here, Mr Seabub. I will arrange a bank transfer for your co-operation if you give me your details.'

Gift horses and their mouths! 'That's very kind of you. The details are on my card,' he said, handing one over. Baz was not a man to be swayed by sympathy or sentiment when bucks were on offer.

He whistled as the rickety lift wheezed and clanked its way to the ground.

Lost and anonymous in the crowd on the pavement opposite, a man watched Baz Seabub leave the building.

7

'Motive! That's the key!' Baz sat with his feet up on his desk; Sheila listened patiently, having heard little else since Seabub took on the case. 'Money. Sex. Jealousy. Money.'

'How about secrets?' Sheila offered. 'People kill to keep secrets secret.'

'Bugger me! Secrets! You're right.'

'Well don't look so surprised. I'm not just a pretty face. I got a degree from Woolamalooga Community College.'

'It was in media studies. Watching soaps all day. *Neighbours* - Australia's gift to the world.'

'Still,' Sheila insisted, unfazed.

Baz sighed, shrugged his shoulders and conceded the point. He had tried arguing with Sheila before and found it was like trying to argue with treacle.

'Her latest squeeze, according to her sister, was that MP, Peter Ward. He's on all the news and politico talking heads shows. Tipped for great things, Gawdhelphim. Time to give Ron Greenhalgh a tinkle.'

Ron Greenhalgh. Born in the Tasmanian seaside town of Penguin, a town so twee and touristy that Ron fled to Melbourne at the first opportunity and never returned. Prompted by the Big Burn Ron joined the Aussie diaspora in the UK, getting a job on one of the redtops in the last gasp of the print media. Since then he had moved on to run *Exposed,* a blog whose prime aim seemed to be to dig the dirt on those in the public eye. The site attracted hundreds of thousands of followers and had made Ron a very wealthy man.

'G'Day, Ron,' said Baz into his mobile. They had briefly been flatmates when Ron first arrived in London but Ron had moved on as soon as he could afford it. However, there was no ill will between them and they often met up for a drink, with Ron paying.

'Baz, you old bastard! How's it hanging? What are you after?'

'I'm investigating the death of Sally Effingham.'

'What have you heard?' Suddenly Ron was all ears. This was rich meat and strong drink to his journalistic instincts.

'Nothing specific. Her sister hired me.'

'Surely it was an accident. The silly drongo drove her car into a tree.'

'Her sister doesn't believe it and is paying me to poke around.'

'Have you got anything? I'd pay for something juicy.'

'Not so far, Ron. That's why I'm reaching out to you and your contacts. What have you got on Peter Ward?'

'What's the connection?' Ron's spider sense was tingling.

'Sally was seeing him, apparently.'

'Seeing him as in horizontal jogging?'

'You hadn't heard?' It was not often that Baz had one over Ron and he took a moment to relish his triumph.

'Stone me, he kept that good and quiet.'

'What else is he keeping quiet? Anything he might be prepared to kill to keep under wraps?'

'You knew his rep, a latter-day Saint David and the Blessed Greta all rolled into one. Champion of the environment and all things cuddly and cute?'

'Yeah, of course. He's Minister for Sustainable Development. Never off the telly. Tipped for the top, they say.'

'He's a fake,' said Ron.

'Whaddaya mean?' asked Baz, *his* spider sense now tingling.

'This is on the QT, Baz. Understand?'

'OK,' said Baz, not meaning it for one second.

'No, Baz. Uncross yer fingers. I mean it.'

'Bugger,' thought Baz but Ron was too useful a person to cross and fall out with.

'You telling me about Sally Effingham makes things fall into place,' Ron mused to himself.

'What things, Ron?'

'I got a call from Myra Ward, Peter's wife. She is one pissed-off lady. I didn't know why but Peter playing the two-backed beast with our Sally explains a lot. Myra obviously got wind of it. A woman scorned and all that. Anyway, she shopped him.'

'Peter?' Baz queried to make sure he was still following.

'Yeah. Keep up. He wasn't just in bed with the lovely Sally, he was in Bed with Red River Mining.'

'The infamous destroyers of rain forests and natural habitats the world over?'

'The very same.'

'How.'

'I don't know the details but apparently Myra suspected Peter of doing the dirty deed away from home and checked out his call history one night when he was fast akip. It seems that one number came up quite a lot. She rang it and discovered it belonged to Anderson Quelp…'

'CEO of Red River Mining,' Baz supplied.

'The very man. It was like Hitler phoning Winston Churchill for a chat in the middle of the Blitz. Now, what could they have to talk about?'

'Beats me.'

'Seems Red River had bought up a large tract of the Jurassic Coast in Dorset in the name of a shell company called The Endangered Butterfly Trust that was going to apply to Ward's Ministry for exploitation rights. In exchange, lots of moolah would surface in a bank in the Caymans.'

'How do you know all this?'

'Myra phoned Quelp pretending to be Ward's PA. She might have given the impression that she would be joining Peter in their Caribbean love nest. Anyway, Quelp let enough slip for Myra to know she had Peter by the balls when it came to an uncontested divorce.'

'So, does Myra know *who* Peter was jigging a jig with?'

'No. There Peter was careful. He must have had another phone stashed away that he used to call Sally.'

'Could she have known about his dealings with Red River?' Baz was still in search of a motive for murder.

'Highly unlikely, Baz. It seems Peter kept his todger and his wallet in separate pockets.'

'And how about Myra? Was she after blood?'

'Nah, she just needed ammunition to take Peter to the cleaners. Didn't matter where it came from and the threat of exposure of his double-dealing was more than enough.'

'So, that rules both Peter and Myra Ward out as potential murderers.'

'I'd say so, Baz. Keep looking, and if you hear anything, who ya gonna call?'

'Cheers, Ron. Will do.'

8

The CEO sat at her desk reviewing the quarterly returns. In a business that could be subject to seasonal fluctuations, the quarterlies were strong; there would be a very satisfying dividend pay-out for the shareholders and a nice little (well, actually, not *quite* so little) bonus for herself. Life, she told herself was good. But she mustn't rest on her laurels. Onwards and ever upwards. The world of commerce never sleeps. There are profits to be made by the entrepreneur who seizes the main chance.

She unlocked the drawer where she kept her pristine burner phones, each one used only the one time and then destroyed.

She punched in a number and waited while it rang.

'Yes,' said a voice.

'Anything?'

'Nothing.'

'Excellent. Now, I have a fresh task. Someone very big in the world of popular music. Someone for the girls. I leave it to you.' She broke the connection. The whole conversation had lasted less than twenty seconds.

9

Treloyhan Close, the story of a close-knit South London criminal fraternity, is filmed at the Elstree Studios at Borehamwood, Hertfordshire, usually a couple of months in advance of airing. Baz manages to blag his way into an interview with an assistant producer during a lull in shooting. He takes Sheila along with him as a treat; he *has* been particularly snippy with her of late as all his leads turn to dead ends.

This morning's scenes are set in the *Baby and Bottle* the pub that is the fulcrum of the show. Baz and Sheila are shown onto the set by a minion with a First Class Honours degree in Fine Art from Cambridge who is serving her time as an intern, supported only by her trust fund. To the untrained eye the film set appears to be chaos unleashed: cables, cameras, lights, people performing mysterious tasks rushing hither and thither, many clasping clipboards tightly to their chests. The intern introduces Baz to a small, neat man in his early thirties who is already going bald.

'This is Jerry,' she says with a touch of awe in her voice, 'the Assistant Producer.'

'Yeah,' says Jerry in his best drawl. He thrusts a hand in Baz's direction. 'Thank you, Anita.'

'It's Alice, actually.' She replies in a cut-glass voice. 'But close enough.' She will remember him when her father's influence in the business allows her to rise to a position of power.

'Baz Seabub. We spoke on the phone.'

Jerry looks blank; he has many weighty matters on his mind and cannot be expected to remember every phone call he takes.

'About Sally Effingham,' Baz prompts.

'Dear, dear Sally. Such a talent; such a waste.'

'Her sister thinks she was murdered.'

'Murdered!' His mouth forms a perfect O and his eyes sparkle. *How delicious*, he thinks.

'I'm looking for a motive,' Baz admits. 'Her sister mentioned some sort of rivalry between Sally Effingham and Elizabeth Downing. Something about one of them being written out of the show?'

'Can I rely on your discretion. Mr Seagull?'

'Of course,' Baz lied.

'As you may know, the show is recorded some time in advance of transmission. In fact, we still have a couple more episodes with Sally in them. The writers have only just resolved her disappearance but, of course, I can't tell you the storyline.' He gives a little chuckle and looks around himself nervously to check that he has not been overheard by anyone who matters.

'And, so?'

'So, it's not just Sally.'

'What is not just Sally?'

Jerry is bobbing about like a meercat on the lookout for an eagle. '*Absolute discretion*,' Jerry warns.

'Yeah,' Baz is getting impatient.

'The bitch has jumped ship. There, I said it.' Jerry fold his arms, draws himself up to his full five foot four inches and swells out his chest. He is *important* and privy to insider knowledge. Baz is reminded of the gnomic utterances of messages to the French Resistance in the Second World War: *The chicken has landed tonight; tell Jacques it will soon be autumn; the moon wears an overcoat.*

'I'm sorry?' says Baz.

'So are we.'

'No, I mean I have no idea what you are talking about.'

'Elizabeth Downing! All the time her agent was fishing around over the pond.'

Baz is now frankly lost and shakes his head.

'*LA*' Jerry hisses. 'Lalaland'

'Oh, you mean Hollywood.'

'Yes. As soon as her contract came up for renewal she was off.'

'So, she wasn't about to be written out of the show?'

'Good God, no.'

'So, it wasn't a case of her or Sally?'

'Absolutely not. This show has an audience of eight million viewers on a regular basis. Now we've lost two of our key characters…' His voice trails off, the thought too terrible to finish.

Bugger! Thinks Baz. That's another motive gone down the dunny.

Bells are shrilling; people are moving onto the actual set. The First Assistant Director is shouting and pointing. Baz guesses filming is about to start.

'I've got to go. Nice meeting you, Mr Seesaw.' Baz is getting the brush-off. He looks around for Sheila who seems to have wandered off while he was talking to Jerry. He finally spies her in the distance, deep in conversation with a thickset man with a beard and a ponytail and thick, square-rimmed glasses. Baz goes over just as the man walks onto the set.

'Who was that?' Baz asks, although he is not really that interested.

'That was Dave Ivanovitch,' says Sheila in a star-struck voice.

'Oh, yeah?'

'The Producer!'

'Not an Assistant, then?'

'No.' Sheila shuffles her feet. 'He's offered me a job,' she blurts out.'

'*What!*'

'Assistant PA.'

Baz starts to laugh. 'He just wants to get into your pants,' he scoffs.

'So how does that make him different to you?'

Baz has no answer and for once in his life feels just a twinge of shame.

'And he calls me Ninette! I'll be round to pick up my stuff.'

'You can't just leave,' Baz wails.

'Just watch me!'

10

Boyz2luv take their final bow as the audience scream and weep and howl for more. They make their way, high on adrenalin and adulation to the VIP dressing rooms where the post-show party is waiting – a gaggle of young groupies, booze, drugs of choice, a selection of vegan dishes for Jamie, cold lobster salad for Zeke, a Kobe beefsteak specially flown over from Japan for Thaddeus and fish 'n' chips for Pete (the one the mums love!).

'Great show tonight, boys!' says Lester Pine, their manager and producer, the man who put the band together out of the TV show *Pick Me!* And is fast on his way to becoming a billionaire.

'Yeah, whatever,' says Zeke, cracking a lobster claw and sucking out the meat. A moment later he starts to choke and his face goes bright red. Thaddeus slaps him on the back, to no avail. Lester shouts for a First Aider. Zeke is on the floor, convulsing, his heels drumming a rhythm of death. The Duty Nurse rushes to pump at his chest, starts to give him CPR. It is fruitless. A doctor pronounces Zeke dead twenty minutes later.

Lester Pine starts to call the Media.

*

'Nice work,' the CEO says into the burner phone. 'Remuneration in the usual way.' She breaks the connection and sets the mobile aside to be destroyed.

11

Donald Antrobus had a secret vice – he gambled and like most people addicted to betting, he was lousy at it. He lost money hand over fist. He lost his own money and he lost other people's money. He lost money to legitimate gaming outlets and he lost money to well-dubious sources, the sort that believed that broken bones encouraged prompt repayment of debts (with interest, naturally). His vice had lost him his prestigious office space in Soho Square and had lost him a slew of lucrative showbiz clients; he now rented a shared office space in a building in Acton with a middle-aged lady who served as secretary/receptionist/PA to half a dozen other down-at-heel businesses. She it was who invited Baz Seabub to take a seat in the shabby waiting-room with the promise: 'I'll see if Mr Antrobus is free.'

Surprise, surprise, he was.

'I'd like to talk to you about one of your clients,' Baz told him.

Antrobus, who was down to representing 'actors' in the world of adult entertainment films and going nowhere musical wannabes, sighed. He was a cadaverous looking creature, more sixty than fifty with thinning hair and a sharp nose and pale, bloodless lips. He wore a pinstriped suit that looked like it had come out of an undertaker's dressing-up box and a clip-on polka-dot bow tie.

'Sally Effingham.'

'Sally?' Antrobus's face lit up. She had been his star. He had nurtured her career from the outset and in return she had made him a rich man. He had had, and still had, a very soft spot for Sally. He felt a tear form in his eye and his lower lip trembled.

Baz was having none of it. 'According to her sister, Sally was about to dump you. She thought you were ripping her off. She was going to hire forensic accountants to go through your books.'

'She'd have been right,' Antrobus sobbed, tears now running freely down his cheeks.

'You admit it?' Baz asked, incredulous.

'I've been bad. I'm weak, weak. A slave to my lusts. What can I say?' Years of representing theatricals had rubbed off on Donald Antrobus: the histrionics came naturally and easily.

'Er.'

'But,' said Antrobus, miraculously switching off the tears, "I can make it up to her.'

'No, you can't. She dead.'

'To her estate, then.'

'I had a win. Just before Sally so tragically had her accident. I opened an account for her. One that I could not touch. I know my failings. But...' He fished about in his trouser pocket, found a large, grubby handkerchief, blew his nose loudly, briefly inspected his effort and returned the handkerchief to its hiding place, '...I loved Sally. Like a daughter. I felt so *guilty* borrowing her money.'

'Yeah, but you still took it.'

'*Borrowed* it. I replaced it but she died before I could tell her.'

'Can you prove it?' Baz asked. It was looking like his last suspect had no motive for murder.

'Yes. I can show you the details of the bank account.' He rummaged around in the top drawer of his desk and produced the documentation of an account in Sally Effingham's name.

And with that, Baz was stymied.

12

Jane Stamford once more sat in Baz Seabub's office, now bereft of Sheila who had abandoned Baz for the glitter of showbiz.

'I've investigated them all, Miz Stamford. None of them have a motive. None of them stood to gain from your sister's death. I've come to the conclusion that the Police got it right. Your sister died in a road accident. Who knows why? A momentary lapse of concentration? A deer running across the road. We'll never know. I can't do any more for you.'

'You are sure?' Jane Stamford didn't want to believe what she was hearing.

'I'm sure. It's as clear as a creek after a rainstorm.'

'Then I must thank you for your efforts and settle my bill.'

'That would be fair dinkum. Thank you kindly, ma'am.' I'll put that down to The Murder That Never Was Baz thought as he showed her out into the busy sleaze of Southwark.

He contemplated giving DI Effie St John a ring, maybe ask her out for a drink. You never know!

*

The assassin stretched out on a lounger by his pool, a sunshade angled just so. A long drink sat on a table close to hand. He could hear his wife clattering around in the kitchen, tempting smells beginning to waft in his direction. Another half hour and the kids would be back from the International School in Marbella and that would be the end of his peace. He had checked through a series of cut-outs and satisfied himself that his £25,000 fee for killing Zeke from *Boyz2luv* was resting in his account in Grand Cayman. Easy money for injecting a traceless poison into the lobster claw. As easy as shining a lasar pointer into the eyes of a motorist, causing her to crash into a tree. Life was good.

*

The CEO had come up with The Idea when she was a branch manager in the North-West of England. Her industry was a year-round business but with two great spikes – Mothering Sunday and Valentine's Day, rather like the Christmas spike in other retail sectors. For the rest of the year business was steady but not spectacular. How to drive up demand was the question that obsessed her. Driving around in the towns and countryside she noticed the memorial bouquets left by the side of the road, against fences in accident blackspots, piled up in cemeteries and crematoria. And then she had The Idea. She made very discrete inquiries amongst ex pupils of her old school in a part of Liverpool famous for its skallies and made contact with a lad smart enough not to have a criminal record. She sounded him out, liked his response and put The Idea to him. He agreed to give it a go and on August 31st 1997 rode a motorbike into the Pont de l'Alma road tunnel in Paris, causing the car he was chasing to swerve and crash into the wall.

The subsequent outpouring of grief on the death of Diana, Princess of Wales and the ocean of floral tributes that flooded the nation made millions for the florists of Britain and cemented the CEO's business model as she rose to the top in the cut flowers industry, earning a Damehood for services to the economy on her way.

Life, the CEO reflected, was good. She would never again suffer from the money worries that blighted her childhood and left her prey to insecurities.

She fired up her desktop and went hunting on social media for her next celeb to die in a couple of months' time. Although she was unaware of it, she was whistling a little tune.

She loved her work.

The Kidnap Kaper

1

I woke up to find myself slumped over my desk, a small pool of drool under my cheek. I felt like a whole bunch of salamanders had thrown a wild party in my mouth and left me to clean up the mess. I risked opening an eye and winced as the light stabbed at it. I could see the blurred shape of a bottle three inches from my face. A pessimist would say it was three-quarters empty; an optimist would say it was a quarter full. Me, I'm a realist – you have to be in my job – I would say that I had drunk too much last night.

It took me a full minute, although it seemed like a whole lot longer, to realise that the banging wasn't only in my head. There was someone at the door doing their best to batter it down. I could see a blurred outline through the frosted glass window. Hell, the way I felt any outline was going to be blurred.

'Le' me 'lone,' I croaked at the party trying to kill me with decibel overload but the party went right on hammering.

Somewhere in the foggy reaches of the back of my mind the survival instinct kicked in. You never lose it, that feeling in the gut that you have to take *action*, that you have to *move*, that you have to do *something* and that you have to do it *now*. Hell, another few bangs on the glass and the party would be waist-deep in broken glass. I'd only just had the pane fixed after I threw The Dirty Rat's gat after him as he stumbled out of the office. I'd had to smack him around a little when he got fresh. He got sore and made a play with his heater. Punks like him, they're a dime a dozen. Think they're tough but they ain't so tough without a piece. I took the rod off him before his dumb brain could register what was happening and gave him a little tap on the head with it to drive the lesson home. He left and I threw his toy after him. Maybe he learnt the lesson too good because he shut the door nice and polite and five pounds of blued steel went through the window after him. I'd have to remember to send him a bill for the repairs.

And here was this party pounding on the glass and probably smudging the new paintwork which read:

Bernie Zeebarb
Discreet Investigations

I got myself vertical and shuffled to the door. I may have called something. I don't know what but the banging stopped and the feeling that I needed very badly to throw up receded. As I got closer the blur acquired curves. Maybe it my bloodshot eyes, maybe it was the light but the curves looked good and in all the right places.

The key was still in the lock. I turned it. The party was sure in a hurry. The door flew open, cracking me on the wrist but I'm tough. I can take pain. Hell, in my line of work I've had a lot of practise.

The party sashayed into the office in a swish of silk like she owned the joint, giving me the once over as I stood there rubbing my wrist. Maybe she liked what she saw, maybe she didn't. I don't apologise to no-one. Sure, I hadn't shaved too much lately and so what if my eyes were a little blood-shot and maybe a little baggy but I'm four foot six and lean and mean with it and I've been around the block with more than my share of dames.

But this one... Well, maybe *she* didn't like what she saw but I certainly did. She was class. She was a Babe dressed all in pale blue silk. Neat, petite with the curves in *all* the right places. When she tilted her head to look into my eyes with those baby-blues the light struck highlights off her auburn hair that sent my heart into my mouth. You think I'm being slushy? Hell, who can be tough with a Babe like that sharing air with you?

'Mr Zeebarb?' She had one of those contralto voices that make my knees forget they are supposed to hold me up.

'Yeah. At your service,' my voice came out a cross between a croak and a rasp. I shuffled back to the shelter of my desk. She followed close enough behind me for me to get a good whiff of her perfume. Flowers of Gold if I wasn't mistaken at $50 a very small pop. Without waiting to be asked she sat down in the battered leather swivel chair that I keep for clients. I like a woman who can think for herself.

I swung my legs up onto the desk, remembered the hole in my shoe and swung them back down again. She didn't need to know that times could be better for Bernie Zeebarb, Private Investigator of this burg. But from the look of her, in her long silk dress that shrieked designer, the matching ribbon in her hair and her few pieces of discrete jewellery that were definitely *not* costume, she hadn't seen a hard day in her life.

'What time is it?' I asked, just to get the conversation going, not that I really cared.

'Why, Mr Zeebarb, it's quite eleven o'clock.

I shook my head to clear the last of the fumes and swept the bottle off the desk and into a drawer. I hoped she hadn't noticed.

'Late night meeting with a client,' I offered by way of an explanation, giving her my best boyish grin but she didn't seem to be listening. She musta had something pressing on her mind to resist the flash of my pearly-whites. Not many broads can.

'It's my son, Mr Zeebarb. He's missing.' I clocked a glance at her third finger, left hand. Sure enough, there was the wedding band. How had I been so dumb as to miss it? Hell, I prided myself on my ability to notice details. In my work, noticing details can make the difference between life and death but she didn't look old enough to have a kid. I guess that is what the up-market beauty parlours charge the big bucks for. And besides, those curves of hers were *firm*!

'Yeah?' I pulled a scrap of paper over. It was my laundry list but she wasn't to know. I flipped it over and saw that I hadn't used the other side. That would do fine. I licked the stub of my pencil. 'Tell me about it,' I said.

'It was yesterday. Last night. My husband and I were out at a charity function. We go to a lot of those.' Her smooth contralto washed over me like I was taking a bath in honey. 'I bet you do,' I thought but had the good sense to keep my trap shut. I nodded to encourage her to go on.

'And when we got home…' She paused to give her eyes a dab with a little lace number'…he was gone.'

'Did you leave him home alone?'

She was shocked and showed it. 'No, *of course* not, Mr Zeebarb. What *sort* of parents do you think we *are*? Why, I'm shocked you could even ask such a thing!' That was me told.

'So, who *was* in the house?' I started again.

She paused and picked at the bright red lipstick that coated her mouth. Impure thoughts smashed through my head like a runaway express train going down the side of a mountain with the whistle blowing and the steam escaping. 'There were the maids, of course.'

Regretfully I dragged my thoughts away from bright red kissable lips and back to the matter in hand.

'And the cook. The gardeners don't live in the house, naturally and the coachmen and the footmen were out with us. But they don't live in the main house. They have accommodations in the stables.' She paused again. 'Fairchild's nanny, of course. She has a room in the main house. Next to the Nursery.' It was beginning to sound like a small town.

'Fairchild?' I asked, scribbling the name down on my scrap of paper, trying to look like I was on the ball but I had a pretty good idea.

'Fairchild's my dear little boy, Mr Zeebarb. He's…he's…' Her lower lip trembled and those beautiful baby-blues misted with tears.

'Hey…hey…lady.' I pulled a handkerchief out of my pocket and shoved it in her direction. I hate to see a dame cry. It gets to me every time. I guess I'm just a pushover for a babe in distress.

She looked at the handkerchief, pulled a face and produced her little lacey number. OK, so my handkerchief was what you might call a little grimy in that it hadn't seen the inside of a laundry tub for several weeks. What the hell, it was the thought that counts. I tried to sooth my hurt feelings.

'You were saying?' I prompted.

'I'm sorry, Mr Zeebarb. I'm upset.' She sniffed and attempted a brave face.

'Yeah,' I said, all concerned, 'I understand. Just take your time.' I looked at my pocket watch. 'I'm free for the next hour,' I lied. Hell, I hadn't seen a client in days. Business wasn't exactly hammering on the door.

'I really appreciate you giving me your time,' she coo'd, batting those baby-blue eyes at me and I decided there and then that I'd walk to hell and back for her.

Some Babes get you like that, know what I mean?

'So, tell me exactly what happened Mrs…uh…Mrs…?'

'Sylvester. Mrs Faunus Sylvester.'

I whistled. I couldn't stop myself. Faunus Sylvester was Money with a capital M. Money *and* Power. His uncle on the distaff side was the Duke. Sylvester's father was already a major league money man when he married the Duke's sister. He wouldn't have got a look in otherwise. Like I said, Money and Power. And it all came to Faunus. And here was his little lady sitting in my crummy office telling me her kid was missing.

It didn't make any kind of sense.

She could have had every cop in the city out looking for him. Hell, she could have had the Army out. So why me? Why come to a (let's face it) none too successful private eye with something this big?

Something stank of none too fresh fish and it wasn't yours truly. I decided to mention it upfront, get the elephant out of the room.

'Mrs Sylvester, why have you come to me with this thing? Look around you. Let's quit kidding around. What have I got that the cops haven't?' I stopped short. I hadn't asked her the obvious question. I narrowed my eyes. I like doing that. It makes me look as if I'm on top of things. At least, I like to think so. 'Mrs Sylvester, have you told the cops about your son's disappearance?'

'I…I…we…' She couldn't look me in the face. Those lovely eyes took a real interest in my threadbare old rug.

'Mrs Sylvester, level with me. What's the beef?'

Her eyes travelled all the way up from the floor until they met mine. They widened just a fraction on the way to let me know she was giving me the real gen.

I waited. I had nothing better to occupy my time.

'Last night my husband and I came home late. I told you we were out at a function. Some charity of which my husband is a patron. The nanny put Fairchild to bed before we went out. I...I went in to his nursery myself and kissed him goodnight.' She found her little lacy number from where she had tucked it away in her purse and dabbed at her eyes, clutching it tightly in her hand ready for further use. 'We came home and I went into his nursery to check on him as I always do before I go to bed. He was gone. The covers were folded back and the window was open. Nanny said she looked in on him during the evening and that he was sleeping peacefully. But...but... when I...when I looked in...he was gone.' Her handkerchief was doing sterling service.

'What did you do?' My pencil was scribbling this all down.

'Why, I called my husband, of course.'

'Yeah? Then what?'

'We questioned Nanny and the other servants. The maids and the cook had finished their work and were in their own quarters. The Major Domo had the evening off and had gone into town. No-one heard anything. The coachman and the footmen were with us. Not at the function, of course,' she added quickly lest I assumed the help were mixing with the makers and shakers. I hadn't assumed that for a moment but it was good of her to straighten that out. 'No, something was arranged for the servants.'

Yeah, like polishing up their master's money while they were waiting for him to finish having a swell time.

'How old is your son, Mrs Sylvester?' Kids sometimes wander off at night. They do it for kicks. Maybe hide out in the garden in a den they've made in the bushes. Have an adventure sleeping in the broom closet. Curl up with the dog in his kennel.

'He's six months old, Mr Zeebarb. Such a sweet little baby boy. Why?' Her face had gone all dreamy-looking.

'Just getting the low-down, Mrs Sylvester.' That was my wandering-off theory shot to hell and back. 'So,' I was all hard-headed business even though this Babe was doing things to my mind that no other dame had done before. 'what happened after you'd questioned the servants?'

'We searched the house, of course. And then the grounds. By the time we had finished it was very late. I was frantic. I still am, as you might imagine. But my husband insisted that I have a bath and get some sleep.'

I tried hard not to picture her in her bath wearing nothing but soap suds: it was a losing battle so I gave in to a little bit of speculation.

'Mr Zeebarb, are you all right?'

I snapped out of my fantasy. I could always go back to it later.

'Why haven't you call the cops in?' I asked her, cutting through to the chase.

She started. Her hand jerked tightly around the handkerchief and she looked away from me in a swift movement.

'Mrs Sylvester. Your son is missing. He is six months old so he couldn't have gone off under his own steam. You didn't come here just for me to tell you someone took him. You know that. So, let me ask you again: why haven't you gone to the cops?'

'They always say don't tell the police,' she replied in a small voice.

'"They" I snapped back at her. 'Who are "they"?'

'Kidnappers,' she whispered as if she were afraid to utter the word; afraid maybe they could hear her. I had to strain *my* ears to hear her but I already knew where she was coming from.

'Has this happened before?' I couldn't keep the surprise out of my voice.

It was her turn to look surprised, like she'd been given a jolt of the juice. The sort they keep up at the Big House for use with the Chair.

'Of course not!' Now she was indignant. Her eyes flashed at me. My heart did a somersault.

'Then how come you know all about the routine?' Oh, I was merciless in my search for truth.

'I read it in a book. Sometimes I read…I like true crime stories.' It came out aggressive with just a smidgen of apology for seasoning.

I like a woman who is not afraid to have and opinion and stick up for it.

'Has there been any contact?'

'Contact?' she asked vaguely as if that had never come up in her stories and she was coming to terms with the idea for the first time.

'A letter, a ransom note, demands for money, instructions? The stuff kidnappers do.'

'No.'

'What does your husband think?'

'He agrees with me. He doesn't want any fuss. If we call the police in to investigate the newspapers will find out. His uncle…' She didn't need to say any more. The newspapers would make their lives hell. All the scum and the low lifes of the city would crawl out of their holes like iron filings drawn to a magnet. The Sylvesters would be deluged in phoney ransom notes from chancers hoping to get a slice of the pie. And the real kidnapper might well be frightened off by all the publicity with only one possible outcome. I certainly understood why she didn't want to involve the cops.

'So, you want me to find him,' I guessed. I'm a P.I. That means I can usually spot the blindingly obvious. 'No publicity. No embarrassment for City Hall. Just nice and quiet.'

You'd have thought I'd given her the world. When it came down to it, she was only really a kid and so far she was handling the situation pretty good.

'That is exactly so, Mr Zeebarb' she said with a kind of dignity. Then, for good measure she added a lie. 'You come highly recommended,' she said, and managed not to blush.

I didn't push it. Who knows how or where she'd heard of me. Not at the Country Club or the Ladies Debating Circle. You can bet your last nickel on that!

I got down to the nitty-gritty. Did she have any enemies? No. Did she have *any* idea at all who might want to snatch the kid? No. Did she know anyone who had had the opportunity? No. Any servants recently fired? No. Would she like to leave her husband and join me in a life of squalor? Just kidding. I may have fantasied that last thought but I'm not dumb enough to kiss off a client who dripped money. Somethings are more important than a life of unbridled lust. I hadn't been eating too well lately and most of what I *did* eat came out of the neck of a bottle.

When it came down to hard facts she was no help. Let's face it, if the Sylvesters knew anything they would already have done plenty and not come to me. They were stymied and I was their last bet. I told her my *pro diem*, chucked in a fee for a successful conclusion that resulted in baby Fairchild being restored to the loving arms of his Mama, not a hair on his head suffering hurt. And then, just for good measure, brought up the subject of expenses.

She didn't bat an eyelid. I was used to a bout of protracted haggling with my clients and I must say I found her approach to business strangely refreshing.

She apologised for not having any small change with her with which to cover my advance and pulled out a bank note that would more than cover everything for a week. Great! Who did I know that could make change for a Big One? If I went to the bank where I kept what I laughingly called my 'Business Account' they would take the lot to cover my overdraft. And I would still be in hock.

I'd find a way. I'm a private dick and we can do these things that the average Joe Citizen doesn't even dream of.

She left. I promised I'd get onto the case right away. She had the decency not to ask about my next appointment.

Or maybe she had other more pressing things on her mind.

2

I changed the note into more modest units of currency. Don't ask me how. I'd be a rube to tell you.

I also had a shave and a splash down in the tin bath I keep for special occasions. If you are going to mix with the likes of Faunus Sylvester it helps to look presentable. But don't get me wrong, I didn't go as far as clean linen and a tux. I'm a private eye – we're *supposed* to look seedy. It comes with the job. Seedy and tough. Goes hand in hand with the image. Seedy and tough. Yep, that about sums me up to a T.

But presentable seedy when I'm on a big case like this.

I allowed myself the luxury of a hackney up to the Sylvester place – what the hell, he was paying for it as part of my expenses. The estate wasn't exactly Downtown, although I'd guess that he must have had a nifty little *pied de Terre* tucked away somewhere discrete and opulent for those times when a man wants to be alone. Or, at least, away from prying eyes.

A high wall that disappeared away into the distance to right and left was pierced by a wrought iron gate with a neat little gatehouse tucked in behind it. I peered through the bars, which for some reason gave me an uncomfortable feeling in my stomach. All I could see through the gate was a road that vanished into a park. Trees, lawns, bushes, ornamental borders. Probably a lake or two hiding out in the forest. My main impression was that there was plenty of cover for a low-life to sneak about in. A rope ladder with grappling hooks and you could be over that wall in a flash and in the cover of the trees.

I wondered if the house was any better protected. Probably

not. The rich think that isolating themselves from the common herd ensures their safety and feel snug and warm under the delusion. Not that I'm on nodding terms with that many rich folk. Not *rich* like the Sylvesters.

A burly type was nosing out of the gatehouse to see what the hackney had deposited on the doorstep, so to speak. He gave me the once over and was definitely not impressed. I was disappointed; I'd had a shave and all.

'This is the Sylvester Estate. Are you lost, pal?' I bet he graduated top of his class in one of those fancy charm schools.

'Bernie Zeebarb to see Mrs Sylvester.' I gave him one of my cards to look at and to see if he moved his lips while he read it. He didn't so I guess reading was a skill his charm school had left off the curriculum. I flipped the card back into the pocket of my waistcoat. Cards cost money. I don't give them away if I don't have to. And No Way was I giving one to this bum.

I watched him go through the painful process of thinking. Generally, I hate to see a man suffer but in his case I was willing to make an exception. I don't usually form instant dislikes but one thing I hate is being looked at like something the cat has vomited up on the kitchen floor.

'Yeah. OK. You can go up,' he said reluctantly. Like it made a difference to him. 'Don't leave the path.' He made a major production about opening the gates and gave me a smile like a hungry owl spotting a nice fat vole. He stood there watching me as I set off for the house. Probably checking I didn't steal any trees on my way.

I had been walking for five minutes and still hadn't caught sight of the house. But I was right about the lake. There it was through a break in the trees. I was watching the sunlight do sparkly things off the water when I saw the movement in the trees out of the corner of my eye.

At first it was just shadows flitting in the trees, nothing distinct. Then the leader broke out of the trees, paused to sniff the air and suddenly become very interested in yours truly. I've hated them ever since I was a kid and lived in the country. I hate the way they hunt in packs like feral children. I hate the way they howl in the moonlight when people are trying to sleep.

Wolves.

There must have been six or seven of them. A full pack with me as the Joker.

Maybe Sylvester got his jollies from having a pack of wolves roaming his park. Trophy pets of the very rich. Or maybe they weren't pets. Who needs fancy-schmancy security when you've got a wolf pack patrolling the grounds? An interesting problem in need of an answer. Right now.

If I made a break back down the path to the gatehouse they would easily out-run me and pull me down. Not a prospect that filled me with glee. On the other hand, I had no idea of how far or even where the main house was. Things looked less than good.

There was a beech tree near the drive. I was up it and hanging onto the highest branch I judged would take my weight faster than a squirrel with its tail on fire. Like I said, I lived in the country when I was a kid. We did stuff like that all the time.

The wolves snuffled round the tree for a bit, growling and yipping and glaring up at me. I'm sure there was some licking of chops at the prospect of nice, fresh Zeebarb but I didn't actually see it; I was too busy hanging on. After a while the wolves settled down around the tree in a circle and sat on their haunches watching me with those terrible yellow eyes.

It was a stand-off.

I was being paid by the day but, somehow, I didn't think that included hanging around in trees to amuse the pets. I tried shouting for help. Nix. I tried breaking off bits of the tree and flinging them at the wolves. They thought we were playing 'fetch' and kept bringing the branches back and wagging their tails.

After twenty minutes of crouching in the upper reaches of the tree I started to get cramp. I knew that all to soon the cramp would get the better of me and I would fall off my perch into a nightmare of yellow teeth and bloodied muzzles. I tried to think of all the really good things I had done with my life but couldn't come up with that many. Then I started to feel very sorry for myself and promised myself that if I survived I would become a new and better person.

I do that a lot when I find myself in a tight spot. I'm pleased to say the resolution lasts about as long as a resolution made at a New Year's party after strong drink had been taken.

Just as I was about to pitch to the ground in a bundle of knotted pain there was the blast of a whistle from the direction of the gatehouse. The wolves jumped up and loped off following the sound, just like good doggies.

That *ratfink* of a gatekeeper! That was the reason for his smile. He must have known the wolves would give me a hard time. What he couldn't have been sure of was me surviving the encounter. In my book that went down as attempted murder. Of me. That made it personal.

I dropped out of the tree and ran up the drive as fast as my legs could go in the opposite direction to the one the wolves had taken. I was beginning to pant and suck in lungfulls of air when I got to the fence. It was high, over six feet, and made of strong wire links and disappeared away to right and left into the trees. Sylvester obviously didn't want his pets roaming about unchecked near the house. I guess it wouldn't do his rep as a society host any favours if his guests got eaten while out for a moonlight stroll in the grounds (or a little illicit nooky in the summerhouse).

There was a gate with a latch across the road. I lifted the latch, went through and carefully shut the gate behind me.

At last I saw the house. It was a Spanish ranch-style rustic affair and then some. My entire neighbourhood could live comfortably in that house and never bump into each other. I walked up to the door and yanked on the bell pull. Somewhere deep inside a bell tolled.

I was beginning to think there was no-one home when the door opened. Standing in the doorway was a short, fat man wearing a green and yellow striped waistcoat and a natty pair of red trousers. On his feet he wore a pair of shoes with long points that curled back on themselves in a style fifty years out of date. No cigar for guessing this had to be the Major Domo.

I identified myself and was allowed to wait in the hall. Inside, the house was cool, even chill. Or maybe it was just the sweat drying on my body after my run up the driveway.

After a good wait the Major Domo rolled back into the hall. 'Sir and Madam will see you now. Please follow me.' He'd tried to sneak up on me but the flap-swish of his shoes gave him away. Judging by what I had seen so far, Sylvester sure like to employ wisenheimers with elevated ideas of their own importance. I wondered what they were like around the Class. Smarmy as hell. That type always are. Screw 'em!

He led me into a room the size of a football pitch. It had sofas the way other rooms had armchairs. Large, expensive (of course) carpets made floral islands on the floor giving the impression of walking through a meadow where you sank up to the ankles into the pile. There were painting on the wall, mainly of people who must have died a long time ago. Antique vases perched precariously on plinths. If ever there was a break-in at the City Museum this would be the first place I'd check out. At the far end of the room a fire burnt in a fireplace. I half expected to see scullions turning an ox on a spit in it. It was big enough.

Sylvester was standing in the centre of the room with his arm draped over his wife's shoulder. I felt a stab of jealousy in the pit of my stomach and had to give myself a stern talking to. She was way out of my league and married to boot. Still, that doesn't necessarily mean a broad is outta commission.

I had seen Sylvester's image in the papers many times and not just in the society pages but I didn't expect him to be so tall. He towered over me by a good three inches. He was lean and tanned by hours spent by his swimming pool or sailing on his lake and toned by time spent with a personal trainer in a gym. His dark hair was cut by a master and his fingernails glowed where they had been buffed up. He wore elegantly 'casual' clothes, purple chinos and a check golf shirt, that a designer had sweated over for hours to create the look.

Class, Money and Power – the magic Trinity.

He hiked over in my direction as the Major Domo announced me in his squeaky little voice, his hand thrust out to shake mine in his firm grip as if we were old friends.

'I'm *so* glad you could come, Mr Zeebarb,' he greeted me as if I were some house guest up for the weekend instead of hired help. Gracious. I liked that. It was an act but he didn't need to do it, 'Please.' He waved me in the direction of a convenient sofa. I plonked myself down and very nearly disappeared into its depths. Sylvester and his lovely lady wife sat gingerly on the edge of a sofa within hailing distance of me. Obviously, they knew their own furniture and were wary of it.

They held hands and she looked adoringly up at his face. A poster image of a happy marriage.

'I gather my wife told you everything this morning?' He raised his eyebrows at me to make sure I understood it was a question. I did. I'm quick like that.

'Yeah. I think so.' Just to make sure I did a recap of what she had told me earlier. He nodded along with the story to show that he agreed and was paying attention.

'We are both frantically worried,' he said when I had finished to his satisfaction. 'There has been no word, no new developments since my wife spoke to you. It's been…' He paused to consult a wafer-thin pocket watch which he conjured out of a pocket in his chinos '…nearly fifteen hours. Find my son for me, Mr Zeebarb and you will have a powerful and very grateful friend for the rest of your life.' A bit dramatic but I appreciated the sentiment.

'Yeah, well, I'll certainly give it my best shot.' If only for those baby-blues. But I thought it wiser not to tell *him* that. He might not understand.

Or then again, he *might* and I didn't want to make a powerful *enemy* for life.

'Please, Mr Zeebarb.' She spoke for the first time. The strain was showing on her. Her mouth was drawn and there was a suspicion of dark lines under her eyes.

'Can I see your son's room?' I asked to show that I was on top of the job and also to break the atmosphere that was building up like a storm front.

'There's nothing...' she started to say.

'Of course, if you think it will be useful,' Sylvester interrupted her smoothly. 'Come with me. I'll show you.' To his wife he said: 'You stay here, darling. I can manage.'

He led me out of the room and down about half a mile of corridors that seemed to twist and turn on themselves. Left to myself, I'd need a map to navigate my way. I wondered how the kidnapper or kidnappers had fared. Sylvester was explaining that he didn't want his wife going back into the Nursery as she became very upset. 'Hysterical' was the word he used. I thought that might be a little harsh but then again, I was biased.

The Nursery turned out to be a small suite of rooms, bright and sunny with murals of happy bunnies and pixies gambolling in the woods. Not good role models for a young child, I thought. In my experience pixies *always* cheat. Expensive toys that the child was far too young to play with littered the floor of the playroom. Sylvester led me to an adjoining room – Fairchild's bedroom. He assured me that nothing had been touched. The cot had the feather duvet thrown back. The window over the cot was open and the curtain fluttered uncertainly in a slight breeze.

I examined the window closely. It was a double window that opened into the room with a latch to close the two sides together. Just where the latch was I noticed marks consistent with someone forcing a thin strip of flexible metal up between the frames. So, that was the point of entry. I drew Sylvester's attention to it to let him know I was on the ball and earning my retainer.

The window was some two and a half feet from the ground. High enough for someone of average height to jump down from carrying a small child. Looking very carefully I could make out the two indentations where his heels had hit the ground. I pointed these out to Sylvester as well. I was on a roll.

'He came in here through the window, took your son and then jumped back out. The extra weight of the boy made him land heavily, as you can see, but apart from that he seems to have been careful not to leave tracks. What I'd like to know is how he got past your pets. They had me up a tree. Someone blew a whistle and they took a powder. Otherwise I'd've been doggie dinner.'

'Gilbert!' Sylvester exclaimed as if he had just discovered the secret of the Universe. 'I'm terribly sorry. Mr Zeebarb. He should never have allowed you to try and come up to the house by yourself. I shall speak to him about it myself.' The way he said that almost made me feel sorry for Gilbert. I'm pleased to say the feeling didn't last longer than a heartbeat.

Something nagged at the back of my mind, something I was missing.

Then I got it.

'Mr Sylvester, does Gilbert control those wolves?'

'What? Well, yes. He is responsible for the security of the estate. The wolves were his idea. I think he reared them from cubs. His father was a woodsman and Gilbert grew up in the forest. I think he rather ran wild.'

'Do they obey anyone else?'

He saw the way I was thinking and looked rattled. Sylvester was a smart cookie all right.

'No, Mr Zeebarb, they do not. He keeps them in a pen when the gardeners are working on the estate outside the fence.

'So, no-one could get in and out of the estate on foot if he didn't want them to?'

'That's right.' He was completely with me now. That's a strike for Zeebarb! I thought. We have a suspect!

'How do you and your lady wife and the servants move about if you want to leave the estate?'

'Have you ever heard of a motor car, Mt Zeebarb?'

'A what?' I had no idea what he was talking about.

'It's a very new invention. A carriage that is driven by an engine. A machine. There are not many in the world but I have one.' He sounded like a proud father. I wondered if he talked about his son with such pride in his voice. 'At present we just use it to drive around the estate. It's not perfected yet.' He laughed. 'In fact, it keeps breaking down so we can't use it for longer journeys, just to drive around the estate. But it will improve.' He dropped his voice to a confidential whisper.' In fact, I have shares in the company.' He winked at me. I might have been one of his cronies at his Gentleman's Club getting the low-down on a hot tip. I felt honoured. This was how life for the top people worked. Back scratching all round. 'But if we want to go on longer journeys, into Town, say, we still use the traditional horse and carriage combo. Gilbert keeps the wolves in so as not to frighten the horses. If the servants want to leave the estate the coachman takes them down to the main gate in the motor car as a treat. They can catch an omnibus not far down the road.'

'I think I'd like to ask Mr Gilbert some questions, Mr Sylvester.'

'I think you should,' he agreed. 'I'll have the coachman get out the motor car.'

Sylvester and I waited by the front door. He'd told his wife that we might have a lead and some of the strain had gone out of her face to be replaced by a look of hope that I did not share. Sure, I had a lead. But it was a slim one.

I heard a series of loud bangs like a barrage of musket fire and a cockamamie looking contraption hauled itself round the loop of the drive from the rear of the house where I guessed the coach-house and stables were located.

The back end of the thing resembled a normal carriage resting on a pair of high wheels but the front, where the horses should be, had a long metal snout resting on a pair of much smaller wheels. Wisps of black smoke were escaping from under the snout. A man stood on a narrow platform forward of the carriage holding onto what looked like a ship's steering wheel. He was flanked on both sides by large levers, whose function was totally beyond me but certainly looked impressive. I had never seen anything like it. Sylvester bestowed the smile of a proud father on me as the gizmo banged to a stop and the coachman leapt down to open the carriage doors.

'The wolves are terrified of it,' Sylvester informed me.

And that was another surprise: I never thought I'd have sympathy for a wolf.

Sylvester ushered me in and we sat down on the plush seats. The thing gave a bang and lurched slowly down the drive. I could have walked faster. We stopped at the gate in the fence while the coachman lifted the latch, climbed back onto his platform, lurched through, got down, closed the gate and climbed back to the controls. I could've happily taken a nap if it hadn't been for Sylvester chattering away trying to explain how his toy worked.

Like I could care less!

The coachman gave a blast from a foghorn. Any wolf within hearing distance would be heading for the hills.

So, it turned out, had Gilbert.

3

I questioned the other servants up at the house but they didn't know anything. But one of the gardeners, an old guy in blue trousers, red jacket and a floppy hat, mentioned a bar in Town where Gilbert sometimes hung out. I'd heard of it but had always given it a wide berth. The cops never went there less than twenty strong. It was that kind of bar – sawdust and teeth on the floor. Not promising but it was the only lead I had.

Sylvester laid on a carriage to take me back to Town. It was swell. I could very easily get used to this high living. Ah, who was I kidding? I couldn't say my life was a bundle of laughs but I rubbed along OK, all things considered. I was my own boss and as such I was prepared to cut myself a lot of slack. No 9 to 5 for me. Only thing was, the money could be better. And regular. That would be peachy.

I got the carriage to stop a couple of blocks away from the bar. It was the kind of neighbourhood where they play tag with hatchets and I didn't want to frighten the horses. I also didn't want to give the clientele of the bar any ideas by arriving in style. At the sight of a carriage and horses they'd be queueing up to mug me.

The name of the bar was *The George*, named after one of the Duke's ancestors whose idea of a political campaign to win the hearts and minds of the people was wholesale rape and murder. Politicians tend to be more subtle nowadays. Just. But I dare say they miss the Good Old Days.

I walked in through the batwing doors like I was a regular. The bar was a long, windowless, rectangular room. At the far end was a stage lit by a few spluttering candles. A girl was lethargically dancing on the stage. She wore a pair of scruffy high-heeled shoes and some tired feathers in her hair and that was her entire ensemble. She exuded a palpable air of boredom but then so did the two jerks who made up her audience.

The actual bar counter itself ran the length of one side of the room with booths for the discerning drinker. The tables and chairs were bolted to the floor. In the middle of the room stood a couple of pool tables. If you were lucky, you played on the table nearest the door where the light from the street allowed you to actually see the balls. Lack of clarity didn't seem to bother the trolls who were hunched over the stained baize, their glasses balanced on the table rims.

There were a handful of drinkers in the booths, leaning in to each other, their heads almost touching, discussing nefarious matters, shooting suspicious glances around the gloom. Hustlers in gaudy satin perched on barstools like vultures, waiting to pick up a John. *The George* rented rooms by the minute on the upper floor.

Nobody stopped talking when I came in. The trolls didn't pause in their games. No heads turned to stare at me, not even the hookers. It wasn't that kind of a place. They'd just ignore you until someone decided for some reason that they didn't like you. *Then* they'd stomp you. If you were lucky you might actually learn what you had done to cause offence as the paramedic loaded you into an ambulance.

I drifted over to the bar and hauled myself onto a barstool, ignoring the purring noise from the raddled old trout next to me. When the barman condescended to acknowledge me I ordered a shot. Hell, breakfast time had been long ago and I didn't remember drinking any. I sat and sipped and declined various interesting offers involving one on one, two on one and some kind of combo that involved the active participation of a goat. Finally, the message got though that I wasn't a punter and the girls gave up on me and went back to their glasses of neat gin and exchanging whore stories.

Noticing that my glass was empty and that I could be spending money, the barman sidled over to offer me another shot. I let him hit me with another and then said, real polite: 'Hey, maybe you can help me out.' I saw his guard go up, something came over his eyes like someone pulling down a steel shutter. Out of the corner of my eye I noticed that the pool games had stopped and that the trolls were standing very still.

I had to play this *very* carefully. I can handle myself pretty well when it comes to the rough stuff but I can also gauge the odds. They were definitely *not* in my favour.

'Yeah, I just blew in to Town. I been *away*. Know what I mean. I gave him a meaningful wink and made sure at least some of the pool players saw it. If he wanted to draw the conclusion that I had recently been a guest at the Duke's pleasure in the Big House, that was his right.

'Oh,' he grunted helpfully. Like this guy was a real conversationalist. A sympathetic ear for all your troubles. One of the world class barkeeps. Right!

'I'm trying to find Gilbert. I heard he's got a sweet little number up at some bigshot's spread.'

'Never heard of 'im.' *Of course* he hadn't. He probably deny his own name if asked.

'Sure you have,' I persisted. 'Frankie Fingers tol' me he always drinks in here.' Frankie Fingers was doing five full-tariff Life stretches up in the Big House and was never going to be in a position to call me a liar. But he was well respected by certain citizens of this burg and the hint that we might be acquainted carried a lot of weight.

Truth be known, I had only met him the one time while he was on the outside and that was when I was still on the city's payroll and investigating a series of homicides. Frankie was our prime suspect but we could never get the goods on him. People were terrified of him and would sooner eat their own tongues than grass him up. Even sheltering behind my badge and the whole Murder Squad he scared me more than any one person had the right to. He got his sobriquet from his habit of biting off the fingers of people who upset him. It was said we could never find any bodies because he ate his victims. Often before they were quite dead. Not a guy you would want to cross.

'You know Frankie?' asked the barkeep, a mixture of respect tinged with terror in his voice. I nodded. The pool game picked up where it had left off.

'What can I say? We, er, shared accommodation for a while. He tol' me you'd see me right, Whayne.' Using the name was a long shot but Whayne was a very common name around this part of Town.

'Hey,' he said quickly, 'Whayne's the night man. I'm Paulie.'

'Hi, Paulie,' I said and then clammed up, leaving the play to him. Let him mull it over for a while. I could almost hear the cogs grinding.

'Any pal of Frankie's is a pal of mine.' Yeah, I thought that might be the case.

'So?' I demanded and tried that trick with the narrowed eyes and the hard stare.

'Gilbert...?' He pretended to think but he didn't fool me. 'Gilbert, eh?' Dawning recognition crossed his face. He was wasted serving suds in this crummy bar. This kid had a brilliant future on the stage. 'He stays with some moxie over on Canard Avenue. Jillie, Julie. Some name like that.'

'Jennie,' said one of the hustlers, who'd been earwigging. So much for solidarity among the sorority!

'Know where I can find her?'

'Well...' she said, rubbing her fingers together. I kinda got the message what was expected. A note changed hands and I had the address. 'Sure there's nothing else I can do for you?' She shimmied her hips at me and made a production number out of licking her lips. 'You just out an' all.'

'I'll take a rain-check, sweetheart. Business before pleasure,' I told her and left.

4

Smack opposite Jennie's address on Canard was a bar/eatery with a long bow window onto the street. I sat and nursed a jar of suds while I eyed the comings and goings across the street. As a bar it was a step up from *The George* but that's not saying much. Here they probably changed the sawdust once a month. I watched a young bimbo go in and out of the gaff a couple of times. From the way she was dressed – bustier, stockings held up by suspenders, black velvet choker around her neck -I guessed she was Jennie.

To kill the time and to keep the beer company I forced down a plate of steak and fries. The menu claimed it was beef and who am I to argue. I'm no biologist. I was mopping up the greasy gravy when I saw Gilbert come out of the building looking shifty. I threw some money down on the table and hightailed it out of there after him.

It was dusk and the light was uncertain. Streetlights in this part of Town were non-existent. No sooner did the City install them than the locals smashed them, preferring to do their business in the anonymity of the dark. Pretty soon the City got the message and stopped wasting the taxpayers' money.

I kept pace with Gilbert on the other side of the street. He was a man on a mission, in a hurry to get someplace and was not taking a great deal of notice of fellow pedestrians.

We walked some ten blocks, heading downtown to a more salubrious commercial district where the lights *were* working and the crowds were thicker. The pavements were busy with working stiffs hurrying home, people doing a little shopping after work, guys drifting in to bars for a little R and R after a hard day on the treadmill, people waiting at the omnibus stops. I slackened my pace, hanging back while still keeping him in sight. Night was falling and soon the creatures of the night would come crawling out from under their stones to take over the streets from the upright citizens.

I wanted to talk to Gilbert alone. No witnesses. But I also wanted to see who he met as I was sure he was on his way to a meet.

I almost missed it.

I crossed over the street and tucked myself onto the flow of moving bodies about fifty yards behind him. Not close enough. I moved closer in. Thirty yards. I saw him barge into a citizen in the crowd, apologise or curse (I was betting on the latter), and keep on walking.

I thought nothing of it as I walked by the same man myself. He was a small, wizened gnome of a person wearing a sour expression and long, hooped-striped stockings of red and white that disappeared into his leather shorts. On his head was a hat with a turned-up brim and a large feather stuck in the hatband. Judging by his expression, Gilbert must have cursed him. I congratulated myself on winning the bet.

I hurried on. I could see Gilbert's head and shoulders but not the rest of his body but there was something different about his gait; some change in his posture. Most people wouldn't notice a thing like that but then, I'm not most people.

I pushed through the throng until I was within five feet of him. He was carrying a leather hold-all in his right hand and it was heavy enough to drag his shoulder down.

I spun around, searching for the feather in the hat but the

gnome was gone, lost in the crowd, the feather and the hat no doubt discarded now that the switch had gone down. Gilbert was now my best chance.

Just up ahead I saw the dark outline of the entrance to an ally. I drew up alongside of Gilbert just as we reached it. I pushed him, hard, sideways. He stumbled into the ally and I followed close on his heels.

I smacked him twice, hard, on the side of his head while he was off balance. I hit him for two reasons: first, to show him I meant business and to soften him up for later; and second, because the rat had let me walk into the wolf-pack. I don't forgive and forget things like that.

Gilbert was down on his knees, shaking his head to make the stars go away. I kicked him in the back and sent him sprawling onto his face. The floor of the ally was none too clean and I almost felt sorry for the sap. *Almost.*

'Hello, Gilbert. Remember me?' I asked.

He turned his head to look up at me and tried to get up. There was something very nasty smeared on his face and it didn't smell too good.

I gave him another sharp tap at the base of his spine with my steel reinforced toecap and he stayed down like a good boy who knows what's best for him. Just for good measure he gave a little whimper that cut no ice with me. I mean, *wolves!*

He had dropped the hold-all when he'd gone down. I stooped and picked it up and grunted with the effort. I was right. It was *heavy.* I opened it up while the hard-case lay in the filth and groaned. No sympathy from me, bub.

The hold-all was packed to the brim with what looked like drinking straws. The sort they serve you in upmarket, swanky bars so you don't have to wrap your kisser around the neck of the bottle. The thing was, they were made of gold. I extracted one and tossed it in my hand. Gold. I bit it. Gold. I bent it. Gold. No question. With this much moolah Gilbert was set to be on Easy Street for the rest of his life. Even if he lived to be five hundred years old.

'Who was the gnome, punk?' I snarled at him.

By way of a reply he suggested I should attempt to do something anatomically impossible.

I thought I had asked him politely and that my question did not deserve such a response. It was rude and uncalled for.

To underline my point, I gave him a kick in the ribs. I heard a rib snap with a loud report. Gilbert screamed and called me a name that was totally inaccurate to my gender.

Don't get me wrong, I abhor all forms of violence but, sadly, it's the only language some people understand. And I'm good at languages.

'We can do this the easy way,' I suggested, 'or the hard way. Makes no difference to me. Either way you'll end up talking and I'll get my fee. You ever see the "Interrogation Chamber" those guys Downtown have got? Uh-huh.' I gave him a demonstration shudder. I let him think about it. And the beauty of the thing was, I wasn't bluffing. I've still got friends on the Force that owe me a few favours, including Toby the Torturer, a man so skilled at his craft that he could wring a plausible confession out of inanimate objects. I could get Gilbert booked on any number of charges, no questions asked and lodged in for a session with Mr Pain. Frankie Fingers was the only crim I've ever heard about who didn't break after a round with Toby. That was what made him so scary.

Gilbert sensibly wised up.

'His name's Stiltskin,' he spat.

'What's the spiel?'

I let Gilbert drag himself to a wall and prop himself up. It seemed to help him think.

I'm good like that. A real humanitarian, me.

'I met him in a bar.'

'*The George*?' It didn't hurt to let him know I was on top of the game.

'Yeah, yeah. *The George*. He musta been asking around about me. Knew I was working up at the Sylvester place.' He paused to wipe some of the gunk off his face. I guess the stench must be getting to him.

'Go on.'

'He wanted to get in there. Asked me all about the security set-up. I told him about my wolves. Said no-one got in there without my say so.'

I resisted the urge to give him another kicking for re-kindling disturbing memories. Instead I said: 'So you offered to help him find a way in?'

He nodded and I could see the light of realization dawning in his eyes. He'd been had.

'Look, what did I know? I thought he just wanted to knock the place over. It's full of valuable stuff. Antiques an' art an' stuff. He said he'd make it worth my while and gave me a handful of gold straws as a down payment. He said I get a lot more after the job was done. I thought he was going to fence the gear and give me a cut.' He cast a look at the hold-all that lay open on the ground. 'I guess he wasn't after the loot,' he said ruefully. His tone changed to desperate pleading. 'I didn't know nothing about no kidnap. You gotta believe me. Hell, you know what you get if you kidnap from the Class.'

I did. I never understand why a hanging, drawing and quartering attracts so many spectators. It turns my stomach. I suppose that is the whole point of it. A lesson in retributive punishment. Yet the hot-dog sellers and the pickpockets rate a hanging over the attractions of a ball game for good business.

Funny old world.

Enough of pondering on the strange ways of the world. Back to the matter in hand.

'So why did you skip? Why did you try to kill me? Why didn't you just sit it out and play the innocent?'

'When the Sylvesters didn't immediately call in the cops, I figured something funny was going down. Like Stiltskin had some kinda edge. Then when Mrs Sylvester tol' me to expect you, I panicked. You've got a rep.' If he hoped to flatter me, he'd made a positive start. Then he went and spoilt it all. 'When I didn't see no blood on the wolves I figured you'd got out of it an' would be coming for me. I blew outta there. I'd done what Stiltskin asked and went for the pay-off.' He indicated the hold-all. 'An' he came through.'

I thought about his story; it hung together, sure enough.

'Where do I find Stiltskin?'

'I don't know.'

'The thing about those thumbscrews in the hands of a master like Toby,' I mused. 'What they can do to a knuckle...' I let it hang and gave his imagination time to work on the image.

'Look, Zeebarb, I'm levelling with ya. I only seen him the two times. Once in *The George* and jus' now. He tol' me to meet him here in the street for the pay-off when he was settin' the job up in *The George*. I don't know nuthin' more.'

His story rang true, Gilbert was strictly small potatoes, a necessary cog in the commitment of the crime. Stiltskin was clever, leaving no clue behind that could lead me to him. But he was wrong. I had a name and I had seen his face, even if ever so briefly. I could find him.

Before he saw it coming, I kicked him on the knee with those steel toe-caps to discouraging him from trying to follow me. I slung the hold-all over my shoulder and legged it out of the ally fast.

Criminals shouldn't profit from their crimes and cheap hoods like Gilbert shouldn't be allowed to keep their ill-gotten gains.

I heard him howl as I disappeared into the crowd.

Let him try to find me at my old address. I was rich and outta there.

Hello and welcome to the good life.

5

Very late that same night I rode a hackney Downtown to Police Headquarters. With my new-found wealth I could afford to pay the after midnight excess fare! Years of experience had taught me that the graveyard shift was the best time to get things done at Headquarters for a PI calling in favours. Very few cops were around and the civilians who shuffled the files and did the forensic work were safely tucked up with the Sandman. And so, I hoped, was police captain Ed Dickenson. He and I had had a disagreement about the way he was making his graft by putting the squeeze on widows and orphans. Don't get me wrong, all us cops at the time had side rackets – City pay was lousy but what he was doing was plain *dirty,* praying on the vulnerable and defenceless. The upshot was that I left the Force on the understanding that the City dropped the assault charges and I promised not to talk to any member of the fourth estate about what I knew. Right now, I *really* didn't want to bump into Dickenson. I might be tempted to hit him again.

I snuck into the imposing building by the side entrance used to sneak in prisoners away from prying eyes, slipped through a series of doors, up the back stairs and found the squad room I was looking for: the night shift of the Serious Crim Unit.

Through the fug of tobacco smoke I could make out half a dozen officers seated at desks scattered around the large room. Most had their feet up on their desks, reading the early editions of the papers, cigarettes burning in ashtrays. There was the aroma of coffee and sweat in the air. I breathed it in. Hell, I missed it.

'Bernie! Come to give yourself up,' a joker called out when he saw me.

'Hi, Mickey! How's it hangin'?'

'Zeebarb! Long time no see. Keepin' honest?'

"Bout the same as you, Jonesie,' I replied.

'Arrest that man! He's a crook!' Jones shouted and everyone laughed and crowded round me, patting me on the back and shaking my hand. Somebody gave me a cup of the disgusting coffee that cops drink and I sipped at it happily, lost in memories. Happy times.

We chewed the fat and kidded around for a while for old times' sake before we got down to business.

'I got a little present for youse guys,' I said. 'Maybe you can help me with a little problem that's buggin' me.' I pulled up my trouser cuff and fished half a dozen of the gold straws I had stuffed into my socks. I'm tough but I ain't stupid. If you're out and about on the streets at night it's only prudent to hide your portable valuables. I dished the straws out to the guys and they disappeared like magic. I didn't insult their intelligence by warning them to ask no questions.

'What can we do you for Bernie?' asked Mickey, a lad with a basic education but who knew the meaning of *quid pro quo* well enough.

'I'm trying to trace a joker called Stiltskin. A gnome. About yea high.' I held my hand up to indicate his size. About shoulder height to me. 'Fifty, sixty. Difficult to tell. Sour face, long, pointed nose. Drip on the end of it. Big hands. Wart under left eye.' Although I had only brushed past him in a crowd I have a *very* good memory for faces.

You gotta give these guys credit. When there is paid work to be done they just get right down and do it. And when are being paid by the City on top of the bung, they work twice as hard.

There was a result but it was bad news.

'He's political, Bernie,' O'Roark told me. He handed me a file with the toe rag's picture stapled to the inside cover. It was him, alright. The file held a single sheet of paper. On the paper was a name:

Stiltskin, Rumple

and the message, in large red letters

Political: Refer to Dept C

For those who don't know, Dept C is the law within the law. They have very few dealings with humble cops unless they need back-up bodies. They come and go in and out of Police Headquarters and answer only to themselves. Even the ordinary laws regarding the treatment of perps are suspended when it comes to Dept C. Even more suspended than for ordinary cops who know better than to kill their suspects. Someone arrested by Dept C may well never be seen again and heaven help you if you start asking dumb questions about suspects.

What could I do? Not a lot. I thanked the guys and left. Back to my royal suite in the best hotel in town. And the ministrations of a couple of high-class bimbos who would not have acknowledged that the scrubbers in *The George* were in the same business.

But no goats.

Call me an old fuddy-duddy.

6

What with one thing and another (I think her name was Lizzie) I didn't get a whole lot of sleep but I woke up early with that tired, smug feeling you get after a good workout in the gym. I was worried how Mrs Sylvester was holding up. It was thirty-six hours now since little Fairchild was snatched. And if was going to crack the case and earn my fee, I needed Sylvester's connections.

This time I hired a hackney to take me *all* the way to the front door of the house. There was a new man on the gate and I didn't see any signs of the wolves but I was taking no chances. I went through the same runaround with the Major-Domo and ended up in that same vast room.

She was sitting by the fire. The day was warm so I guess it was a comfort thing. She was very pale and there were black rings under those beautiful eyes that tore at my heart-strings. But she seemed to be holding up well. Tough *and* beautiful.

Her husband joined us, creeping up behind me silently and announcing his presence with a discrete cough.

'I know who snatched your son.' I came right out with it. No pussyfooting around. She gave a sort of gasp and sprang to her feet. Sylvester gripped my arm just above the elbow. His grip hurt, but I forgave him in the circumstances.

'Who?' she faltered, her hand fluttering to her mouth as if to catch the question.

'A low-life by the name of Stiltskin. Know him?'

I thought she was going to faint. Sylvester still had hold of my arm and his grip was cutting off the supply of blood to be done they just get right down and do it. And when are being paid by the City on top of the bung, they work twice as hard.

There was a result but it was bad news.

'He's political, Bernie,' O'Roark told me. He handed me a file with the toe rag's picture stapled to the inside cover. It was him, alright. The file held a single sheet of paper. On the paper was a name:

Stiltskin, Rumple

and the message, in large red letters

Political: Refer to Dept C

For those who don't know, Dept C is the law within the law. They have very few dealings with humble cops unless they need back-up bodies. They come and go in and out of Police Headquarters and answer only to themselves. Even the ordinary laws regarding the treatment of perps are suspended when it comes to Dept C. Even more suspended than for ordinary cops who know better than to kill their suspects. Someone arrested by Dept C may well never be seen again and heaven help you if you start asking dumb questions about suspects.

What could I do? Not a lot. I thanked the guys and left. Back to my royal suite in the best hotel in town. And the ministrations of a couple of high-class bimbos who would not have acknowledged that the scrubbers in *The George* were in the same business.

But no goats.

Call me an old fuddy-duddy.

6

What with one thing and another (I think her name was Lizzie) I didn't get a whole lot of sleep but I woke up early with that tired, smug feeling you get after a good workout in the gym. I was worried how Mrs Sylvester was holding up. It was thirty-six hours now since little Fairchild was snatched. And if was going to crack the case and earn my fee, I needed Sylvester's connections.

This time I hired a hackney to take me *all* the way to the front door of the house. There was a new man on the gate and I didn't see any signs of the wolves but I was taking no chances. I went through the same runaround with the Major-Domo and ended up in that same vast room.

She was sitting by the fire. The day was warm so I guess it was a comfort thing. She was very pale and there were black rings under those beautiful eyes that tore at my heart-strings. But she seemed to be holding up well. Tough *and* beautiful.

Her husband joined us, creeping up behind me silently and announcing his presence with a discrete cough.

'I know who snatched your son.' I came right out with it. No pussyfooting around. She gave a sort of gasp and sprang to her feet. Sylvester gripped my arm just above the elbow. His grip hurt, but I forgave him in the circumstances.

'Who?' she faltered, her hand fluttering to her mouth as if to catch the question.

'A low-life by the name of Stiltskin. Know him?'

I thought she was going to faint. Sylvester still had hold of my arm and his grip was cutting off the supply of blood to my hand. I pulled myself free, ready to catch her if she went down. Sylvester's face was set, like it was made out of poured concrete. His expression made me glad I was not in Stiltskin's pointy shoes. Something very nasty lay in store for Mr Stiltskin if Sylvester caught up with him. I repeated my question.

'No,' replied Sylvester firmly. 'Should I?'

'Mrs Sylvester?' I asked, ignoring him for the moment.

'I…I'm not sure.'

'Darling?' Sylvester lost his composure for a moment. I saw something flash in his eyes. What might be buried in his wife's past? I wondered then, for the first time, about her back story. He was a straight-A blue-blood, that I knew. But her?

'No, of course not.' She straightened her back and looked him in the eyes. 'I don't know anyone of that name.' He seemed relieved to hear it.

'And where is my son, Mr Zeebarb,' he asked.

'Ah, that's the problem. I know *who* took him but I don't know *where* he is being held. There is a problem you can help me with, Mr Sylvester.'

'Anything. Name it.'

'I saw a police file on Stiltskin.' I held up a hand to ward off any questions. 'Don't ask me how. I just did. The file was marked "Political". Have you ever heard of Dept C?'

'Isn't that some sort of branch of the police that keeps an eye on disaffected anti-social elements?'

Yeah, I thought, you would say that if you were a member of the ruling elite and were above the messy little details of how your life of privilege was sustained against any whispers of opposition.

'Something like that,' I agreed.

'What about this Dept C?'

'Basically, Mr Sylvester, you have two options. You can hand over what I've found out to the regular cops or even Dept C. They'll listen to you.' Of course they will: his uncle ran the whole kit and caboodle. 'Or you can clear the way for me to have a look at the Stiltskin file and trust me to finish the job.'

He mulled it over for a moment, came to a decision and asked me to leave the room. The Major Domo left me hanging about in the hall like a spare Christmas ornament. If ever he needed a job after I'd laundered my new-found wealth I'd be happy to give him one. Just to give myself the pleasure of firing him.

After ten minutes they called me back into the salon. She was back sitting by the fire, her head nestled in her hands, her shoulders slumped, in an attitude of defeat. I guessed they had been doing some hard talking. I wondered what she had told him. By now I had figured out that she knew more about this whole thing than she had let on to me.

'I think, Mr Zeebard, that it might be a good idea for you and I to pay a visit to Police Headquarters,' Sylvester informed me.

I nodded and waited to see which way he had decided to play it.

'I'll get you access to that file.'

It took him a couple of hours to get but get it he did. I waited for him in a ritzy place downtown near Police Headquarters. To pass the time I tucked into a steak as big as my head and a bottle of something so good I didn't believe it could come out of squished grapes. All on Sylvester's dollar. I *really, really* could get used to this.

He came in and slid the file across the table to me. He didn't say a word as he did so but he looked mighty troubled. I guess now he'd been putting two and two together and didn't like the number they added up to.

I'd never seen an actual Dept C rap sheet before but if this was a typical example they were masterpieces of laconic prose. The file consisted of a single sheet of paper in a red cardboard folder. It had Stiltskin's name printed on the outside. I opened the file and read the page. It took me all of ten seconds to read it, but then, I'm a careful reader and pay attention to details.

Name: Stiltskin, Rumple
Nature of Offence: Counterfeiting
Sentence: Indefinite detention
Last known address: Straylingdorf Forest
Known associates: Alice Corbulo

'Mean anything to you, Mr Sylvester?'

He shook his head but he wouldn't look me in the eye. That set alarm bells ringing in my mind.

'What now, Mr Sylvester? Still want me to keep at it?'

'Yes.'

'And no cops?'

'No. Leave the Police out of this.'

'What about the pussy cats in Dept C?'

'They have been notified of the circumstances and have been advised to take no action for the moment.' He gave me a straight look and I saw Power burning in his eyes. I felt a sudden chill in the room but none of the other diners seemed to notice. I realised that Sylvester was not a man to cross. Mr Nice Guy was a mantle he wore when it suited him that could be shucked off if the situation warranted. I had been frightened by Frankie Fingers but compared to Sylvester Frankie was just a school-yard bully.

'So, how come this low-life is on the lam?' I tapped the file with my finger. 'It says 'Indefinite Detention' here.'

'He bribed a warder to help him escape. That warder no longer has a job.'

Or a life, I thought. I felt that chill again.

'Straylingdorf Forest is a pretty big place,' I pointed out. 'It's going to take me a good while to check it all out.'

'The officers from Dept C have been busy searching for him since his escape. They've narrowed the search area down.'

'Are they still searching the Forest?'

'Not any more. I asked them to give you twenty-four hours. I didn't go into any details as to why you were searching. They don't need to know.'

'And if I don't find Fairchild in time?'

'Then they go back on the case. I don't want that to happen. Mr Zeebarb. Find my son for me before that.' There was a threat implicit in his words: 'or else'. I didn't like the sound of that one little bit.

'Yeah, well. Sitting around here ain't gonna get that done.' I dabbed at my lips with my napkin and pushed my chair away from the table. Ready for action!

'Precisely.'

As we walked to his carriage he filled me in on what Dept C had told him about their search for Stiltskin. They had been working their way methodically into the Forest from the outside. Straylingdorf Forest was a pretty scary kind of a place. There were no roads through it, only around it. People didn't venture in there unless they *absolutely* had to. What with the wolves and the bears and the odd desperado outlaw like Wilfred and his Happy Band it was not the most welcoming environment for your average Joe Citizen.

I was brought up in the country in somewhere very similar. It's where I learnt to give wolves a wide berth. I didn't relish the idea of going in there but I was going to do it. For her.

I didn't think she could hang in the game much longer; I had seen the strain she was under.

7

I went back to my office to pick up my equalizer from the bottom drawer of my desk. I don't often carry a gun but it would be dark by the time I got to Straylingdorf Forest and no way was I going in without some degree of protection. Did I mention wolves and bears and bad guys? I also picked up a bull's eye lantern to light my way with a focused beam. Next, I visited a man I know and bought a short machete which I carried wrapped in a cloth under my arm.

I found a cabbie who was prepared to take me as far into the Forest as we could go at night. It cost and arm and a leg but, what the hell, I was on expenses and Sylvester could pop for it. It was loose change to him.

It was very nearly dark when the cabbie dropped me off in the Forest. No sooner had money changed hands than he was off back to the city like his horse was a contender for the 2.15 Breeder's Cup. I figured I had about five miles to cover, say two to three hours along game tracks. I lit the lantern and unwrapped the machete. The gun was tucked into my belt, within easy reach. I practiced my quick-draw technique a couple of times to make sure it didn't snag.

I set off down the track using the machete to blaze a trail on the trees and to clear away hampering undergrowth in case I had to beat a hasty retreat. Generally, I have a good sense of direction but the darkness in the Forest was almost total. The canopy overhead blotted out any light from the moon and stars, which didn't help matters.

I only had the vaguest of notions where I was going. If it

was easy Dept C would have already apprehended Stiltskin. I knew the general area where they had yet to search and it lay deep in the bowels of the Forest. That's where I was headed to conduct my own sweep. It promised to be a long night. I promised myself not to think about the wolves. The bad guys I could handle. I was probably on first name terms with most of them after my time on the Force.

Two hours of exploration later I was roughly where I wanted to be. Whenever there was a break in the tree cover I orientated myself by the stars as best I could. I was brought up in the country, remember.

The outlaws must have figured that no-one in their right mind would be wandering around the Forest in the dead of night and had all gone to bed. I frightened up a deer a couple of times that went crashing off through the trees and the night birds hooted at me to complain I was scaring away their supper with the noise of my passage. But, all things considered, I made good time.

It was the light that gave him away.

That and the singing.

I was edging carefully along a track that, for a change, was clear of undergrowth and brambles when I saw the gleam of light through the trees. I immediately killed the light from my lantern and hooked it onto my belt, leaving my hands free. I might never have found this place in the daylight. I could see a little hut made out of woven branches that blended perfectly into the background tangle of vegetation. He had a small fire going inside the hut and the light was flickering through the gaps in the weave. He was crooning some song in a high, cracked voice.

Moving as stealthily as I could, I circled the little clearing. It took me fifteen minutes as I moved slow and quiet. I used the light from his fire as I felt for tripwires fixed to alarms. Nothing: he was an amateur.

Gradually I made out the words. It was not so much a song, more a litany of words:

Oh they won't find us here, my dear
Safe and snug in the forest.
She thought she could cheat me,
Yes she did,
Yes she did!
But now who's the sorriest?
She is!
She is!

Right, I thought. Here's another of life's walking wounded. If he were a political party he'd be ten votes short of a majority.

I got down onto my belly and crawled up to the hut, hoping I wouldn't bump into any snakes on the way, and peered through a gap in the foliage. It was him alright – the gnome I'd seen do the switcharoo number with Gilbert. He was prancing around the fire rocking a baby in his arms. His crazy crooning was not my idea of a lullaby but the kid must've liked it well enough because he was fast asleep.

I didn't think a whole lot to his idea of interior decoration either. There was your basic dried grass on the floor and two nests of grass, moss and ferns by way of a bed and a crib and of all things, an old-fashioned spinning wheel. Maybe he was some kind of eccentric antique collector.

And, oh yes, did I mention the pile of gold?

There it was just heaped up casually in the corner reflecting the firelight and minding its own business. With that much gold to hand, I didn't see why he wasted his time counterfeiting. Maybe it was his hobby.

Time to do what I was being paid to do.

I worked my way to what might pass for a doorway, got to my feet and burst my way in, the machete in hand to show I meant business and was no slouch.

He froze in mid-caper. His face showed disbelief rather than fear.

'The jig's up, pal. Give me the kid!' I shouted. Not full of the social niceties I know but direct and to the point.

'NO,' he screamed. 'He's mine. She promised me.' He clutched the sleeping kid tightly to his scrawny chest. The kid woke up and started crying. I was worried that the racket would stir up who knows what unpleasantness. Just now the last thing I wanted was any aggravation. I just wanted to get the job done and get back to the nice, safe city with its dark alleyways and muggers. Sylvester hadn't said anything about me taking Stiltskin in. I figured my job was to get the kid back safe to his parents. That's what I had been hired to do. Let Dept C reap the glory for capturing their counterfeiter.

'Cool it. Just give me the kid and I'll be outta here.'

'We had a bargain,' he whined. 'She said her firstborn would be mine.' His eyes were going wild, darting from side to side. Saliva flecked his lips. A real live wire. He stamped his little feet in a paroxysm of rage. '*We had a bargain! I spin the gold!*'

I saw him tense up, ready to make a move on me. I moved in first. I dropped my machete and palmed his chin with my left hand. With my right I grabbed at the kid.

He was off balance and started to fall, flung out an arm instinctively and lost his grip on the kid, who was now exercising his lungs to their full extent.

When he hit the floor, I was holding the baby and moving back out of the hut.

He sort of bounced and started to come back at me, shrieking like a banshee.

There was a flash and a roar that nearly ruptured my eardrums.

Stiltskin was in a much worse state: the top of his head was splattered against the wall of the hut.

'I'll take my son now,' Sylvester said.

At least, I think that's what he said. My ears were still ringing from the gunshot.

'I thought I heard something behind me.' I said as I handed over the screaming child to his loving father. 'I'm glad it was you and not a pack of wolves.'

'You didn't really think I would want to miss the kill, did you?'

'I didn't think there *was* going to be a kill.'

'That creature stole my child. He deserved to die.

I bit my tongue. I still have old-fashioned ideas about the due process of the law. But I kept forgetting. This guy *was* the law.

'What did he mean about a bargain?'

'Why don't you fill your rucksack with gold?' he said, neatly sidestepping my question. 'Think of it as a bonus. What you can't carry will go to the Exchequer.' Less, I was pretty sure, a recovery fee for one F. Sylvester. You can never be *too* rich

I did just that.

I know when not to ask any more fool questions.

8

Together the three of us made it back to the edge of the Forest without being mugged or eaten. Baby Fairchild quietened down in his father's arms and eventually fell asleep again. I guess the man had a way with children.

I tried to pump Sylvester once or twice on the way back for the story. It wasn't important anymore but I was curious and I hate loose ends. He wasn't playing ball and just clammed up on me. I resigned myself to never knowing the truth. Maybe it was just as well. I didn't want the sweeties from Dept C knocking on my door one day. Not now that I was a solid citizen with a stake in the good life.

With all the gold I had distributed about my person, I could hardly walk. Hell, better it went to me, a deserving citizen than to the State. They'd probably waste it building an orphanage for foundling children.

Sylvester had a carriage waiting. He must have had me followed to know where the hackney had deposited me.

It was dawn when we got back to the city and the early birds were stirring in search of that elusive worm. I realised I would never have to work again, what with the gold I picked up from Stiltskin's liar and what I had relieved Gilbert of earlier. This caper had set me up on easy street for the rest of my life.

Sylvester had his coachman drop me off outside my hotel. The hotel doorman sprang to open the door of the carriage for me, yanking at his forelock in the approved manner.

'My wife and I thank you once again, Mr Zeebarb.' Sylvester murmured as I went to get out. 'I doubt we will meet again in person but I will arrange to have your fee sent to this hotel. Is that in order?' So those were my marching orders. The Help was not to pester the Class. 'I know I can rely on your discretion in this matter.'

Was that a threat veiled I velvet or was I imagining things?

'Yeah. Glad it all turned out OK and the little boy is safe.' Except it didn't turn out so well for Stiltskin.

Sylvester shook my hand, gave the word to his coachman and clattered off to his mansion to tell his distraught wife the glad tidings.

I dragged myself off to the joy of my feather matress and a new life of wealth and ease.

9

A month later I was back at work in my old, crummy office. I didn't *need* to work. Hell, if I declared my wealth up-front to the Taxman I'd be listed in Fortune 500. But I'd probably be locked up in an expensive sanitorium for the hopelessly stupid. I wasn't about to go flashing it around. Those guys from the Tax Office can get mighty nosey and had a tenacity to investigate that made Dept C seem like rank amateurs. They got paid by results.

I set up lots of nice little accounts and investment portfolios with company addresses far away overseas with boards of directors who existed only in my imagination and sat back to watch my money grow.

I moved to a better neighbourhood, nothing too flash and bought myself (through an off-shore shell) a pleasantly modest town-house that had hot and cold running water and absolutely *no* running rats. Then I partied hard for a fortnight without stopping and suffered a two-day hangover when I did stop.

And then I got bored.

I missed the life.

It came as a shock to me. I'd always figured I was cut out for the life of an idle rich playboy but I soon found out the *idle* part of being idle rich was a drag. Even the idle rich find things to do. Often it involves making more money; sometimes it involves finding ways of giving it away.

So here I was, back doing the only thing I knew how to do.

But there was a difference. Now I had a secretary/receptionist/dogsbody. Although her *body* was all girl. Curves in all the right places. That first day when she started working for me I kept inventing reasons for her to come into my office just so I could look at her. But I just looked in admiration. No way did I want a sexual harassment suite filed against me. I'm a modern liberated man, me.

And then a week after I opened up again *she* showed up. The secretary/receptionist/dogsbody announced her and she waltzed into my office like the sun outshining the moon.

'Mr Zeebarb. I was in town and just wanted to call in and thank you personally for what you did for us.'

'It was my pleasure, Mrs Sylvester. Or may I call you Alice?'

'What?' A worried expression had crept into those lovely blue eyes.

'Mrs Alice Sylvester. Nee Corbulo. I'm on the button, aren't I?

She sipped at her coffee. That's another good thing about having a secretary/receptionist/dogsbody. I make lousy coffee.

'How much *do* you know, Mr Zeebarb?'

'I know some. I'd like to know the rest. Tie up the loose ends. I'm kinda curious. It's like an itch. I need to know the facts.'

'This goes no further?'

'With your husband's connections? I want to stay free and I kinda like breathing.'

'I owe you my son's life, Mr Zeebarb. If my story repays that debt I think we are even and quits.'

'Yeah, we'll call it quits.'

'When I was much younger I was poor. Really poor. My family lived on a tiny smallholding. We scratched a living off the land but it was a bare existence at best. I hated it. I wanted better. I'd do anything to escape and I mean *anything*. My father knew Rumple Stiltskin. I don't know how. Even then he lived in the Forest. I think he was happy there. He didn't get on with people, as a rule.'

'Go on,' I encouraged.

'He had this amazing ability. He could spin straw into gold. He could have been fabulously rich but he wasn't interested in money. He lived a very simple life, all alone. But the one thing he *did* want was a son. Not a wife – he could have had any woman he liked with his wealth, even though he was not exactly what you might call handsome.'

I could think of any number of dames who would overlook a little thing like that in return for a life of utter luxury. The ladies of *The George* for a start.

'Anyway,' she continued, 'I got this crazy idea. I wrote to the Duke and told him that *I* could spin straw into gold. Of course, he didn't believe me.'

'Who would,' I agreed.

'So, I got the Duke to supply me with a bundle of straw and took it to poor Rumple. He'd always had a soft spot for me ever since I was a little girl. Like I said, he didn't have many friends and our family was the nearest thing he had to a family of his own. Long story short, he spun it into gold and I presented it to the Duke. The next thing I know the Duke has shut me up in the Castle with a whole *bale* of straw and a spinning wheel. He said I had two options: one spin it into gold and be well rewarded for my efforts or, two, be executed for wasting his time. Nobody, me least of all, had thought it through. If I could spin straw into gold why would I involve the Duke? I was in a fix.'

'I'll say.' I could picture it. A girl from the boondocks

desperate to get out and willing to risk everything for a better life. Why didn't she just get good ol' uncle Rumple to whip her up the odd haystack of gold baffled me. I asked her about it.

'He wouldn't do it. Just flat out refused. All he wanted was a son.' She blushed. It was cute. My heart went out to her. 'I don't think he could have one in the normal way.' So, she had considered it, then. Of course she had. She was desperate.

'So, you made a deal. If he spun you out of trouble you'd be set up tight with the Duke. The *quid pro quo* was that you'd give him a son as and when you produced one.'

'Something like that,' she admitted. 'You see, I didn't just want money, I wanted a position in society. That was what the Duke offered. I was to marry his nephew. It was the dream catch of a lifetime for me and as far as the Duke was concerned, it bound me to the ruling house where he could keep an eye on me. And we love each other.' She sounded almost surprised at this unplanned outcome. Stranger things happen.

'Anyway, I smuggled Rumple into the palace. He spun the gold but the Duke got greedy. He put me in another room with more straw. Rumple helped me again. Then the Duke made me do a repeat performance, only this time he spied on me. He saw Rumple at work and had him arrested when he finished the job. The Duke realised that Rumple could destroy the entire economy of the Dukedom. He could make gold valueless. He had Rumple shut up in prison, safely out of circulation.'

'Right. I can see that the Duke might have concerns.'

'But the Duke kept his bargain with me. He made me promise on pain of something nasty never to speak of or to Rumple again. I married Faunus and in due time we had a baby.'

'And somehow Stiltskin got to hear of it and wanted his side

of the deal. I guess he bribed is way out of jail.'

'I think so. But I couldn't give Fairchild up. He's my baby.' A tear graced her eye.

'Did your husband know all about this?'

'No. At least, not everything. He knew I had made the Duke very rich. Some of the money came with me as a dowry. He didn't know anything about Rumple and the agreement we had.'

'But when he saw the Dept C file on Stiltskin with your maiden name on it, he put it all together.'

'Yes. His uncle must have told him some of it.'

And now Stiltskin is dead and you've got your baby back and everything is tickety-boo.'

'Yes,' she said and smiled the smile of a girl from the boonies who was willing to do *anything* to get out and stay out. For a fleeting moment I wandered just *whose* idea it was to have Sylvester follow me into the Forest and blow Stiltskin's head off.

'I love a happy ending' she said as she walked out of my office. She paused by the door and winked at me.

I never saw her again.

The Fabulous and Wonderful Frowla

1

'The very *worst* thing that could happen to us,' said Snatterjee, 'is that we could be killed.'

The Frog gave his companion a *look* out of the corner of his eye. There were many and varied ways of being killed and from what he had heard, he didn't fancy any of them, thank you very much indeed. The Frog was not an actual amphibian as such, it was just that he exuded a certain air of froggishness. Perhaps it was the wide mouth, the tongue that flicked over his lips, the slightly bulging eyes (in his defence, it can be argued that they bulged no more than the eyes of your average sociopath on a murder rampage). And while it was true that he had been known to eat the occasional fly, that could be ascribed to absent mindedness. Neither his hands nor his feet were unduly webbed. Just what it was that about him that conjured up the impression of a green croaker was hard to define but was an unfailing first impression on everyone he met.

'You don't know the Houmjars as well as I do,' replied The Frog, who had come to terms with his nickname almost to the extent that he had forgotten the name given him by his parents. 'Being killed might just be the best thing that could happen to us. And if being killed is going to be the best thing to happen to us, you can count me out! It's not my idea of a bundle of laughs.'

'Have you ever met a Houmjar?' Snatterjee demanded, his tone heavy with scepticism. Where The Frog was prone to a certain squatness, Snatterjee was tall and thin with a shock of ginger hair standing upright on his head. He reminded people of a pencil, crowned with an eraser. He had put it about that he was related to the Bunyip on his great-great-great *grandmother's* side but was never believed. Snatterjee's more indulgent friends reckoned amongst themselves that he had invented the story to account for some of his more bizarre habits and to make himself more interesting to girls.

'No…' answered The Frog cautiously, 'but I *have* heard an awful lot of awful stories about them. And,' he added defiantly, 'I've lived on the edge of Sloo Swamp a lot longer than you!'

'Humph,' Snatterjee grunted, as he always did when a snappy and crushing riposte failed to come to mind. He shuffled about a bit and looked up at the sky for want of something better to do. The clouds that rolled (actually, oozed might be a more accurate description) out from the interior of Sloo Swamp always had a sickly greenish tinge to them. This was said to be caused by the reflection of the endless miles of slime, spirogyra and sphagnum that covered most of the swamp. From the position of the miserable looking sun, he guessed that the evening was on the point of packing it up for the day.

'I suggest we make camp,' he said to The Frog, scratching his chin with an incredibly long, dirty and horny fingernail.

'*Here?*' said The Frog in a tone that suggested his companion was not quite all there in the marbles department. 'You mean "here", as in right where we are? Here?'

'Well, where would *you* recommend?' demanded Snatterjee, fixing The Frog with a baleful stare from his yellow eyes. 'Going on into Sloo Swamp in the dark, perhaps?'

The Frog let the sarcasm flow off his back. 'How about turning right around and going back the way we came? There was a nice little inn a bit back. You remember?'

'Oh, yes. *The Gibbeted Ferret*. I'd prefer to take my chances in the Swamp.'

'I thought it was rather nice. Rustic. Unspoiled.'

'Unspoiled! Unspoiled? There was nothing there to spoil in the first place. The food was inedible, the beer was sour, it was crawling with vermin, the landlord was a miserable devil who was about as jolly as a week-old corpse and the two other customers who were mad or desperate enough to be in there must have been on the run for some years by the look of them.'

'I liked it.'

'Yes, you would. That's your idea of the high life, isn't it? I mean, that's where you'd go for a good night out. And you worry about the Swamp and the Houmjars?'

The Frog took this chiding to heart and went and squatted down in an untidy heap by the edge of the Swamp, sulking. It was not, he reflected, his fault that he had never had the opportunities in life to better himself and he thought it most unfair for Snatterjee to throw his lack of *savoir-faire* in his face. He squatted and muttered and listened to the sounds of the Swamp mud sucking and oozing and the strange shrill, chittering cries of the Swamp Madgers (which were the only creatures desperate enough – apart from the Houmjars- to live in Sloo Swamp).

(*Swamp Madger* (n) a small six legged mammal that lives in Solo Swamp. It uses its long, bushy tail as a blanket.)

He was definitely NOT HAPPY.

Snatterjee shrugged his shoulders and stoically got on with the task of pitching camp for the night. The sun, having resolved to go, was not hanging about. Snatterjee was aware that twilight didn't last long in this part of the world and he was very anxious to have his bed set out before darkness fell. Snatterjee knew it to be an incontrovertible fact that nasty things that went bump in the night could never get you once you were safely tucked up with the covers pulled up to your chin. He shouted to The Frog to help but was ignored while The Frog was having a lovely time sulking and ignoring the world. Muttering vague threats in The Frog's direction, Snatterjee started to unload their backpacks and fuss about erecting the tent.

By the time he succeeded in erecting their heavily patched tent dusk had indeed fallen.

The Frog stirred himself out of his sulk to inquire about the status of supper, the rumblings of hunger in his fat little tummy drowning out the whine of the maggot of anger writhing in his brain.

'We might have had a fire going,' Snatterjee snapped at him,' if you could have been arsed to go and look for kindling. But, oh no, not The Frog. Heaven forfend *you* do any work. I'll just sit here and sulk, shall I, while poor Snatterjee toils away for the both of us.'

His sulk forgotten, The Frog was magnanimously willing to forgive and forget. 'Right,' he said, 'I'll just pop off now and see what I can rustle up.'

The barren fringes of Sloo Swamp was not an environment rich in multicellular flora, slime being the vegetation of choice. However, The Frog did find a patch of gnarled and twisted, black, leafless bushes that grew to the height of about a metre. The Frog, who could see surprisingly well in the crepuscular gloom, shuffled his way over to the nearest clump and broke off a branch. At once, a foul stench filled the air. Snatterjee was reminded of a very dirty henhouse stuffed with unwashed socks, angry skunks and old fish. All this during a heatwave for good measure. He gave a little choking gasp and pinched his nostrils tight shut with the fingers of one hand while clamping the other hand over his mouth to stop himself retching. The smell was unpleasant.

To his horror, he heard The Frog snapping away at other branches and marvelled yet again at his companion's insensitivity to all things truly disgusting.

'Frog…' he gasped, his voice muffled and distorted.

'Is that you?' called The Frog.

'Yiz.'

'Then why are you talking funny?'

'Iz de smell.'

'Smell?' asked The Frog in all innocence.

'Dose bushiz. Dey shtink.'

The Frog considered this for a moment. 'They do niff a bit,' he conceded. 'That's why they are called Bog Bushes. They say you get used to the pong in a couple of hours. Me, I don't see what all the fuss is about. Doesn't worry me at all. Some finicky, picky people say that you can taste just a teeny taste on your food if you use Bog Bush to cook with but I can't say I've ever noticed. S'pose it depends on what your cooking. Probably improve Swamp Madger. Besides, the smoke is good for keeping insects away. It stuns 'em in mid-air,' he informed Snatterjee as he returned to the camp with a bundle of branches cradled in his arms and mere inches from his nose.

'Gah,' said Snatterjee as the full force of the Bog Bush's odour struck him. 'I'm going to be…' But it was too late and he threw up behind the tent. That helped. A bit.

Somehow, The Frog had got a fire going with bright green

flames leaping high into the night and was rummaging around in a pack for food.

Earlier in the day they had come across a Zingba (*zingba (n)* a creature very like a goat but only the size of a large hare) that was clearly unwell. The Frog had been all for eating it there and then but Snatterjee had insisted on killing it first and then skinning it and keeping it for their evening meal if nothing better turned up. And nothing had.

Zingba, when casseroled in red wine, a clove of garlic, a bay leaf or two, a little thyme, rough sea salt, black pepper, shallots, carrots, thinly sliced potato, a dash of tomato paste, slow cooked and served with fresh crusty bread, can be delicious. Eaten half-alive and raw it is *not* so good as it tends to be tough, noisy and the fur gets stuck between your teeth and tickles your throat on the way down. The Frog had had to console himself with a quick snack of raw Zingba liver while Snatterjee wrapped the rest of the carcass in fresh leaves and popped it into his pack.

And now a food-maddened Frog was rummaging through the pack, hurling its contents aside in search of his dinner. With a triumphant cry he drew the dead Zingba forth and tossed it straight onto the fire, racking the ashes over it.

The Frog danced in a half-crouch, half-shuffle around the fire uttering disturbing grunts for the whole three minutes he judged was needed to cook the Zingba. The he snatched it out of the fire, burning his fingers in his haste, tore it apart and offered a barely singed leg to Snatterjee while sucking up the juices from the remainder of the creature.

Snatterjee, all appetite long fled, disappeared behind the tent to void the contents left in his stomach. The sound of his heaves in no way diminished The Frog's enjoyment of his dinner.

Doubled up, groaning and feeling utterly wretched, Snatterjee cursed the fate that had teamed him up with his uncouth guide. Were it not for the lure of the Fabulous and Wonderful Frowla he would chuck in this quest and go back to his Gyroscope, Salt Pork and Amber Curios Emporium in the exceedingly pleasant and civilized town of Minfadlek.

As it was, he had Fallen Foul to Frowla Fever.

2

It all started with an overheard conversation, furtive whispers between two strangers seated in a dark corner table in John's Frothy Cocoa Shop. As the great foaming flagons of frothy cocoa were rushed to thirsty customers by the smiling (and sweating) Beverage Beauties in their flat wooden clogs, their ornate rainbow-hues hairstyles and their charming lack of clothing, Snatterjee and his friend Two-Fingers Earnold sat quietly earwigging.

'I tell you, he's just come from there,' hissed one of the men. He was hunched up under a long black cloak and wore a floppy black felt hat pulled down low over his face and could not look more suspicious if he tried. The other, dressed exactly the same as his drinking companion except for the thigh-length fisherman's waders that he wore rather than the silver platform-heeled shoes favoured by the other, clapped a hand over his companion's mouth and darted a furtive glance around the room. Snatterjee and Two-Fingers Earnold smiled and waved at him to let him know he was amongst friends but the man had narrowed his eyes to such tiny slits that it was unlikely he saw *anything* at all.

''S true,' asserted the first stranger. 'I tell you, he knew someone who had heard of it first-hand.'

'Garn,' scoffed the second stranger. 'No-one's *ever* seen it. Nor will they.

'Have *you* seen it?' Snatterjee asked Two-Fingers Earnold.

'Can't say that I have.' Two-Fingers replied.

'Nor have I,' confessed Snatterjee sadly.

'Er, what *exactly* are we talking about?' wondered Two-Fingers Earnold but Snatterjee hushed him quickly because the strangers had started to speak again and he was desperate to hear what they had to say. Snatterjee *loved* a mystery (and poking his nose in other people's business).

'Have you ever heard tell of the Houmjars?'

The second stranger instantly made the sign to ward off the Evil Eye and drew in his breath with a sharp hiss.

'Them as live in…' he paused, as if the very act of uttering the name brought doom on the utterer, '…Sloo Swamp.' He made the sign again, narrowed his eyes to the merest slit and stared around the room.

'Ahrr. The very same. The Sloo Swamp Houmjars. Them as would eat the very eyes right out of yer head just fer lookin' at 'em'

'Them as would pull the very tongue out of yer mouth just fer darin' to speak?' asked Slitty-Eyes by way of confirmation.

'Aye. Them as would stamp on yer toes jist fer walkin' near 'em,' the first stranger confirmed.

'You mean them as would rip yer stomach out jist fer bein' hungry,' Slitty-Eyes checked.

'Ahrr. Them.'

'What about them?'

'Well, they know where it is,' confided the first man. 'The Fabulous and Wonderful Frowla.'

'Did you hear that?' Snatterjee demanded.

'I did. I did,' replied Two-Fingers in a voice filled with wonder and awe. 'The Fabulous and Wonderful Frowla!'

'Sounds good,' Snatterjee murmured with bated breath, straining at the same to hear more of the strangers' conversation.

'But who'd be daft enough to risk askin' 'em?' the man with the waders was saying. Not me, that's fer sure. Not them Houmjars. I respect my neck too much.'

'Ahrr,' growled the first stranger, darkly, 'tear yer throat out jist fer swallowin'.'

Abruptly, as if by prior agreement, the two men lifted their flagons to their lips and drained them in long, noisy gulps. Snatterjee mused that all this talk of throat-ripping had prompted them to make full use of their throats while they could. With two simultaneous bangs they crashed down their empty flagons down onto the table and rose to their feet in unison. Slitty-Eyes tossed a handful of coins onto the table in payment. Swirling their cloaks about their shoulders they strode out of the Cocoa Shop, casting menacing looks at the assembled company, who for their part mainly ignored them. They paused by the swing doors, bestowed parting scowls and swirled away into the night.

'I must have it,' Snatterjee announced in a far-away voice. His eyes seemed to be focused on something a long way away.

'Have what?'

'The Fabulous and Wonderful Frowla.' Snatterjee's voice sounded dreamy and distant whilst at the same time carrying an overtone of scorn that Two-Fingers Earnold had failed to grasp the bleedin' obvious. To be fair, Two-Fingers was not the sharpest tool in the box. Not everybody can manage to get their fingers bitten off by shoving them into a donkey's mouth to get their carrot back.

3

And that was how the whole thing started. That was the first step on the road that led to the fringes of Sloo Swamp; to the stomach-churning sight of The Frog wolfing down the singed remains of a diseased Zingba by a stinking fire and sucking grease off his stubby little fingers.

The one and only consolation that Snatterjee could console himself with was that noxious smoke from the fire seemed to have discouraged every biting insect within the radius of a mile.

With a weary shrug and a heart-felt sigh, Snatterjee crept into the tent to escape from: 1) the cares of the day; 2) the stench and; 3) his equally loathsome guide.

Taking care to make no sound he pulled a slice of salt pork out of a side pocket in his backpack, rubbed it on his sleeve and nibbled at it as he crept into his sleeping bag.

As he drifted off to sleep he hoped that the Fabulous and Wonderful Frowla was worth all the trouble.

He was sure it was.

*

Snatterjee shot out of John's Frothy Cocoa Shop like a cork out of a bottle of champagne in the hands of a Formula One podium winner and, like fizzing champagne, went bubbling on a round of his friends, associates and casual acquaintances. For three days he made a nuisance of himself with the same question, over and over:

'What do you know about the Fabulous and Wonderful Frowla?'

A sample of the answers he received:

'What about it?' Dog John;

'Wonderful what?' Banjackle Smeed;

'Great, man!' Rollin' Robin Rawlins (who had ambitions to be a Heavy Metal star and said 'great, man' to everything);

'Don't be a silly boy, Snatterjee,' said Aunt Leah (who always suspected that he would Come To No Good).

But when he asked: 'What about Sloo Swamp and the Houmjars?' peoples' reactions were uniformly consistent: 'FORGET IT!'

But Snatterjee could not forget it. The more he asked around about the Fabulous and Wonderful Frowla, the more obsessed he became. Nobody seemed to know what it was or how valuable it was or what it was for or where it could be found or if it could fit in a pocket or even what it actually looked like. This made it very definitely a MYSTERY.

Snatterjee had worked hard now for several years to build up his Gyroscope, Salt Pork and Amber Curio Emporium and, to tell the truth, he was bored rigid with the whole business. A shop selling gyroscopes, salt pork and amber curios might, at first hearing, sound a little unusual, perhaps even a little bit weird and hardly a successful commercial venture. Not so. There was a good reason behind the establishment of Snatterjee's business enterprise which harked right back to the days when Snatterjee first set up in the cutthroat world of retail commerce.

Minfadlak (the place of Snatterjee's birth) is the last town you come to travelling east before the Great Flat Nothing, where the calaphel caravans halted before making the crossing.

(*Calaphel* (n) Mammal. A cross between a dromedary, a

giraffe and a llama with excellent stamina and water retension. The calaphel can spit with great accuracy to a distance of fifty metres. During the closed season for crossings of the Great Flat Nothing calaphel drovers organising spitting contests (for the calaphels – not the drovers) where fortunes can change hands on a gob. A good, accurate calaphel with an active saliva gland is worth its weight in all sorts of precious goods.)

Snatterjee was a bright-eyed youth who had just banged together a hand barrow and stocked it with bits of junk and tat that the good folk (and some not so good, in fact, definitely dodgy) had heaved out into the street in the best tradition of Minfadlek. He had grand dreams of selling his wares to a passing merchant for a handsome profit. His greatest dream was to use his profit to kit himself out as an artist and sell hand coloured pictures of Minfadlekian places of interest of which there were not many, hence his fall-back side-line of a range of postcards of Beverage Beauties in 'artistic' poses depicting scenes from classical literature from a time when clothing seemed to be optional.

Business was, surprisingly, slow and Snatterjee lay dozing under the handcart when he saw feet shod in expensive shoes approaching. He scrambled out from under and was brushing the dust off as a very smartly dressed man came to a halt by the barrow and cast an eye over the pile of cast-off junk. Snatterjee's heart beat faster; his dream was about to come true. He bit his lip to stop it trembling and twisted his mouth into his most sincere smile: he looked like a game-show host.

'See my wares, Sir. Something for that special person? Something for *everyone*. All good stuff, Sir. No rubbish.' This in a sing-song, best market-trader, cheeky-chappie voice.

'I seek a gyroscope, young man. Name your own price.' The man hefted a large purse that clinked and clanked and chinked with coins.

'Er,' said Snatterjee, not at all sure what a gyroscope was when it was at home but sure he did not possess such a thing, 'I've just this moment run out. Sold the last one not ten minutes ago. How about some nice second-hand marbles? Hardly used. The glass is a *bit* scratched but not so's you'd notice. See,' he held an opaque ball of glass up to the light, 'you can still see the twisty bit in the middle.'

'Alas,' said the rich stranger as if he really was sorry, 'not today. However, I *will* take all the salt pork that you have. In barrels or jars, it makes no difference.'

Snatterjee rummaged around in the junk on his barrow as if he were seeking out lost containers of salt pork among the detritus of broken bed-springs, chipped chamber-pots, headless dolls and rusty cutlery.

'I've got some coconut shells,' he said, hopefully.

'Ah,' said the man with a rueful shake of his head and a wan, sad smile. He gave Snatterjee a long, hard, quizzical look. 'Do you, by any chance, have any amber? I am a collector of unusual pieces. My collection excites the admiration and envy of kings, viziers, beys and Chancellors of the Exchequer.'

Snatterjee was almost in tears. As a final desperate attempt to sell the stranger *something*, he held up a cracked glass snow-dome of the Unsafe Tower of Minfadlak that had lost most of its snow.

'If you shake it, Sir, you will get a snow storm, or a dust storm or something. It's a collectors' item, Sir.'

'But, sadly, outside my sphere of interest. I wish you Good

Day, young man and success in your enterprises.'

As the merchant walked away, taking his money with him, Snatterjee swore an oath that he would never again be caught out. He devoted all his energy, time and money to build up the best (and only) Gyroscope, Salt Pork and Amber Curios Emporium in all of Minfadlak and the surrounding territories. And because he had no competition in those early days, much to everyone's surprise, he did well and prospered in this rather niche market.

Now, however, Snatterjee was restless, ready for a change, a new challenge and the Fabulous and Wonderful Frowla was just the spur he needed.

*

He tried to persuade his friends to set off into the unknown with him is search of the Fabulous and Wonderful Frowla but with a singular lack of success. As soon as Sloo Swamp and the Houmjars came up in the conversation, everyone suddenly remembered that something urgent that they just *had* to do and could not be put off any longer. In most cases, this urgent business would occupy all of the foreseeable future. Snatterjee soon became used to the sight of his erstwhile friends ducking into doorways as soon as they spotted him coming. Even Two-Fingers Earnold could not be tempted and he was very much Snatterjee's last resort. At that point, Snatterjee had not yet met The Frog and so did not know what the last resort was *really* about.

So, at last, despairing of the cowardly stay-at-homes, Snatterjee shut up shop and steeled his heart to undertake the Great Adventure all alone.

4

Snatterjee shut up his shop. He packed a goodly ration of salt pork (think: soggy pork scratchings), a gyroscope and a couple of fine pieces of amber for possible trading purposes. Amongst the latter was a new example, just recently come into his possession. It was very unusual or, as Snatterjee's sales patter would have it: 'Take a good look at this, sir. Have you ever seen the like? Came from a Nemperor's tomb, that did. Unique, that is!'

Quite often amber contains the perfectly preserved body of an insect or spider that was unfortunate enough to get trapped in the stick goo excreted by pine trees. The better the state of preservation, the better the ghoulish attraction of the piece and hence, the greater the value and this piece was a doozy, a curious beetle with an iridescent carapace that had escaped the ravages of time, encased as it was in amber. The other two pieces, an ant and a wasp, whilst very fine, were not quite in the same bracket. Altogether, to the serious collector and concessioner, they were worth a good chunk of dosh and were Snatterjee's fall-back plan. All he had to do was *find* said collector when needed. He hadn't really thought the plan through, but that was Snatterjee all the way.

He harboured a secret fantasy that he would run into the wealthy amber collector again and amaze and impress the man by whipping out a valuable chunk of amber and nonchalantly saying: 'You might be interested in this? Make me an offer! Oh, *and* I just happen to have a gyroscope about my person.' *YES!* Fistpump!

Armed with these essential supplies he slung a homemade tent and sleeping mat from the bottom of his backpack, packed a couple of clothes changes inside, wrapped up some coins in a handkerchief which he stuffed into a leather bag which he hung around his neck and tucked into his shirt. A Minfadlekian Fire Brigade knife (eight blades and gadgets) completed his kit.

Cocking a snoot at the miserable gits of Minfadlek who would not know an adventure if it bit them on the bum, Snatterjee set off round about lunchtime and headed west.

No-one came to see him off or wave him goodbye or wish him luck (or even to have a last snigger at his folly). As far as his friends were concerned, Snatterjee was a dead man walking and it only remained for the Houmjars to formalise the fact.

To give them their due (his friends, not the Houmjars), the wake they held for Snatterjee at John's Frothy Cocoa Shop went down in the social history of Minfadlek as AN EVENT NOT TO BE MISSED. Even people who were miles away at the time later claimed to have been there. Many of the Beverage Beauties who subsequently gave birth to male offspring named the baby Snatterjee in honour of the night and not, as scurrilous rumour had it, in ascribed paternity.

*

Snatterjee strode out along the Great West Road with his pack on his back and his hands in his pockets whistling a merry air in the approved manner of people setting out on great adventures. He walked for about three miles without meeting anyone and began to get fed up. Solo Swamp was said to be some one hundred and thirty-four miles, seven hundred and fifteen metres away from Minfadlek (give or take). Just how big Sloo Swamp itself was, none could tell him or even tried to hazard a guess. But everyone he asked were unanimous in their opinion that it was big and nasty and, of course, there were the Houmjars…

By the end of the first day Snatterjee had covered all of twelve miles. It was further than he had walked since he gave up pushing his street barrow around the mean streets of Minfadlak and his cocoa gut was feeling the strain, not to mention his feet, calves, thighs and hips. He had not had the nous (being new to this adventuring malarkey and all) to wear proper hiking boots as he thought that an adventurer cut more of a sartorial dash in dayglo orange wellies. These he had bought with the express purpose of wading gamely through Sloo Swamp, his chin held high, his brow noble. Not for one minute had he given any thought to what it might be like to tramp one hundred and thirty-four miles, seven hundred and fifteen metres in loose fitting wellies and now he was paying the price for his lack of foresight. He stopped and sat by the side of the road, pulling his wellies off to inspect the damage. His feet were puffy and swollen and gave off a nasty niff that was *definitely not* wholesome.

He set up camp by the side of the Great West Road as dusk was falling, lit a bit of a fire and sat down to wait for other travellers to keep him company.

None came.

All in all, that first night out alone by the Great West Road was a bad night for Snatterjee. He tossed and turned in vain trying to find a comfortable bit of ground to sleep on. His feet hurt; his legs ached. He was miserable and downhearted and came very close in the wee small hours of chucking the whole mad idea in and going home like a sensible sausage. Here he was, he ruminated, setting off to a certain nasty death at the hands of the Houmjars looking for something he had heard about while eavesdropping in a bar. He did not know just *what* he was seeking, only that he would recognise it when he found it. He did not even know what it was *for*. Somehow the Fabulous and Wonderful Frowla had enchanted him and robbed him of the little sense he had.

Then came the thought or returning to the daily tedium of retail life and the jibes and jeers of his friends.

He could not face the prospect. Somewhere round about three forty-seven in the early morning his resolve to go on with the quest hardened and he drifted off into an uneasy sleep.

*

In the morning he was up early, stiff and with feet still slightly niffy. He made himself a hasty breakfast of salt pork, checked that his belongings had not been stolen in the night, tied his wellies together with a bit of guy rope, slung them around his neck and set off before he could change his mind.

Towards noon he was passed by a caravan heading towards Minfadlek and the East. Forty or fifty heavily burdened calaphels stamped their feet in unison. They threw their long necks back and gathered up the saliva in their throats, making noises like water running out of a sink and tried to spit at their drovers.

Snatterjee hailed the Caravan Master as one seasoned traveller to another.

'How far to Minfadlek?' asked the Caravan Master, a small man, seemingly completely wrapped up in lengths of cloth from head to toe.

'Er, eighteen or nineteen miles,' Snatterjee guessed. 'How

far to…Sloo Swamp?' he asked in return, hoping to impress the Caravan Master.

'One hundred and sixteen miles, one thousand and forty-seven metres,' the Caravan Master replied without missing a beat.

'Oh,' said Snatterjee and ducked as a spray of calaphel spit came flying in his direction.

5

The days followed each other and were much the same. Snatterjee made slow progress as he dawdled along the Road. Occasionally he would stop for a long lunch in a roadside inn and try and persuade a likely lad to accompany him on his Quest (every hero needs a sidekick) but without any takers. Most people with half a brain cell edged away from total strangers raving on about a fabled treasure (exact nature unspecified) to be found in Sloo Swamp, home of the Houmjars. In the grubby little town of Lakh the Constable threatened to throw him in jail if he so much as mentioned Sloo Swamp and the Houmjars in public again. He didn't linger long in Lakh. It was a nasty place, anyway.

Three weeks to the day after leaving his home in Minfadlek he arrived at the village of Mud Wallow. The topography of the land had been gradually morphing from the gentle green hills covered with shade trees that cradled Minfadlek in their soft bosom to flat, soggy fens crisscrossed by drainage ditches, home to millions of blood-sucking insects that had decided Snatterjee was a moveable feast. Seen from a distance, Snatterjee resembled a windmill in a gale in his attempts to swat his tormentors away.

This interesting sight drew the attention of the half a dozen or so feral dogs that lived under the hovels of Mud Wallow. These hovels were built on rickety stilts to keep them from blowing away in any kind of wind, slippery mud not being the most firm of foundations.

The dogs barked and snapped at Snatterjee's feet. The

increasing bogginess of the land had made squelching along barefoot a chore. Snatterjee had smugly congratulated himself on his foresight and donned his wellies again in a 'I-told-you-so' way. A few well-aimed kicks, a flash of orange rubber and the dogs slunk back to their gloomy lairs under the houses and watched his progress with baleful yellow eyes.

Seeing an inn sign half way along the squalid street, Snatterjee broke into a stumbling run in a desperate attempt to outpace the mosquitoes that orbited his body in a humming cloud of voracious blood-lust. He fell through the door of the inn, slamming it shut behind him. His momentum propelled him forward, crashing him into a bench. It did not help that the place was in almost total darkness with only a single guttering candle perched on the bar for illumination.

'Yerst?' inquired a creaky voice like a rusty hinge from somewhere in the gloom.

Snatterjee panted, trying to get his breath back and orientate himself to his surroundings. His knee throbbed from its collision with the bench.

'Is it always this dark in here?' he asked, mainly for something to say.

'No,' creaked the voice, 'it gets darker when we blows the candle out. Anything else?'

Snatterjee peered into the gloom, trying to make out some clue as to the speaker. He blinked his eyes, trying to get them accustomed to the lack of light. Something glimmered in the flickering candlelight. Suddenly he realised what he was seeing – the bald dome of a head protruding just above the level of the bar counter. When he looked carefully he could make out a pair of glittering eyes exactly on a level with the edge of the bar. A great hairy hand like an enormous black spider stole into view from the depths behind the bar and made vague mopping motions on the bar top with a rag that had seen better days but not soap and water for quite some time.

'Well,' ground out the voice, 'are yer stopping?'

'Erm,' Snatterjee was somewhat at a loss for words. He was no stranger to bars, inns, taverns and frothy cocoa shops but this place was *definitely* a first. 'Er, what have you got?'

'What does yer want?' countered the landlord, quick as a flash.

'Hot cocoa?'

'Nah.'

'Cold cocoa?'

'Nah.

'Talabousch?' Snatterjee offered.

(*Talabousch* (n) A drink made from the roots of the Injib bush and seasoned with the dried seeds of the Lablab flower. It is often served with Zingba milk. Because of its horrendous effects it is, quite rightly, banned in most parts of the world and shunned by all who would prefer to stay in their right mind)

'Talabousch! Talabousch!' mimicked the landlord in his rust hinge of a voice. 'Oh! Oh! The fine gentleman wants talabousch!'

The landlord's performance was acknowledged by a series of wheezing grunts emanating from a pitch-black recess of the room. Snatterjee stared about wildly in an effort to see who or *what* else was in the room but the darkness was impenetrable.

'Well,' he said, his voice rising in anger, 'what *have* you got?'

'Don't be getting all aeriated, young fella,' cautioned the landlord.

Snatterjee swallowed his wrath and counted to ten. His eyes

were becoming used to the gloom. As far as he could judge, there was not a bottle, barrel or glass in evidence in the whole place. He could have sworn the building had advertised itself as a hostelry on the outside. A terrible suspicion took root in his brain. Could it be that innocent travellers were lured inside only to be foully murdered and robbed of all they possessed? He had read of such places in the *Minfadlek Almanac*.

'Tell me, mine host,' he purred with honeyed tones, 'what would *you* recommend. I am but a simple stranger travelling through these parts, although,' he added quickly, 'there are any number of people fully aware of my movements and will trace my path if I am never seen again.' *That should cover it*, he thought. 'Is there, perhaps, some local speciality of which I, as a humble stranger, am unaware?'

'Nah,' croaked the landlord.

'Fine,' said Snatterjee, gathering up his pack. 'It was a pleasure and a privilege to meet you. And you, sir,' he said nodding in the direction of the patch of darkness.

'Are you orft, then?' asked the landlord.

'Ah, I see you have accurately perceived my intention, sir. Very astute of you, if I may say so. There's not much slips by you, is there?'

'No call to be like that,' muttered the landlord in a voice like a rasp on a very hard plank of wood. 'Not when we was jerst getting friendly, like.'

'Friendly!' screamed Snatterjee in disbelief. 'You call this place *friendly!* I just hope the Houmjars aren't this friendly.'

'Houmjars, yer say?'

'Indeed.' Snatterjee straightened his back and squared his shoulders in what he hoped was the posture of an intrepid adventurer. 'I am bound for...' A little pause for maximum dramatic effect, 'Sloo swamp.'

'Sloo swamp, he says,' creaked the landlord into the darkness and was rewarded by another series of grunts.

Somewhat deflated that his statement had not had the result he hoped for (shock and awe and the landlord begging him not to go on) he said, somewhat anticlimactically, 'I don't suppose you know of a local guide I might hire to show me the way?'

Silence.

'No? Well, I'll bid you good day again and take my chances all by myself.' Snatterjee hoped he wasn't laying it on too thick. He started to grope his way in what he thought might be the direction of the door. And at that moment, the door (which was nowhere near where he had thought it was) opened and the murky interior of the inn was illuminated by a brief shaft of light. Snatterjee spun around and caught a glimpse of a long, thin figure sprawled out on a bench. Turning like a flash to the doorway he had the impression of a squat, solid shape, like the after image in flash photography.

A whine about his ears alerted him to the presence of a mosquito, drawn to him like iron to a magnet. He shuddered at the prospect of the swarm of bloodsuckers awaiting him outside and lingered a blissful moment longer. He heard, rather than saw, the newcomer weave a path towards the bar. Snatterejee was intrigued to discover how any transaction might transpire.

''Lo, Jelliot,' said the newcomer, leaning confidently on the bar with the assured air of a regular visitor to the inn. 'Cup o' finest, if you please.'

'My pleasure, Ned,' Jelliot ground out and as if by magic a hairy black paw crept onto the bar wrapped around a large earthenware cup. A coin danced on the counter and fell with a clink. The hairy black hand crept out and snaffled it, reminding Snatterjee of a moneybox he had once had on his barrow. A hand at the end of an arm deposited a coin into a box, only it didn't because the arm was broken.

Snatterjee swallowed his pride and crept back to the bar.

'A cup o' finest, if you please,' he tried, standing next to Ned in a companionable sort of way. Ned ignored him, engrossed as he was with his drink.

'If that's yer'd been wanting, why didn't yer jerst say so,' demanded Jolliot, slowly producing a cup. Snatterjee had heard neither the sound of a bottle being opened or liquid being poured. He supposed Jolliot must keep a supply of ready-filled cups beneath the bar and even this close to the bar all Snatterjee could see of mine host was that dome of a head and the two twinkling eyes that slid in Ned's direction having served Snatterjee.

'Gentleman was talking o' Sloo Swamp,' said Jolliot to Ned as if Snatterjee had up and left.

'Was 'e? Sloo Swamp yer say?'

'Wants a guide, he said.'

'A guide?'

Another burst of grunts came from the long figure on the bench, now back in the dark.

'That so, Mr Bates?' said Ned.

Snatterjee felt his head start to spin. He was reasonably sure that there was nothing wrong with himself and therefore all the weirdness was with the others. Classic inbreeding, he decided. To steady himself he raised the cup to his lips and took an experimental swig. Who knew what might be in the cup? The liquid was thin and tasted basically of muddy, slightly slimy water. He gave an involuntary gasp and pulled a face. Jolliot misread his reaction.

'Good, eh? It's the finest we have. They all comes here to drink. All o' 'em.' Who *they* were was not explained. 'That'll be a half-glimp, please.'

(*glimp* (n) unit of currency. Thirty-six *fertles* make one glimp)

'*Half a glimp*! It tastes just like water.' Snatterjee was forever frugal around drink.

'Yerst. It *is* water. Finest. Half a glimp.' The black paw crept out onto the counter again and lay there, palm uppermost like something nasty that had just died there. Snatterjee noticed, hardly surprised, that the palm, too, was covered in black hair.

Beside him, at the bar, Ned turned to face him, arms hanging free at his sides, a clear sign that he was ready for trouble if this outsider tried to bilk Jolliot for the price of a drink. Reluctantly, Snatterjee fumbled out a coin from the wallet around his neck and deposited it into the hirsute palm that folded over it like a Venus Flytrap over a fly.

Snatterjee raised the cup to his lips again and bobbed the water against them, making sure not to swallow.

'Hmmm. Yes. Lovely. Don't get water like that everywhere.'

Ned gave him a funny look, no doubt trying to work out whether Snatterjee was being sarcastic but the task was beyond him so he went back to his conversation about Snatterjee with Jolliot.

'Bain't goin' to find a guide hereabouts in Mud Wallow, is he?'

'Nah,' agreed Jolliot.

'Not to go to Sloo Swamp,' Ned persisted, as if Jolliot had

disagreed with him.

'Nah.'

'Not with they Houmjars!'

Snatterjee had had enough of the delights of Mud Wallow. Much more of listening to these two and I'll be as terminally strange as they are, he thought. He placed his barely touched cup of water on the counter and hitched up his pack. 'Well, goodbye then, gentlemen,' he said.

They let him grope his way almost to the door.

''Corse, he might try…'

'Nah,' said Jolliot

'It'd be his best bet.'

'What?' said Snatterjee before he could stop himself.

'Nothing,' said Jolliot and tried a little whistle that sounded like a mule choking.

A burst of grunts came from Mr Bates.

'I agrees with yer, Mr Bates. He might be the very chap yon daft stranger is looking for.'

'*WHO?*' Snatterjee screamed.

'Now don't yer be getting' yerself all excited like. It's bad fer yer health.'

'I'm sorry. But please, please, if you know of someone who might serve as a guide in my Quest, then please direct me to his door.' Snatterjee had learnt long before that there was no shame in begging and whining to get what he wanted; it cost nothing and gave the other party the illusion of superiority that soon wore off.

'Happen Rat Worrier might…'

'Rat Worrier?' gasped Snatterjee, '*Rat Worrier?*' Of course, what else in this madhouse.

'Yerst, the Rat Worrier', Jolliot confirmed now that the secret was out.

'Have yer finished with yer drink, stranger?' asked Ned hopefully eying up Snatterjee's abandoned cup o' finest on the bar counter. "Cos if yer have, I'll be glad to finish it up fer yer. That's Finest, that is. Crying shame to let it go to waste. You having paid for it an' all that.'

'Take it, take it, you're welcome to it.' Snatterjee waited until Ned had raised the cup to his lips and had his eyes shut in anticipation of ecstasy and then added: '*If* you take me to find this person to guide me to Sloo Swamp.'

'Oh, he's a sharp one and no mistake,' croaked Jolliot in admiration.

'Yerst,' said Ned. 'Alright, I takes yer.'

And with that he drained off the cup in one long, blissful draught of pure lip-smacking pleasure.

'Aarrh!'

6

Ned led Snatterjee about a mile and a half out of Mud Wallow until they reached a copse of stunted thorn trees growing reluctantly out of the mud and huddling together for company. Brackish, stale water hung about in great flat puddles all around and gave off a distinctly unhealthy niff. The track – a generous naming to be taken with a fist-full of salt – was slick with yellow mud the colour of pus that made the act of walking, or, more often, sliding, a hazardous and noisy business as their feet kept sinking down and had to be dragged out of the mire with disgusting slurps.

Ned had barely said a word to Snatterjee since leaving the darkened inn taproom and Snatterjee had soon given up the fruitless task of trying to strike up conversation to make the journey pass in convivial banter. Topics of mutual interest were exhausted almost as soon as Snatterjee thought of them. Overhead ominous looking black birds wheeled against the bruised sky and uttered great gasping croaks. Snatterjee kept a mistrustful eye on them whenever he felt it was safe to look up from picking his way along the track.

'Swamp Nasties,' said Ned, suddenly breaking his silence and pointing at the birds with his chin. "Strip a body clean o' flesh quicker'n it takes yer to drown.'

'Hmm. Nice,' replied Snatterjee, reluctantly prepared to indulge in conversation about the life and times of carrion-eating wildlife but Ned had lapsed back into a morose silence. Snatterjee tried a different gambit: 'Much further?'

No reply.

'Oh, well,' he thought, 'never mind then.'

It had crossed Snatterjee's mind that Ned might be leading him out into the wild grey yonder in order to slit his throat and rob him but then he dismissed the thought almost as soon as he thought it: Ned probably didn't have the nous to think out such a complicated plan for himself. Nevertheless, Snatterjee made sure that Ned was always a good five yards ahead and had even gone so far as to loosen the Minfadlek Fire Brigade knife in its sheath that hung around his neck along with all the other bits and pieces suspended on bits of string and tucked inside his shirt.

If the truth be known, Snatterjee had never once in his life been involved in any activity more violent than wresting the cork out of a bottle but he was pessimistically confident that violence was only to be expected if you set off on quests to strange foreign parts. Nonetheless, the prospect of foreign violence was not top of his bucket list.

While he was chasing these thoughts and feeling quite sorry for himself, Ned suddenly stopped and Snatterjee almost slid into him. For a moment he thought his worst-case scenario had come true and he panicked. He fumbled with the snee, (familiar term for a Minfadlek Fire Brigade knife once opened with the knife bit out) that had become caught up in his clothing and fell over into the squelchy embrace of the mud. He lay there for a moment, his eyes pressed tight shut as he waited for death to claim him. When nothing happened he open one eye a crack and saw Ned watching him impassively. Snatterjee managed to extract himself from the grip of the mud with an obscene sucking sound, now fully caked in his own share of mud.

'There 'im be.' Ned's greasy chin poked forward.

'Eh? What? Who?' spluttered Snatterjee, his wits befuddled by his near escape from cruel death.

Ned gave him what might almost be called a pitying look.

'Yon fellow whom yer wanted ter guide yer to Sloo Swamp,' he explained in a voice much slower than his usual tone, as if addressing a listener who was not quite as sharp in the comprehension department as himself. He accompanied his speech with encouraging little nods of his head. 'Remember? That's why'm we be here. Ter see 'im?'

'Yes, yes,' Snatterjee snapped impatiently, having realised that he was not, in fact, about to be foully robbed and murdered and his corpse left for the Swamp Nasties' supper. 'Of course, I know why we're here.' He attempted to restore some dignity and authority to his appearance by brushing his hands down over his clothing but only succeeded in sending a stream of filthy water gushing down his legs.

'It's jerst that I wondered, like,' replied Ned, unconvinced.

Many years before, another stranger had made his way to Mud Wallow and the villagers still spoke in hushed tones of his strange ways and daft manner. Ned was confident that the recounting of the behaviour of *this* particular stranger would stand him in good stead and free drinks for many a year.

Foreigners, eh?

Snatterjee squinted in the direction Ned had indicated. He could see nothing at first in the mirk that passed for daylight but then he made out the shape of a mean hut built, or rather, heaped together, of rushes, very like a small and untidy haystack. It was set on a small rise in the ground some two hundred yards further down the track from where they stood.

'I'll be leavin' yer, then,' Ned called over his shoulder, already some way down the track leading back to Mud Wallow.

Snatterjee had been too intent on staring at the alleged dwelling to notice Ned's departure. He had fully intended to press some small coin upon Ned in appreciation of his services and as an unspoken reward for Ned not murdering him and leaving his bloodsoaked body to be pecked over by the Swamp Nasties.

'Too late now,' thought Snatterjee, with no real regret. Ned would only fritter it away on best water!

Ned himself was moving with astonishing speed for someone of his compact build and the unforgiving nature of the track. It suddenly struck Snatterjee that there just might be *something* out here that Ned was afraid of and that that was the reason why he wasn't hanging around in hopes of a tip. Snatterjee instantly convinced himself that he was staring horrible death in the face again.

After a couple of minutes of uninterrupted life with a complete absence of death, Snatterjee opened his eyes again and gazed upon an empty, uninspiring landscape of mud, puddles, stunted trees and reedbeds with the reed hovel on the slight rise. No apparent danger loomed. He told himself for the three hundredth and sixty-eighth time that faint heart never won fair Frowla and gave himself a good shake.

However, the was no sense in being recklessly foolhardy. He shucked off his pack so that he might run more easily if there was the faintest sniff of danger. He cupped his hands around his mouth and shouted:

'Hello! Hello!'

But answer came there none.

He shouted again, peering in the direction of the hovel.

Then, just out of his line of vision, he became aware of movement. At the same instant his ears registered a squishing sound. He snatched at the hilt of his snee and whirled round to confront who or what it was that was creeping up on him. The immediate effect of his action was to send his feet shooting in opposite directions on the slippery mud and for the second time in ten minutes to land him on his arse in a rain of mud and filthy water.

As he tried to struggle into a sitting position and wipe mud out of his eye at the same time he was vaguely aware of a *prowling* all around him. The mud held him fast, giving off horrible gurglings and farts as he tried to escape its clutches.

When he finally managed to clear one eye of mud, he risked a peep at the world, expecting to see a band of desperadoes making ready to plunge their weapons into his body.

7

What he *did* see was a figure squatting in the mud close to his head. There was something vaguely familiar about it. Or, rather, it reminded him of something. He raised his head out of the mud and squinted.

'Don't say it,' the figure said in a voice that was more of a croak. 'Everybody does. Don't ask me why. *I've* never noticed the resemblance.'

'Well,' thought Snatterjee, 'it's a start. It doesn't *sound* hostile and I can't see any sign of a weapon. What *does* it remind me of, though?'

The figure stretched out a scrawny arm, clasped Snatterjee's wrist in a surprisingly strong grip and helped him to his feet.

'A frog!' said Snatterjee suddenly and very loudly.

'I said:"don't say it,"' chided the figure mournfully, turning away.

'I'm sorry. Er, you see, I'm looking for someone. Someone who is supposed to live out here.' He gestured around the barren mud flat as if to demonstrate the unlikelihood of anyone *actually* living in this desolation. 'Someone called the Rat Worrier. Er, have you…? Do you…?'

'That'll be me, then,' confided his rescuer with a distinct note of pride in his croak. 'Rat Worrier to Mud Wallow. Appointed by Mr Bates hisself.'

'Mr Bates? Yes, I think I've met him.'

'Very important man, Mr Bates. Very powerful. You don't want to cross 'im. He's the Grand and Worshipful Mayor of Mud Wallow and Surrounding Ditches and Fens. Yerst. A great man indeed.'

'Oh, really.' Snatterjee tried to sound impressed but failed utterly. Was he not a cog in the great mercantile hub that was Minfadlek? The doings of the yokels of Mud Wallow had as much clout as a nest of clippersnappers.

(*clippersnapper* (n) a species of eight-legged [three on one side, five on the other], bright blue beetle that, because of the unevenness of their leg distribution, mainly rushed around in confused circles, getting nowhere .)

'Yerst! Indeed!

'And he appointed you Rat Worrier, did he?' Snatterjee was trying to think of a way he might broach the subject of his search. He had met with so many outright rejections (not to mention a number of threats of bodily injury if he didn't push off sharpish) in his search for a guide to Sloo Swamp that he had learnt circumspection.

'That he did. Bless His Glorious Name!'

'Rat Worrier? Sounds important, not to say impressive. Is it ceremonial?'

'Ceremonial? Ceremonial? No, it is not,' replied The Frog, hopping about in the mud indignantly. 'I'll have you know there's lots of hard graft involved.'

'I beg your pardon, I'm sure,' said Snatterjee with a transparently false humbleness that was completely lost on The Frog (as the creature was now and forever fixed in Snatterjee's mind). 'And what, pray, if you will forgive my ignorance and curiousity, does a Rat Worrier *do*?'

'Worry Rats,' said The Frog.

'Ah, yes. Stupid of me not to have guessed. The clue's in the name, I suppose,' snarled Snatterjee as he hunted around for his pack and tried to wring the cold, muddy water out of his clothes.

'I thought so, too,' said The Frog with a smug smile.

Snatterjee, emboldened by the suspicion that he was not in clear and present danger of being murdered, shot The Frog a venomous look. The Frog ignored it and set off towards the reed shack. Snatterjee squelched furiously after him. 'How?' he asked.

'How what?'

'How do you worry rats?'

'Do you know how to worry sheep?' The Frog demanded over his shoulder.

'Well…' muttered Snatterjee, playing for time and desperate not to be bested by this apology for a yokel.

'You shout *Mint Sauce* at 'em'

'I should have guessed. I really should.' Snatterjee cupped his hands around his head, for all the world like a man hearing a terrible scream of unreason echoing over the mud flat and trying to block it out.

'That's how I worries rats,' explained The Frog as he reached the heap of rushes he called home.

'What? You shout *Mint Sauce* at them?' Snatterjee was beginning to fear he was losing his hold on reality. A sneaking suspicion grew on him that Mud Wallow and its immediate environs was some sort of open reserve for the Terminally Confused.

'Don't be daft,' came The Frog's muffled voice from inside his hovel. 'Why would *Mint Sauce* worry rats?'

'Search me,' confessed Snatterjee, stooping to peer through the crawl hole. The rushes that formed the very fabric of the hovel were very loosely woven and admitted the sullen grey light of the mud flat. A heap of rushes were piled up against one wall which Snatterjee took, correctly, to serve for a bed. Yet another pile in the centre of the hovel served for all the rest of the furniture. Rushes were strewn over the mud floor but did little to disguise the ooze of water that seeped in.

'Nice place you have here,' Snatterjee said.

'I expect you *are* somewhat overawed,' The Frog said in all seriousness. 'This is the finest dwelling hereabouts.'

'Not that there is a lot in the way of competition,' Snatterjee muttered as he crept through the opening and went to sit down on the rush bed.

'Hoy! Watch the mud. You're covered. That's my bed, that is.'

'Terribly sorry.'

'Yerst. Sit on the couch.' The Frog pointed to the heap of rushes in the centre of the (for want of a better word) room.

Snatterjee sat.

'Now, why were yer looking for me?'

'I'm looking for a guide.'

'A guide? I'm not a guide. I'm a Rat Worrier.'

'Ned thought you might be able to help me out.'

'I shouts *atouille* at 'em,' said The Frog mysteriously.

'Snatterjee stared blankly at him, remembering his recent theory about the Terminally Confused.

'The rats. I shouts *atouille* at 'em.'

Snatterjee was none the wiser and shook his head. Perhaps there was something wrong with his hearing? A build up of mud in the earholes?

'It's a local dish. Great delicacy. Ver' tasty if yer can gets it.'

(*Rat atouille* (n) a local dish of the district of Mud Wallow.

Rat boiled in puddle water with *bog weed cv.*

Bog weed (n) a weed that grows in a bog. Tastes pretty much like it sounds. An acquired taste if there is absolutely no vegetable alternative.)

'Sounds delicious. I must try it.'

'Frightens the life outta 'em. You should see the little buggers run when I shouts *atouille, atouille* ats 'em.' Spoken with all the pride of a true craftsman.

Snatterjee decided it was high time he took back control of the conversation while he still had a semblance of his wits about him.

'Look. I want *you* to guide *me* to Sloo Swamp.'

A look of disbelief stole over The Frog's face. 'Did you say Sloo Swamp?'

'I did.'

'Nobody goes to Sloo Swamp.'

'I am.'

'The Houmjars live in Sloo Swamp.'

'I know. That's why I'm going.'

'To see the Houmjars. Do yer know what they do?'

'I've heard.'

'And yer *wants* to go there?'

'Yes. And I want *you* to guide me. The road runs out here at Mud Wallow.' He paused for a beat and then dangled his bait. 'I'll pay you, of course.'

'Ah,' said The Frog.

This was by far the most encouraging response Snatterjee had encountered since he had set off on his quest. He pushed his advantage.

'Minfadlek money…'

'Money?'

'Coin. Minfadlek pfenning.'

The Frog looked at him blankly.

Quick as a flash Snatterjee changed tack. Skills honed in the mercantile hurly-burly of the retail jungle that was Minfadlek kicked in.

'Or these.' He fished about in his pack which he had recovered from the mud and produced the pieces of amber and the gyroscope that he had had the foresight to pack from his stock in the Emporium back home.

The Frog's eyes bulged. Never in his life had he seen such treasures and he was quite sure that not even Mr Bates owned anything quite as marvellous as these. He reached out his hand to touch the shining piece of amber that encased the body of the beetle with the iridescent carapace but Snatterjee snatched it away and popped it back in its pouch.

The Frog was making clicking sounds with his tongue and muttering to himself, his eyes slightly glazed over. Snatterjee recognised the signs. 'He's hooked,' he thought and chuckled inwardly. He had no intention whatsoever of paying The Frog for his services with such an obviously valuable specimen. He tried a distraction.

'Here,' he said,' hold the end of the bit of string.'

Holding the other end in his own left hand, Snatterjee pulled the string taut, spun the gyroscope with his right hand and dropped it onto the string. It balanced perfectly, spinning along its axis with a faint humming sound.

The Frog shrieked and let go of his end of the string as if it were red hot.

'Good, eh? Magic!' This was like taking candy from a baby,

and a not very bright one at that. 'The pretty jewel shall be yours and I'll throw in the enchanted spinner as a bonus when we get to the Houmjars. How about that, then?'

'I'll take you as far as the shores of the Swamp,' agreed The Frog, greed overcoming his reticence. 'It's about a three day journey from here, depending on the rain. There's an inn fairly close to the Swamp. It's The Last House and is very highly thought of in these parts. Mind you, not many people go there, on account of its so near the Swamp and the Houmjars an' all.'

'Good. When can we start?'

'How about next week?' replied The Frog cautiously.

'How about tomorrow?'

'If you insist. What's the hurry?'

'The Fabulous and Wonderful Frowla!'

'The wha?'

And so Snatterjee was forced to tell The Frog the bare facts of his mission.

And once he had heard the story The Frog became infected by Snatterjee's enthusiasm and in the first flush of his excitement agreed that they should set off the very next day.

*

And so here they were, after three days of tramping and slipping and sliding through mud and bogs (not to mention a *very* brief visit to the Last House which boasted an inn sign proclaiming *The Hanged Ferret*) onto the edge of Sloo Swamp with night rapidly falling.

*

With the last morsel of Zingba picked clean and the last embers of the noisome fire damped down, The Frog crept into the tent and snuggled up on the floor next to Snatterjee. The Frog had an odour uniquely his own and after three nights of sharing the tent Snatterjee was just about getting used to it, so much so that he hardly gagged when The Frog crawled in and soon fell back into an uneasy doze.

Within moments The Frog was asleep himself, his belly stuffed full, lost in a world of wuffling snores and grunts which jerked Snatterjee back into wakefulness. He lay on his back, hands cupped behind his head, staring at the roof of the tent where it snapped and cracked in the stiff breeze coming off the Swamp.

Tomorrow, whether The Frog realised it or not, their path led into Sloo Swamp.

Snatterjee was terrified.

8

Dawn arrived washed out and pale, the sky featureless, cloudless, offering no hint as to the day to come. Both Snatterjee and The Frog slept right through the dawn, perhaps, subconsciously not in any great hurry to face the day. When they awoke the sun was already high in the sky and heating up the wilderness of mud, slime and fetid water.

Having eaten the Zingba for supper, there was, ostensibly, nothing left for breakfast. Snatterjee was not about to tell The Frog of his emergency supplies of salt pork hidden in his pack. The Frog, on the other hand, knew well enough where to forage for food on the shores of the Swamp but was blowed if he was going to share his knowledge with Snatterjee (who would most likely turn his nose up at whatever it was The Frog judged to be edible unless driven to do so by the last throes of starvation – and only then under protest).

The result of this stand-off was that both declared they would go off in search of food and rapidly went off in opposite directions to eat. After about twenty minutes both wandered back to their camp and reported to each other, with profuse apologies that they had been unable to find anything in the way of sustenance. Strangely enough, both were wiping their mouths and patting their stomachs and The Frog gave a loud belch and looked guilty.

The Frog kept finding little make-work jobs to do around the camp as Snatterjee struck camp ready to set off but there came a time, inevitably, when he could procrastinate no longer. Snatterjee waited by the track, tapping his foot and with his pack on his back looking expectantly at The Frog who shuffled his feet and hung his head.

'What's the matter?' asked Snatterjee, who knew full-well what the matter was.

'I'll be getting' back to the rats now,' The Frog muttered and held out his hand.

'Nonsense,' cried Snatterjee in a voice full of bonhomie and joviality. "If you remember, our agreement was that you guided me *into* Sloo Swamp, not just to the outer fringes. So, come on, old chap, let's be off.'

The Frog had only the dimmest of recollection of what he *had* agreed to, his wits being turned by his lust for the shining piece of amber (but not so much for the gyroscope, which he mistrusted as being some form of magic that might well turn on him and destroy him). This lust still burned brightly in his soul. With a resigned shrug he shouldered his own pack and set off gingerly along the track. He debated whether it was only fair to explain to Snatterjee that he had only been here on one previous occasion and that he had not gone more than a quarter of a mile before his nerve had failed him and he had legged it back to Mud Wallow at full pelt.

He decided it was more prudent to keep schtum.

By contrast, Snatterjee exuded an air of irrepressible confidence and blatant lies about the good fortune that lay just within The Frog's grasp that soon overcame the latter's scruples (not to mention abject terror) and he reluctantly began to inch his way forward along the track, Snatterjee close behind.

Sloo Swamp was a wasteland of mud – black, stinking, sucking, oozing, foul mud- and stagnant water covered by a carpet of green slime. The track they followed was only a couple of feet wide at best and was frequently less than half that. There seemed to be a ridge of lightly packed dirt running into the Swamp and it was on this ridgeway that they gingerly crept along. Whether this was a natural or artificial phenomenon Snatterjee had no way of knowing. When he asked The Frog about it he was given the pessimistic reply that it was an artifice deliberately built by the cunning Houmjars to lure the foolhardy on to a horrible doom.

After a couple of hours of slow and nervous progress the little copse where they had spent the night was well out of sight. The sun rose to its apogee and hung overhead like some vulture in a cartoon, ready to swoop and feed when they inevitably dropped with exhaustion. The reflected sunlight speared off the water and flashed silver and gold spears into their eyes, causing them to squint. To add to their discomfort (well, mainly Snatterjee's, The Frog didn't seem to mind too much) the sun's heat was stirring up the rank, decaying odours of the Swamp that burst on the surface of the water with disgusting pops like a severe case of flatulence.

The Frog grew increasingly fearful. His pathetic moans and whimpers blended with the symphony of pops and gurgles from the marsh gas. Snatterjee trudged along behind The Frog, shielding his eyes with one hand and trying to keep focused on the trackway. His left leg was coated to the knee with drying mud where he had suffered a momentary lack of concentration and stepped off the narrow path. It was only by screaming for The Frog's help that he had managed to extricate his leg from the hungry maw of the Swamp. He had lost his left wellie in the mud and been forced to spend several thoroughly unpleasant minutes groping about under the surface of the mud-bath to rescue it. Sticking his foot back into the boot and whatever might have crept in there to make its home (like some kind of hermit crab) had taken all the courage he could muster.

'I can't go on! I can't. I can't' wailed The Frog suddenly and stopped dead in his tracks. Snatterjee barged straight into him, knocking him face down in the mud. He picked him up quickly before he could drown and set him back on his feet.

'What's the matter now?'

By way of a reply Snatterjee received an incoherent garble made all the more difficult to understand because The Frog's few teeth were clacking together with fear and anyway, he had a mouthful of mud.

'Shut up!' Snatterjee shouted, full of compassion and solicitude, and gave The Frog an encouraging shake. Gradually The Frog's tirade wound down to a low drone. He stood, a pathetic creature, with his head bowed and his long arms hanging limp by his side. His face, through its mask of mud, a picture of misery like a puppy that has been smacked for chewing up the new furniture.

'Now,' said Snatterjee, in a calm and reassuring tone, 'what is *exactly* the matter?'

'Clack, clack, clack, clack,' replied The Frog's teeth.

'You're frightened?' Snatterjee divined.

'Click, click, click,' accompanied by frantic nods of the head.

'And why, precisely, are you frightened?' It was like talking to a small, not very bright, child.

'Hou...hou...hou...'

'Houmjars? Is that what you mean?'

The Frog nodded again and then his knees started to quake so violently that Snatterjee feared he was going to tumble off the path, which was very narrow at this point. It was high time for drastic measure.

'All right. If you are that frightened, you'd better go home. Go on. Go. Shoo.'

The Frog gave him a look of dumb gratitude (c.f. the puppy) and held out his hand.

Snatterjee took it in his own and shook it. 'I shall miss you, old chap.' He said.

The Frog shook his head and held out his hand again. Snatterjee pretended not to understand and looked quizzically at the filthy limb.

'I'm sorry? Do you want something?'

'Payment,' said The Frog, his voice returning to something like its normal whine at the prospect of getting out of the Swamp unharmed and going back to an untroubled life of worrying rats.

'No chance,' Snatterjee scoffed.

The Frog fired off a stream of truly inventive insults and abuse at Snatterjee which failed to move him in the slightest (apart from making a mental note of some of the more choice items for future use). He then tried to edge past Snatterjee but the track was far too narrow and Snatterjee effectively blocked all attempts to get past him.

After five minutes of this fruitless fandango, it dawned on The Frog that he was effectively stymied.

'You said you would pay me if I guided you *to* Sloo Swamp,' accused The Frog, trying to be reasonable. 'You said nothing about going right *in*.'

'I lied,' Snatterjee admitted, shrugging his shoulders and spreading his hands palm out. On his face there was an expression that clearly said: 'Well, of course I lied. What did you expect?'

The Frog's fear was replaced by a burning anger such as he had never before experienced. He turned abruptly and marched forward, leaving Snatterjee to follow through a wake of muttered threats and promises of dire retribution.

9

The track grew narrower and narrower until their progress was reduced to the torturous pace of putting one foot carefully before the other and creeping forwards like very inexperienced funambulists out on the wire without a safety net. The heat and brightness of the day, such as it was, were over and the temperature was falling. Snatterjee was getting worried: if the track did not widen out soon they would be in serious trouble. There was no chance that they could pitch camp or even just lie down where they stood on such a precipitous perch. Yet to go on, weary and in darkness, was rank folly.

He tried asking The Frog for his opinion but The Frog was still in a mega sulk and not speaking to him.

Then, just as dusk was closing in, the track opened up into a large, hard-packed square that just *might* have been custom-built to be a camp site.

Keeping this rather creepy thought to himself, Snatterjee cheerfully called a halt to their march and requested The Frog to halt and assist him make camp.

Now that they had come this far into the Swamp – six or seven miles as far as Snatterjee could judge – there was no danger of The Frog sneaking off in the night and abandoning Snatterjee to his fate. The Frog was far too big a coward to attempt the journey back by himself in the dark. They would have to wait until the following day to resolve their dispute. However, Snatterjee reasoned, now might be the time to offer The Frog a little bribe, a sweetener, an inducement to get him to stay. There was always the danger that Snatterjee would oversleep and The Frog have it away on his toes at first light. If the truth be known, Snatterjee did not fancy travelling alone into the mysterious depths of Sloo Swamp any more that The Frog did.

So, when the tent was up, Snatterjee dug about in his pack and produced a small hunk of salt pork which he waved in the direction of The Frog, who still had not spoken to him.

'Hungry?'

The Frog squinted at the morsel from out of the corners of his eyes but kept his head averted and his back half turned to Snatterjee. He made a series of gestures with his fingers accompanied by mutterings and hisses. Finally, he spat on the ground.

'I'll take that as a NO then? Shame. It's salt pork. The best in all Minfadlek. It's a little bit I've been keep for emergencies or a special occasion. But you can have it. In recognition of your bravery in coming this far.'

The Frog scowled and stamped his feet but at last turned to study the peace offering seriously. Drool ran down his chin. The salt pork of Minfadlek was famous (and expensive!). The Frog had never actually tasted it, only heard its praises lauded. Still without speaking, he stretched out a hand and snatched the titbit from Snatterjee, ramming the whole piece into his mouth until his cheeks bulged and his eyes popped. The salt pork did not disappoint.

The food had the desired effect. The Frog thawed and as they lay in the tent to sleep went as far as to discuss their plans for the morrow. Snatterjee let him ramble on, mostly ignoring what he was saying. His own thoughts were turning over the curious fact of the perfect square of hard earth stuck at more or less one day's march into the Swamp. It was most odd and not a little disconcerting.

Just before he drifted off to sleep, he set his mental alarm clock (which never failed him) for half an hour before dawn. He trusted The Frog about as far as he could comfortably spit him.

*

The night, although cold and damp, passed without incident. Snatterjee was up and about well before The Frog stirred, thus removing any temptation to abscond on his part. The Frog, however, much to Snatterjee's surprise, seemed to be in a much more cheerful frame of mind. He had, had he not? survived a day and a night in Sloo Swamp without having his innards torn out and force fed to him by some terrible being from the outer reaches of the imagination (not all that far in The Frog's case). He was a simple creature and once his initial fears had proven unfounded, he was happy enough to accompany anyone who was prepared to feed him such heavenly delicacies as Mindaflek salt pork. Nothing had struck him as particularly odd about their camp site and Snatterjee wisely skirted over his own disquiet.

Shortly after first light they struck camp and set off again, Snatterjee bringing up the rear. Within a matter of metres the path narrowed again as it, and they, plunged deeper into the heart of the Swamp.

*

The second day and night of their trek into Sloo Swamp was pretty much a repeat of the first. Again, as dusk was falling they came upon another square island of solid ground in amongst the ocean of mud and water that surrounded them.

"You know,' mused The Frog as he sat outside the tent staring up at the stars and wondering if, by any chance, Snatterjee might have another overlooked morsel of salt pork in his pack, 'it's odd about these camping places.'

'Yes,' Snatterjee agreed in a non-comital sort of way. He was wondering how he might sneak himself a snack without The Frog being any the wiser.

'It's almost as if they have been put here on purpose.'

'Hmmm.'

'Do you know what I mean?'

'Hmmm.'

'Well? What do you think?' demanded The Frog, hoping that his worldly-wise companion might be able to provide and comforting and non-threatening answer to the riddle.

'I expect you're right,' answered Snatterjee, who had not really been paying attention.

'Oh,' said The Frog, surprised that Snatterjee had agreed with him, even though he had not provided a comforting and reassuring explanation. 'Well, good night, then,' he said and crawled off into the tent. Moments later he was snoring without a care in the world.

Snatterjee waited another five minutes and then found himself something to eat.

Tomorrow was another day and it might just be the day he met the Houmjars.

*

Despite all the terror tales about just how ferocious they were, very little concrete information regarding the Houmjars was current in the world outside Sloo Swamp. You could never find anyone who had *actually* met a Houmjar. It was true that plenty of people knew of friends of friends who claimed to have met one but to come across genuine first-hand witnesses (who weren't making it up to make themselves seem important and interesting and probably didn't have a girlfriend) was about as rare as finding a waterfall in the desert.

Some folks told that the Houmjars were a race of goblins or pygmies or a hybrid of human and babazel.

(*babazel* (n) a creature like a very angry baboon, only smaller and twice as fierce.)

Others maintained they were stunted giants, just over eight feet tall with red eyes and a spare head. Yet other swore faithfully that the Houmjars had no heads at all, had eyes at the tips of the two fingers on each of their three hands or had a slavering, gaping mouth situated directly over their stomachs.

What is more, no one knew for sure *how* or *where* they lived. All were in agreement that the Houmjars lurked in Sloo Swamp but whether they dwelt in caves, in houses built on stilts situated on lakes or simply in holes in the mud was the subject of much disputed debate. The most fanciful had them living in tents made from the flayed skins of their victims using the backbones of aforesaid victims as tent poles and their ribs for tent pegs.

Snatterjee had discounted the latter theory on the grounds that so few people ever went within a hundred miles of Sloo Swamp if they could help it that ready supplies of tent material to make repairs to the natural wear and tear must be impossibly limited.

Snatterjee told himself to keep an open mind and took himself off to bed.

10

Snatterjee awoke the next morning to find The Frog dancing around on the soft mud at the edge of the campsite. The dance involved much stamping of feet and the occasional dive with the hand that was then brought to the mouth. Snatterjee stared, bemused. Had The Frog suffered some kind of incident in the night? Were his wits scattered to the four winds?

'Do yer want some?' asked The Frog, pausing in his antics.

'Some what?'

'Bog worms?'

(*bog worms* (n) foot-long albino worms that live deep in the mud of wetlands. They can be enticed to the surface by the art of *worm charming (cv)*.

To worm charm (v) the art or practice of enticing *bog worms (cv)* to the surface by causing vibrations in the soil and thus arousing their curiosity. They come to the surface to see what's going on and can then be easily caught as they are confused and blinking in the light.)

'Good eating,' said The Frog pulling a pale worm from the ground and slipping it into his mouth like a strand of wriggling spaghetti.

'I'll pass, thank you.'

'Yer don't know what you're missing.'

Snatterjee had a pretty shrewd idea what he was missing and despite the pangs of hunger racking his stomach, decided to give it a miss. 'When you are ready,' he said and set about striking camp. The Frog captured another couple of bog worms and stuffed them in a pocket for later – who knew where their next meal was coming from?

Snatterjee and The Frog had been in the Swamp for two days and nights and had penetrated fourteen or fifteen miles. So far they had not seen the slightest trace of life (save the bog worms), let alone eight foot stunted giants or villages on stilts. Snatterjee was beginning to entertain doubts as to the very existence of Houmjars as confirmed by anyone who was habitually sober.

Nevertheless, *someone* or *thing* was responsible for the beaten squares of earth. Conflicting thoughts chased around in Snatterjee's head as they prepared to set off on the third day's march.

The Frog, on the other hand, not one of the world's great philosophers, was getting more chipper by the hour. The longer he went without seeing hide or hair (or scale or hard chitinous covering or mottled skin covered with running sores or…) of the Houmjars, the more cocky and confident he became. Already, in his mind's eye he could see the hero's welcome that awaited him back in Mud Wallow and the cups of Finest pressed upon him by citizens eager to hear the saga of his exploits. He was even beginning to regard Snatterjee in a benevolent light for giving him this opportunity to travel and broaden his hitherto limited horizons. He strode along the path whistling and singing (-ish) and tossing small clods of earth into the fetid pools to watch the bubbles burst on the surface and disturb the slime. He could tell by the pained expression on Snatterjee's face that the smell stirred up by his actions was causing his companion grief, which encouraged him to throw all the more. Beneficent to Snatterjee he might feel at this precise moment but the fact that he Snatterjee had tricked him still rankled.

Once again the sun dazzled as it reflected off the water and the green meadows of slime. Somewhere ahead must lay an immense sheet of open water because the glare from that direction was intense. Neither of them could stand to look directly ahead, so bright was the shining light. Consequently, they walked along with their eyes cast firmly down on the path. After tramping through the morass for all this time, the scenery held little in the way of attraction so they were content enough to watch their feet on the narrow path.

Each was set in his own train of thought; Snatterjee on the puzzle of the campsites and whether the Houmjars *really* existed and was he just wasting his time on a fruitless quest when he could be back in Minfadlek making money and The Frog on when his next meal might be and just how much salt pork did Snatterjee have hidden in his pack when the voice came booming out of the Swamp from their left hand side:

'What do you seek, strangers to the Swamp?'

Their heads swivelled left but they could see nothing because of the glare that now enveloped them.

'Who...who are you?' Snatterjee stammered.

'I am of the people of Maston' replied the ethereal voice.

'P...p...p...' was the best The Frog could muster.

'You of the Outside know us by the name of Houmjars!'

The Frog gave a little scream and collapsed at Snatterjee's feet in a dead faint, a nasty wet patch spreading over his crotch.

Snatterjee took no notice. He didn't see him. His eyes were tight shut.

11

How Snatterjee and The Frog got from the path through the Swamp to Dorien was never quite clear. Snatterjee had a vague, hazy recollection, like a thing seen through dense fog, of a machine, a conveyance that skimmed at mind boggling speed over the surface of the water, mud and slime. But his brain, faced with the total incomprehensible, had shut down and taken itself off for a holiday until things returned to normal.

The Houmjar, or to give him the name by which he was known amongst his peers, Elishu Brightstar of the Maston, citizen of the city of Dorien in the Land of the Fanshee, was another matter. Snatterjee had a clear impression of a tall man with long black hair falling to his shoulders. He wore a long flowing robe of purest white down to his ankles. On his head was a headband of brightly coloured beads and around his waist his robe was gathered in by a loose girdle of plaited scarlet leather. His voice, when he wasn't using his megaphone for dramatic effect, was sweet tempered and his cat-like green eyes twinkled with good humour.

All this Snatterjee took in peeping through his fingers because he had his hands pressed over his eyes on the often tried and just as often failed theory of, 'If I can't see you, you can't see me.'

'Help me with your companion,' requested the Houmjar, going over to the prone and unconscious body of The Frog. Snatterjee noticed that he seemed to have no difficulty walking on the mud, nor did the hem of his robe become soiled.

'What are you going to do with him?' hissed Snatterjee,

fearing the worst and not *really* looking forward to a detailed answer.

'Why, I'm taking you both back with me to the city of Dorien to rest and recover from your labours. And find you a change of clothes and a hot bath,' he added, noticing the state of The Frog.

This reply sounded far from the blood-curdling reputation of the Houmjars. Snatterjee risked taking his hands away from his face.

'Darien? What's that?'

The tall Houmjar laughed and his laugh was pleasant and soothing to the ear.

'Darien is the city of the Maston whom you call, for some strange reason, Houmjars. You shall see. It is a city very fair and lovely to look upon.'

'And you are not going to tear our throats out just for swallowing?'

Again came that wonderful laugh.

'Have no fear.'

'How about ripping the very tongues from our mouths just for speaking?' Snatterjee persisted.

'As I said to you; have no fear.'

Snatterjee thought he might have detected just the tiniest note of impatience in Elishu's voice but he still wanted to get everything *absolutely* clear.

'Cut off our feet just for walking?'

'No!'

'Poke our eyes out just for looking?'

'Will you shut up and help me with your friend!' Elishu resorted to using his megaphone.

Snatterjee jumped to obey before the Houmjar took it into his head to cut off Snatterjee's hands just for carrying.

Together they carried The Frog into the silver machine and laid him on a bunk in the spacious rear compartment. Snatterjee thought he heard Elishu mutter about having to get the machine valeted and fumigated.

Elishu went to a bank of lights, switches, buttons and little levers in what appeared to be the front of the machine. Two bucket seats faced the instrument panel and a curved glass windscreen gave a view of the Swamp all around them.

'Come. Sit here with me,' Elishu called and patted the seat next to himself, his voice once again calm and well-modulated.

With his heart in his mouth, Snatterjee shuffled forward and plunked his backside down into the seat. It was made of a shiny black material, the like of which Snatterjee had never seen and with a clunk and a click Snatterjee was secured to his seat by a tough but flexible strap from his shoulder to his waist.

He had been well and truly captured!

All the stories of the Houmjars and their fiendishly inventive cruelty and love of sophisticated and prolonged tortures were true!

His fate was sealed and he was facing a death most terrible just as all his friends back home in the safety of Minfadlek had warned him about.

He felt very sorry for himself and blinked back a great comforting tear of self-pity.

The next instant Elishu's hand flew over the instrument panel and there was a great roar like a thousand isbeks all growling at once.

(*isbek* (n) a *really* frightening creature very like a mole but the size of an Indian elephant. Lives in huge warrens underground)

The machine gave a lurch and tilted forward, Snatterjee fainted. It seemed the wisest thing to do in the circumstances and as he lost consciousness he was aware that he was *well pissed off* that The Frog had thought of it first.

12

When he came round, he discovered that the terrible roaring had stopped and so had the sensation of movement. He risked opening one eye and having a quick squint. He was still strapped to his seat and so his gaze was directed out of the windows. What he saw made proud city of Minfadlek look like one of the most run-down and neglected bits of Mud Wallow.

Heart-breakingly beautiful towers of glass speared into a clear blue sky. Surrounding the towers were swards of emerald green lawns, each adorned with a fountain in the centre – a constant movement of jets and fans of clean, clear water. Rainbows danced where the beams of sunlight passed through the water. Snatterjee thought he had the impression of soft music humming in the crystal air but could not be sure, the whole impression overwealming his perception of reality, one minute in the foul depths of Solo Swamp and the next…here.

He could see small knots of people walking on the lawns, conversing together. They were smiling and laughing and all, men and women both, dressed alike in long white robes, their feet bare.

The sun reflected off the glass towers, turning them into shards of silver and gold yet the glass seemed to have been treated in some way so as not to dazzle the eyes of the onlooker. Snatterjee realised that it must have been this shimmer that he and The Frog had seen out in the Swamp. And of the Swamp itself there was not the slightest trace.

'Whoa!' said Snatterjee at last when his mouth had stopped gaping. He shook his head and rubbed his eyes but the vision did not go away.

A moan came from the rear compartment of the wonderful transportation machine.

'Are we dead?' asked The Frog in a pathetic little voice.

'You've got to come and see this,' Snatterjee urged.

Reluctantly, The Frog came into the control cabin.

It is a recorded phenomenon that members of a particular civilization, when confronted by the artefacts of a totally alien civilisation simply do not, or cannot, see said artefact and this was The Frog's way of dealing with the world outside the window.

He blanked it out.

'What did they do to you?' he asked.

'What are you talking about?'

'How did they kill you? Did it hurt? Was it *really* horrible?'

Snatterjee thought he detected a note of prurient delight in The Frog's tone of voice.

'Kill me? Nobody's killed me. Sorry to disappoint you!'

'Isn't this heaven, then?' The Frog asked in evident surprise.

'Aha, he *is* aware of the great outside. He just can't process it properly yet' thought Snatterjee, who wasn't doing much better, to tell the truth.

'I mean, one minute we were in Solo Swamp surrounded by savage and blood-thirsty Houmjars ready to bury us alive in the mud just for being there and the next we are here.' He waved vaguely in the direction of the window. 'It *must* be heaven. Stands to reason. It isn't Solo Swamp and it certainly ain't Mud Wallow. Where else could it be?'

To be fair, The Frog's experience of the world apart from those two places was limited to zero.

'My friend,' said Elishu, whom The Frog appeared not to have noticed, was sitting right next to Snatterjee, 'welcome to the city of Dorien.'

'Who's he? An angel?' The Frog jerked a thumb in the general direction of Elishu.

'He's a Houmjar,' replied Snatterjee, anticipating The Frog's response with some relish.

There was a thud as The Frog hit the floor in another self-preserving faint.

'Oh dear,' said Elishu, his voice full of genuine concern. 'We really must do something about this poor fellow.' He regarded The Frog with eyes that radiated concern and compassion and then his face clouded over and he scratched his head. 'You know, your friend reminds me of an illustration I once saw in a book in the Great Library that contains All Knowledge. Some sort of aquatic creature that could also live on land. Let me think…'

'I think you will find it was a frog,' Snatterjee muttered.

'That's it! That's it exactly.' Elishu snapped his fingers. 'A frog! What's his name?'

Snatterjee thought for a moment. 'Dunno,' he confessed. 'I call him The Frog. He's the Mud Wallow Rat Worrier.'

'I have no idea what you are talking about.'

'Never mind. It would take too long to explain and anyway, I'm not sure I do it justice. It's a Mud Wallow thing.'

With a shrug to show that he, too, was not terribly interested in The Frog's antecedents, Elishu turned his attention back to his instrument panel and pressed a button.

The door of the vehicle slid open with a sigh of compressed air, admitting subtly perfumed air from outside to flood the cabin, carrying with it the muted sounds of talk and laughter.

Elishu leaned over Snatterjee and snapped the stud of Snatterjee's seatbelt which shot back into its housing, making Snatterjee jump.

'But how ill-mannered of me,' Elishu apologised, 'I have not asked you for your own good name.'

'Snatterjee. From Minfadlek.'

'Then come, Snatterjee of Minfadlek and be welcome to the city of Dorien, fair city of the Maston.

Between them, they picked up The Frog and carried him out of the craft and down the ramp that led to the ground.

A small crowd had gathered, curious for what news Elishu might have brought back from the Outer Reaches. Usually not a lot, but you never knew. And today the crowd had struck lucky. Here was Elishu with *two* strangers. An excited buzz of anticipation came from the crowd.

'Hail to you, Elishu, Warden of the Perimeters!' said an old man with a full white beard and a carmine stripe on his robe, stepping out from the crowd and raising a hand in greeting.

(*carmine stripe*: The Elders of the Maston of the city of Dorien are distinguished by a broad coloured stripe running from top to bottom of their robe. These stripes are in different colours:-blue, green, red, purple, orange, carmine, and denote which clan or sept the wearer is a member of. Different shades of colour indicate the rank of the wearer.)

'Hail to thee, Elder Etheron of the Maston. I bring guests to the city of Dorien. May I present to thee and to those Bretheren and Sisteren assembled here, Snatterjee of Minfadlek and… er…The Frog of…er…'

'Mud Wallow,' whispered Snatterjee, who, now that there

seemed to be no imminent danger of being horribly killed, was beginning to enjoy being the centre of attention.

'Mud Wallow.'

'Hail and Welcome,' intoned the old man.

'Hail and Welcome,' echoed the crowd.

'Which is he that is unwell?' Etheron asked. 'Wait! Don't tell me. That must be… The Frog.

'Got it in one,' said Snatterjee out of the side of his mouth.

'Hail to thee, O Learned One,' chanted the crowd in admiration.

At this point, The Frog woke up again and looked around. Before he could faint again the crowd chanted 'Hail and Welcome' at him. As he took stock of himself and checked that the correct number of limbs were still attacked to their accustomed places on his body and that he not been torn into little pieces of pulsating agony, he managed to fight down his fear and with the greatest control he had ever exercised in his life, keep his eyes open.

'It seems to be OK,' Snatterjee hissed in his ear from between clenched teeth. 'I don't think they intend to do us any harm.'

'Urkle,' said The Frog, not totally convinced.

'Pray, Elishu, O Warden of the Wastes, lead our guests to a place where they may take their ease and partake of such food and drink as whets their appetites. And where they might change their soiled raiment,' instructed the Elder, with a significant glance at The Frog and his piss-stained garments.

At the mention of food, The Frog visibly cheered up and shook off Snatterjee's and Elishu's supporting arms.

'Yes!,' he said, 'take us to the food.'

'I am glad to see that you have recovered from your

unwarranted fear of us.' Elishu noted in a dry sort of voice.

'Wasn't fear, it was the heat,' explained The Frog defensively.

'Ah, yes, the heat,' Elishu agreed in a whisper that only the three of them could hear. 'Not, of course, the fear of having your living heart gauged out of your chest and eaten before your dying eyes.' He winked at Snatterjee as the blood drained from The Frog's face. Snatterjee gave a cruel and merciless laugh. It dawned on The Frog that the others were having a laugh at his expense and he shot them a venomous glare but was not *wholly* convinced that the Houmjar was joking. It might well be a ploy to lull him into a false sense of security aimed at throwing him off his guard. It was a universally acknowledged truth that you could not trust a Houmjar not to do *something* utterly disgusting and violent at the drop of a hat.

Fortunately, The Frog was not wearing a hat.

'Come,' instructed Elishu, 'follow me.'

13

He led the way through the gathering crowd, who gawped politely at the strangers but made no move to molest them or even tear them to bloody pieces just for walking, over to the nearest tower. Snatterjee and The Frog followed like sheep, their eyes big and round with wonder.

Close to, the tower appeared to rise up into the sky for ever. Looking up at its height made Snatterjee feel dizzy and uncomfortable. Minfadlek had its own grand four-storey edifices built of mud bricks but nothing as impressive as this. Snatterjee gave up trying to count the floors when he got confused after thirty-four. Logic told him buildings could not *be* that tall.

They passed through a great arched doorway into a marble atrium studded with shops and a sprinkling of idle people examining their contents through the windows with little obvious intent of making a purchase. As a member of the retail industry, Snatterjee would have like to examine the outlets himself but Elishu hurried them on.

The interior of the building was lit as bright as daylight, the light emitting from some source that could not possibly be candle power.

Elishu hustled them away from the curious eyes of the window-shoppers to a narrow metal doorway with two buttons set into a panel on the right-hand side. He jabbed a finger at one of these buttons, marked with an arrow pointing upwards, and they heard a whirring, whooshing noise in response. Moments later the door opened and they found themselves facing a tiny metal room with no space for furniture of any kind.

Elishu ushered them inside.

'I don't think much of this,' Snatterjee whispered to The Frog.

'I think it is wonderful,' replied The Frog in an awe-struck voice, comparing it, no doubt, to his own rush-hut outside Mud Wallow.

'Well, yes, I suppose *you* would.'

On one of the walls of the tiny room there was a long column of numbered buttons. Elishu touched the uppermost of these (number sixty-four) and the metal door hissed closed.

Suddenly the tiny room seemed to shoot upwards although there was no way of really telling if they were moving. There was a pressure on their ears unlike anything they had experienced before and the room hummed.

They both simultaneously vomited on the floor and farted loudly.

Elishu made a soft noise of disgust and tried to edge away from them as far as the cubicle would allow but in that confined space he could not get very far.

The noise and vibration stopped. Elishu thankfully pressed another button and the door slid open, releasing a miasma of odours.

The atrium had vanished.

In its place was a large room, comfortably furnished with armchairs and a sofa, all sinking into the thick pile of a carpet of purest white that stretched from wall to wall. Doorways led off to left and right. The wall facing the entrance was one huge sheet of glass, trimmed by heavy black drapes.

Elishu hurried into the room and swiftly passed through one of the doorways.

Snatterjee and The Frog stood uncertainly in the middle

of the room, not sure what was expected of them. Then they heard the sound of running water and the sounds of someone washing. Behind them the door of the little room swished closed and they heard the whirring sound again. Snatterjee, the sophisticate from Mindadlek, had worked out that the little room was some kind of mechanical device that saved you the fag of hacking up endless flights of stairs to get to what was obviously the top of the tower. The view of uninterrupted sky out of the window was a distinct clue.

Elishu reappeared, shaking water from his hair, and asked them if they wanted to 'freshen up'.

'What for?' asked The Frog, looking puzzled, while Snatterjee gratefully accepted Elishu's offer. He was shown into a spacious room covered in aquamarine tiles from floor to ceiling and full of strange devices all in a tasteful and uniform avocado. Attached to the ceiling was a bright light in an opaque rectangular box. Along one side of the room was what looked like a calaphel drinking trough, although what it might be doing up here and why it needed to be of such fine quality Snatterjee could not guess. A strange pipe came out of the wall with a watering-can nozzle on the end; a ceramic chair with a lid had a box with a handle suspended over it and next to it was an oval bowl-like object whose use Snatterjee was at a total loss to explain.

While Mindadlek was not the armpit of civilization like Mud Wallow, standards of plumbing and personal hygiene regimes were light-years behind those enjoyed by the good folk of Dorien. Soil outhouse privies were regarded as state-of-the-art luxuries by the affluent of Minfadlek (into which group Snatterjee yearned to be numbered) and buckets were seen as perfectly good all-purpose sanitary systems. It was important, if you were picky, to remember to empty your bucket after use as a bodily-waste receptacle if you were planning to use the bucket to wash your face but apart from that, the system worked fine.

Thus, it was not really Snatterjee's fault that he was bewildered by the choices on offer. He chose the lidded cistern and thrust his head and arms into it for a good splash around. While he was enjoying the clear, cold water washing off the mud and filth of Solo Swamp and the traces of vomit that clung to his chin, The Frog came in behind him.

'What's this for? he asked and before Snatterjee could raise his head, pulled the little lever on the box over the cistern.

A rush of water caught Snatterjee at the back of his head and shoulders and flowed onto the floor. Water gushed into his mouth and up his nose. He emerged, splattering and choking for breath to see The Frog beating a hasty retreat out of the door. He snarled and chased after him, fully intending to drown him but he was too slow: The Frog had taken shelter behind the tall figure of Elishu, who, for some obscure reason, was convulsed with laughter.

'Enjoy your wash? Here, let me show you how the bathroom functions.'

Elishu introduced them to the joys of hot and cold running water, the power-shower, the hot tub, the bidet, the flushing toilet.

Stripped of their mystery, Snatterjee and The Frog wanted to try everything at once. They turned on every tap, ripped off their travel-and-vomit soiled clothes and disappeared into a world of steamy bliss.

'I could get used to this,' The Frog croaked, splashing in

the hot tub, naked for the first time in years and not for one minute thinking the hot tub might be a diabolical Houmjar device for boiling frogs.

Slowly.

14

By the time Elishu hauled them out of the bathroom they were both quite pruney and cleaner than they had ever been in their lives. Snatterjee was experiencing a deep sense of well-being and The Frog was in shock. A large pile of fluffy bath towels had materialised in the living room and their old clothes had vanished. In their place, neatly folded on an armchair, were white robes like the Houmjars wore. Elishu pointed to the robes: 'These are for you.'

Clean, dry and in their new clothes there was only one thing left to take care of and Elishu had thought of that too.

'These are your quarters for as long as you wish to stay with us. Please make yourselves comfortable. The bedrooms are through that doorway there.' Then, from his pocket, he produced a black rectangle that gleamed like glass. He touched his finger to its surface and a glowing light appeared.

'Use this if you want anything,' he said, handing it to Snatterjee, who stared at it. 'It's pre-set. All you have to do is tap the icon here and you will be connected.' He might as well have been talking to the wall for all the sense he was making to Snatterjee.

'Oh, hi, this is the penthouse in Sapphire. I'd like to order some food.' He then issued a list of incomprehensible things that Snatterjee assumed were foodstuffs. There was a strong clue when Elishu asked for *Ten Thousand Tasty Tidbits* amongst other items. 'About fifteen minutes? Great. Thank you.' He flicked his finger over the device and the light faded. With a smile, he tossed it to Snatterjee, who fluffed the catch.

Elishu laughed.

'What *is* that thing?' Snatterjee asked, a terrible certainty growing in his mind. His whole body started to tremble.

'It's a Handy,' said Elishu. 'Haven't you seen one before?'

'And it grants wishes?' Snatterjee was almost beside himself. Was this the end of his quest?

'What? Like that Fabulous Frowla thing you told me about?' asked The Frog, finally beginning to cotton on to the reason for Snatterjee's excitement.

'Shut up! Shut up!' Snatterjee hissed and went to kick The Frog's shin to drive his point home.

'Does it have...' Snatterjee paused and gave Elishu a sly glance, 'another name? Something beginning with...eff?'

'Not that I know of. It's just a Handy. You can use it all over Dorien but you can't get much of a signal out in the Swamp.'

Snatterjee's mind was in a whirl. He was convinced he was in the very presence of the Fabulous and Wonderful Frowla, despite all Elishu's obfuscations. Well, he would deny its true identity, wouldn't he? Snatterjee certainly would.

'How does it work?' he tried to sound both innocent and politely curious at the same time. 'How does it grant wishes? Is it magic? Of course it is.' He was babbling in excitement. This was it, this was it, this was it!

How to get it for himself? But Elishu had already given it to him, hadn't he? No talk of a loan. Oh no. Precious!

But wait. What had Elishu said?

You can use it all over Dorien but you can't get much of a signal out in the Swamp.

That couldn't be right, could it? The Fabulous and Wonderful Frowla was a universal charm so this marvel might *not* after all be it.

Elishu was talking but Snatterjee had been too wound up to listen. Waves of conflicting emotions pulsated through him. High. Low. High. Low

'Sorry, what?'

'I was just explaining. A Handy is basically a two-way radio that can send and receive signals blah blah blah blah…'

Snatterjee had zoned out and let the gibberish wash over his head. Elishu might well have been speaking in a foreign language for all the sense he was making. The Frog was stretched out on the sofa and beginning to snore softly.

'…So, there, simple.'

'OK,' said Snatterjee, cutting to the chase, 'so how does it grant wishes, then?'

'What?'

'Wishes. How does it grant wishes? You wished for food.'

'No, I *ordered* food. From the Takeaway. D'liver2U will collect it and bring it to us. Simple.'

'What about other things?'

'Such as?'

'Riches beyond imagination,' Snatterjee tried, just to test the water. 'Girls?' he ventured, and then couldn't think of anything else.

Before he could reflect on his lack of imagination, the little metal door went *ding* and opened to admit the object of his dreams.

She was wearing a tightly fitting tunic that fell to mid-thigh and was the colour of leaves in May. Across her impressive chest was emblazoned:

D'Livered 2U

For one intoxicating moment Snatterjee thought that fifty percent of his dreams had come true.

'Delivery for Elishu,' she said in the sweetest voice Snatterjee could ever remember hearing. His knees felt weak.

She was wheeling a small cart which she pushed into the centre of the room. She lifted a number of lids and the aromas of paradise flooded the room.

The Frog realised that if anybody's dreams had come true, they were his.

'Tuck in. You must be hungry,' said Elishu as Snatterjee's erotic fantasy disappeared back into the tiny room and swoodhed away out of his life.

Saliva was drooling down The Frog's almost non-existent chin and forming a pool on the floor.

'I don't suppose...' said Snatterjee, tentatively.

'What?'

'Is there anything to drink with the food?'

'I took the liberty of ordering some bottles of wine,' Elishu smiled. 'I thought you might be thirsty.'

'What's wine?' asked The Frog.

*

Snatterjee risked opening one eye. He appeared to be lying on the floor. Something was stuck to his cheek. He explored his face with hesitant fingers and gently prized off a spare-rib bone cooked in Philosopher's Sauce that had dried onto him as he lay face down on it. He gave it a lick, sucked the remaining sauce and flesh off the bone and tossed it away.

He decided to heed the banging in his brain and go back to sleep.

*

Bright sunlight flooded the room. Snatterjee was aware of a terrible pressure on his bladder. He hauled himself to his feet, swayed as his body reached full vertical status, flinched as the sunlight crept under his eyelids like needles of light and tried to orient himself in the direction of the bathroom. He either had to find it *very* soon or not bother. He cranked his eyes open and lurched into a stumbling dash.

He made it just in time.

And in the appropriate receptacle.

*

The room had been so beautiful when Elishu had left. Now it resembled a disaster zone. Plates and dishes lay scattered across the floor; stray bits of food had been trodden into the carpet; empty wine bottles cluttered like corpses on a battlefield; The Frog lay on his back, a wine bottle clutched in his hand, a happy smile smeared all over his face like some demented clown. He alternated between gentle burps and pooping farts.

15

It was morning. Bright golden sunlight streamed through the window. At some time during the night a clean-up crew must have hit the living room for now it was its old, pristine self with no trace of the debauch of the day before.

Elishu arrived in what he called 'the elevator', which, Snatterjee reasoned, was all very well if you were going *up* but what did you call it when you were going *down*?

'Good morning! Did you sleep well?' Elishu was disgustingly cheerful. 'Have you had breakfast?'

A breakfast of various breads and flakey cakey things, along with a selection of fruits and jams had been set out for them during the night, presumably by the clean-up crew. Neither of them could face the idea of solid food and so there it had stayed, untouched.

'Any more of that wine?' asked The Frog, hopefully. For one who had only previously aspired to drink Mud Wallow Finest, wine had had a life-changing effect on The Frog.

'Not for breakfast,' Elishu said primly. 'However, if you are ready, I have been charged to bring you before the Assembly of Elders.'

'Now that I think about it, *perhaps* I *might* be able to manage a mouthful of food,' said The Frog; if they were to be taken somewhere, who knew when the next meal might present itself. No sense in taking chances.

'Then take your ease and refresh yourselves. I will return anon.'

'These Houmjars don't half talk funny, but they seem to be

decent enough,' said Snatterjee after Elishu had left.

'I don't know why you were so scared of them,' The Frog sneered.

'ME?'

'Yerst. You.'

'Who was it that kept fainting at the lightest mention of the Houmjars?'

'That was jerst hunger, that was. An' the heat of the sun.'

'Bollocks!'

'Have yer tried this flaky cakey thing?' asked The Frog, changing the subject. 'It's loverly!'

The Frog was well on his way to single-handedly clearing the breakfast tray when Elishu returned. To take them to the Assembly. With the best will in the world, Snatterjee could not face the idea of food.

'Good nosh,' The Frog smiled a contented smile at Elishu and flicked his long tongue over what seemed to be most of his face. He was a creature of simple wants and a full belly seemed to cover most of them.

'Now that you have broken your fast, the Elder Council of Dorien of the People of Maston wish to have the pleasure of conversing with you. Please, come with me.'

This time there was no backing out. They followed Elishu into the elevator and were whisked down to ground level.

Elishu led them out of the tower and along a wide pathway past several other tower blocks. All were brightly lit inside and thronged with people coming and going, for all the world just like a colony of ants.

They came, finally, to a single storey circular building and entered through a tall but narrow doorway. A vestibule adorned with busts of solemn-face male Maston Elders regarded them gravely from niches around the walls. A gentle slope led into an amphitheatre that had been excavated out of the ground. Glowing sources of light set into the surrounding walls lit the whole and as far as Snatterjee and The Frog could see, every marble seat in the amphitheatre was occupied by old, distinguished men (with only a handful of women scattered here and there on the upper row of seats) with a single bright stripe on their robes.

Elishu led Snatterjee and The Frog down into the pit of the amphitheatre where two seats awaited them. After telling them to sit, he vanished discreetly.

From the front and lowest row of seats a venerable old man rose to his feet. He hooked a thumb into the top of his robe (green stripe), shuffled his feet until he felt he was in the approved stance for public speaking and fixed an unswerving gaze on the two strangers. The hum of whispered conversation died away. The venerable old man waited until there was total silence.

'Hail and Welcome, Strangers to the Land of Fanshee.'

Snatterjee thought hard for a suitable response.

'Y'aw'rih'?' said The Frog.

The venerable old man looked taken aback, shook his head and pretended that he had not heard.

'We bid thee make thyselves at home here amongst us for as long as ye may wish to tarry here.'

'Wha'?'

'He says we can stay.'

'Well, why didn't he just say so.'

'Shut up and listen. Leave the talking to me.'

'What is it that brings you here to the Land of Fanshee where few dare venture?' continued the Venerable Old Man.

Snatterjee and The Frog exchanged glances. The Frog shrugged his shoulders. At the end of the day, he was, after all, only the guide.

'The Fabulous and Wonderful Frowla,' Snatterjee admitted in a small voice.

'The *what?*' demanded The Lord High Elder (for such was the VOM).

On all the seats Elders shook their heads and spread their hands at each other to show that they had no idea what the stranger was talking about. There was a hubbub of earnest muttering.

'The Fabulous and Wonderful Frowla,' Snatterjee repeated in a louder voice in case some of the senior citizen were hard of hearing. A distinct sinking feeling was growing in the pit of his stomach. 'You know, the Frowla. That grants wishes. That Frowla.'

'Never heard of it,' said the Lord High Elder, dropping into a more vernacular form of speech. 'Anyone know what he's talking about?'

His question was met by a ragged wall of negatives and shaking of grey locks.

'But you *must* have heard of it,' insisted Snatterjee, on the verge of tears. 'They said the Houmjars of Solo Swamp knew where it was.'

'And who are "they"?'

'Two men I overheard talking in John's Frothy Cocoa Shop back in Minfadlek.'

'Perhaps if you tell us *exactly* what it is,' another of the Elders (red stripe) spoke up kindly, 'then maybe we can help you.'

'I don't *know* what it is,' Snatterjee wailed. 'I was relying on *you* to tell *me*.' Although, when it came down to it, Snatterjee had not thought out just *why* the Houmjars would reveal *anything* about such a priceless treasure to a total stranger, let alone give it away!

'I don't see how you can expect us to help you if you don't even know what it is you are seeking,' a third Elder (navy blue stripe) pointed out reasonably.

The Frog gave Snatterjee a withering look that said: 'I told you so but would you listen? Oh, no,' and sat back in his chair looking smug.

Snatterjee's face was a picture of woe. To have come so far and to have braved so much only to have his hopes and dreams so cruelly dashed was too much. He slumped in his chair and hung his head, fighting back his tears.

'Er, if I might make a suggestion,' shouted a fourth Elder (lemon stripe, so, quite junior). 'Gentlemen. Gentlemen…er… and Ladies.' Female Elders were a recent innovation and not all members of the Assembly were quite *au fait* to the concept.

The noise of the Members debating Snatterjee's folly died away. The Elder stood up and assumed the position for public rhetoric: one hand behind his back, fingers crossed. He cleared his throat and suggested, a little self-importantly: 'Let him be taken to The Library, for it is possible that there, amongst the Wisdom of the Ages, he might learn of that which he seeks.'

He sat down, beaming to acclimations of 'Hear! Hear!' and 'Oh, jolly good!'.

His political career was made.

The Lord High Elder rose to declare the Assembly was

dismissed but The Frog had a question.

'How come you lot have such a bad name, then?'

'Mastons?'

'Nah. Houmjars. Them as would rather…'

'Ah,' said the Lord High Elder, 'that.'

The rest of the Assembly re-seated itself with a collective sigh.

'We are a peaceful people,' in a tone that suggested he had given this spiel many times, 'who shun war and the hurly-burly of the pitch and toss of life on The Outside. Many, many years ago we retreated from all that into the fastness of this Swamp to what we call the Land of Fanshee. We decided to leave the Outside to its folly and madness and pursuit of wealth and ambition. And yet still we were not left to live our lives in peace as we wished. Men sought us out even here in the Wasteland to steal from us and take our inventions and technology by force. Things we would have shared freely. Many of us were carried off to a life of slavery, a life of drudgery and despair.' Here his voice sank an octave and he placed a hand on his forehead. Cries of 'superb' and 'oh, I say' came from the rapt audience and a ripple of polite applause ran around the chamber.

'Thank you,' the Lord high Elder said, bowing to left and right. 'We were severely troubled. In our most optimistic moments we had thought the Swamp to be sufficient barrier against these incursions from the outside.' He paused. 'But it was not to be. So, we invented the Houmjars.'

'Aha,' said Snatterjee, suitably awed by the cunning plan of the Mastons. 'So all this talk of horrible tortures and hideous deaths were all an invention?'

'Oh, no,' beamed the Lord High Elder. 'We actually did all that stuff. We had to have credibility and it did the trick wonderfully. We were right bastards.'

As the Assembly rose for the second time Elishu was trying to revive Snatterjee and The Frog by pouring cold water over their unconscious heads from a carafe from the Speaker's table.

Just before they had fainted they had turned an impressive shade of green.

16

That afternoon, after a long lunch ('to recover from the shock revelation about the Houmjars'), Elishu arrived back at what they now nonchalantly called 'the penthouse' to take them to the Library. The Frog had spent a part of the morning riding up and down in the elevator and annoying Snatterjee by pressing the button that went *bing-bong*.

Strangely, neither could remember just *how* they got back to the penthouse after the morning's meeting with the Assembly. Snatterejee had a curious nagging niggle at the back of his mind like an itch that desperately needed scratching. He was sure it was some vital nugget of information about the Houmjars but just quite *what* eluded him.

They were walking across an open plaza and waving a cheery 'good afternoon' to the friendly Mastons when the niggle became a naggle and the full horrific memory of the Lord High Elder's closing words hit Snatterjee like a kung fu kick to the stomach.

'This morning,' he began cautiously, 'when the Lord High Elder was joking about the Houmjars and what they used to do to strangers…'

'Alas,' said Elishu, sounding very apologetic, 'it was no joke. It's true.'

'Ah,' said Snatterjee and swallowed. He found to his surprise that his throat was suddenly very dry for some reason. 'But that's all over now, isn't it?' Ending on a hopeful note that came out preciously close to a squeak.

'Have no fear, Snatterjee of Minfadlek. Your position here

is one of honour. Our plan for peace and solitude worked only too well. We have had no visitor, or shall I say, guests, for many a long year. It takes a brave man indeed to find Dorien and such as do come are held in great esteem by us. We ask only one thing of you and that is not to speak of what you have found here to the world Outside. For if you did and we were plagued by the unwanted attention of the masses who sought to take from us that which we have created, we would be forced to re-awaken the Houmjars. And that would cause us great distress, for we are a peaceful people. And by the way, during our long years of uninterrupted peace, our scientists have developed weapons that can destroy whole cities in a single flash. This, of course, we would be loath to do and only use as a last resort.'

Did Snatterjee detect a mad gleam in Elishu's eyes for a second? A slight frothing around the corners of the mouth? He couldn't be sure.

'I'm pleased to hear it,' Snatterjee assured him. 'When it comes to being peaceful, you Mastons certainly do it in style. But don't worry about me, I'll never speak a true word about Darien to anyone. Promise.'

'Me neither,' said The Frog. 'In fact, if you keep feeding me I'd be happy to stay here forever and worry rats for you.'

Before Elishu could comment on The Frog's offer they arrived at a compact two-storey, circular building. Standing waiting for them by the door of the Library was a wizened little man with long white hair that hung almost to his waist. The stripe on his robe was a rich vermillion and he wore knee-length buskin type boots of soft green leather.

'Hail unto thee, Strangers in Search of Knowledge,' he

greeted them in a high and creaky voice that sounded like he had not used it in a long time.

'Why do they always insist in speaking in capital letters?' Snatterjee muttered but The Frog did not seem to think there was anything at all strange in anything the Mastons said or did. He was a little bit in awe of them and a little bit in love with them (and totally terrified of their incarnation as Houmjars).

The Librarian led them into his domain through imposing portals that bore an inscription in an alphabet Snatterjee had not encountered before.

They emerged into a cool, slightly dim circular space. Natural light filtered down from skylights set in the ceiling some thirty feet above their heads. A maze of bookshelves rose from the floor to just below the ceiling. Each stack had a curious mobile staircase attached to it with a platform at eight-foot intervals where a reader could sit and browse. Snatterjee guessed there must be over a million books housed in the Library and was puzzled why anyone would need *so many* books. You couldn't possibly read them all.

'Now,' said the Librarian, fussing with his hands, rubbing them together as if he were washing them and making a sound like rustling parchment, 'let me see. Eff. Eff for Fabulous or eff for Frowler? Is that how you spell it, by the way. F.R.O.W.L.E.R?

'I don't know,' Snatterjee admitted. He had never considered the orthography of the Frowla, never seen the word written down.

Faced with a near-impossible task, the Librarian was in seventh heaven. 'Well then, let's see, shall we. The hunt is ON.'

He scurried off and disappeared into one of the stacks. Now and then they could hear the sound of a staircase being moved about and the rustle of pages being turned accompanied by a constant susurration of grunts, ticks, tongue clicks and hums with the odd exclamation of frustration and disappointment. Mixed into this were a number of words Snatterjee did not recognise but decided they were probably swearwords that he resolved to remember and use when he was back in Minfadlek. Their use, he concluded, would make him sound sophisticated, mysterious and interesting to girls.

By the end of the day, as the light in the Library was fading and reading became too difficult, (artificial light was banned in the Library for fear it might fade some of the more ancient volumes) the Librarian announced that he had consulted a total of three thousand, six hundred and seventy-seven books, all without success. He had found all manner of 'Fabulouses' innumerable 'Wonderfuls' but not one 'Frowler'.

He agreed, reluctantly, that it was time to call it a day and that it was probably time for dinner. The Frog, who had spent most of the afternoon snoozing on a reading platform, woke up and agreed enthusiastically.

'Tomorrow,' said the Librarian, not one whit daunted by his task, we will try F.R.O.W.L.A.R. Then, if we meet with no success, we will go on to F.R.O.W.L.O.R.' And then he started the hand-washing business, much to Snatterjee's irritation. 'I must say, this is fascinating. Fascinating. I've not had so much excitement since I don't know when.'

'Great!' Snatterjee yawned, grateful as ever.

17

And so it went on the next day and into the next. The Frog took to bringing packed picnics with him and perching himself on the uppermost platforms of the stairs, alternatively snoozing and spying out for rats to worry. He had taken the whole idea of settling down and applying for citizenship of Darien very much to heart. With regard to the Houmjars and their terrible reputation, he reasoned that if he *was* a Houmjar, he would be perfectly safe. He rather liked the idea.

Snatterjee, for want of something better to do to pass the long hours while the Librarian ferreted about in the stacks, started browsing through the Library for his own amusement. He looked up *Salt Pork* (there was a whole shelf of tomes devoted to the subject), got bored and had started on a reference to *Gyroscopes* when his eye was caught by *Gyromancy* and from there he set off on a journey into *Magic – Grimoires*. Most were hand-written in an arcane script and in a language he could not read but many also featured illustrations of female demons of the succubus variety and who were frequently depicted naked (but all in the best possible taste – nothing prurient!).

It was, to the Librarian's everlasting annoyance, Snatterjee who made the breakthrough on the third day of searching.

He was idly skimming through Egbert's 'Lesser Appendix to the `Grimoire of Fell" (Vol 1) and had reached page 3,692 when he saw it:

Frowla: the Fabulous and Wonderful

'It exists!' he shrieked. He had been beginning to lose his faith in the very existence of the object of his quest and now here he was, his faith vindicated.

The poor Librarian was right at the very peak of a staircase and reaching out to the top shelf of a stack for a particularly weighty tome and nearly lost his balance in alarm. *Nobody* shrieked in *his* Library.

In order to save himself from a nasty plummet, the Librarian lost his grip on the book he was removing from the shelf and it fell to the ground, narrowly missing The Frog (who had come down off his perch for a bit of a stroll to work up an appetite for his next meal). The book was a copy of *The Principals of Viniculture Among Nomadic Topers* and weighed in at ten kilos.

'Listen,' Snatterjee screamed, totally unaware of The Frog's close encounter with literature (not that he would have been unduly concerned, this discovery threatened to make The Frog surplus to requirements). '"*The Fabulous and Wonderful Frowla, that's F.R.O.W.L.A., is a Talisman of great power. It is said that it hath the ability to grant wishes of whatever magnitude to whomsoever doth possess it. Alas*"' read a note in the margin of the text Snatterjee was quoting from, '"*I do not know what its shape or form it may be.*" How about that, then?'

'Fantastic,' said The Frog, apparently unphased by his brush with a serious head injury, 'Just marvellous. Now we know *what* it is but we still don't know *where* it is or what it looks like.'

The Librarian said nothing: he was sulking because it had not been himself that had found the reference to the Frowla first. After all, it was *his* Library. Librarians and academics can be very petty when it comes to gifted amateur interlopers straying into their fields. Think of bulls or billy goats.

However, the Librarian was swift to score a point.

'So, it's some kind of Magickal doodah, is it. Hmm. Oh

dear...oh dear.' His voice faded away to be replaced by clicking and tutting sounds accompanied by lugubrious shakes of the head.

He was enjoying himself.

'What "oh dear, oh dear?"'

'Oh dear, indeed,' the Librarian paused and climbed down the stair, savouring his revenge in the full while Snatterjee squirmed with impatience tempered with panic: he could feel his prize being snatched away from him.

'You see,' said the Librarian, now with both feet planted safely on the floor of the Library, 'we stopped having any truck with Magick after we discovered Quantum Physics, although, if you ask me, it's much the same thing.' He gave a dry little chuckle in appreciation of his own joke. 'I grant you there is still the odd couple of hundred books on Magick cluttering up the shelves but most of that stuff we cleared out and recycled. It was all too contradictory. So, we opted to go with the physics. Seems to work.'

Snatterjee didn't have a clue what the Librarian was wittering on about but the cut and thrust of the retail market in Minfadlek had taught him cunning. He was too canny to show his ignorance and so he bluffed.

'Ah, yes, of course. I can see that that makes perfect sense.'

'Is there something to eat?' asked The Frog, not wishing to be excluded from the conversation. 'Only, it's been a while.' The other two glared at him. 'Well, I only asked.'

'So,' continued the Librarian, softening a little to see his antagonist obviously crushed, 'you'll have to go and seek out someone who keeps up his studies in all things Arcane.'

'Who do you suggest,' asked Snatterjee, humble in defeat.

The Librarian was fully back on top. *That'll* teach him not to go around shrieking in *my* Library. In victory, he felt magnanimous. 'I'll have to look in Schmetterling's *Register of Practicing Necromancers, Warlocks, Alchemists and Fakirs.*'

'We don't want any fakers,' interjected Snatterjee hurriedly. 'We need the real thing.' A tiny flame of hope was flickering into life in Snatterjee's soul. The Frowla existed. How hard could it be to seek it out. The fact that it might be in the possession of some mighty wizard who might not be inclined to just hand it over to Snatterjee if he asked nicely never entered his thoughts. Snatterjee was an optimist's optimist.

'Fakirs! fakirs! Really,' he muttered to himself, 'I don't know where they dig these people up from, I really don't. The Library is supposed to be for serious scholars.'

With a great swishing of his robe and a shuffling of his soft boots, he made his way along the stacks, still muttering until he found what he was seeking. He took down a large volume bound in Zingba skin and embossed with fancy-looking gold lettering. Checking the date printed on the spine to see if the contents were still fairly up to date, he proceeded to leaf through its pages, all the while making funny little mewing sounds to himself. A solitary life spent in the silence of the great Library had made him unaware of the effect his verbal tics might have on an audience.

His mission accomplished, he closed the book with a bang that jerked The Frog out of his light doze and shout 'Wazzat?' in some alarm.

'I have found someone who *may* be able to help you,' the Librarian intoned with evident satisfaction at having redeemed his credibility as a researcher.

'Who?' demanded Snatterjee

'Where?' asked The Frog, more cautiously, as befitted a guide of his standing.

'M'Fang. Doctor of the Arcane Arts. He lives in the Forest of Grimgristle.'

'Is it far?' asked The Frog

'Many, many leagues to the south of the Fair City of Dorien,' intoned the Librarian in a sing-song voice. 'So, you'd better set off first thing in the morning.'

'Not before breakfast, I hope,' The Frog said to no-one in particular.

18

Next morning, brooking no delay, Snatterjee was up early and raring to go. The Frog demanded a full breakfast before he would budge and so breakfast was conjured up by a D'Livered 2U

Maiden, who also brought ample provisions to stuff their backpacks for the journey ahead. Snatterjee had no wish, if he could help it, for a repeat of the skimpy rations of the first part of their journey.

Snatterjee and The Frog were loaded aboard Elishu's Swampmobile and whisked off to the boundaries of the Land of Fanshee where they were decanted onto one of the square campsites.

Elishu pointed down the track. 'From here it is only about twenty miles or so to the edge of the Swamp. Keep going south for three days or so and you will get to Grimgristle Forest. You can't miss it. It's big and full of trees and things. I'm told M'Fang lives somewhere in the middle. According to the Librarian that was his last known address. He might have moved. Anyway, off you go and good luck. Come back and look us up if you find yourselves back in the Swamp any time.'

'Can't you take us?' asked The Frog, not relishing the prospect of a twenty-mile march.

'I'd love to, Elishu lied, 'but I'm not allowed to exceed my boundaries.

And with these parting words, he jumped back into his vehicle and shot off back in the direction of Dorien, spraying Snatterjee and The Frog with a wave of mud and slime as he went.

And that is when the bickering began.

The Frog maintained that he had only been engaged to guide Snatterjee *to* Solo Swamp and that he had, in fact, guided him *through* the Swamp and out to his next destination and had, therefore, more than discharged his obligation under their agreement. So, could he please have his gyroscope and bit of amber with the beetle in it, 'thankyouverymuch'. He was in a quandary: should he try and make his way back to Mud Wallow or should he try and get back to Dorien and apply for citizenship. He was inclined towards the latter option but not sanguine about its feasibility. Only all in words of one syllable.

To be fair, Snatterjee fully appreciated the justice of what the Frog was saying but (and there is always a 'but') although The Frog was far from his idea of the perfect companion on a Quest (he had in mind, perhaps, a D'Livered 2U staffer), he was better than no companion at all. After all, he reasoned, if they met with a pack of wolves, it was better to have someone to throw to them than the alternative. And Snatterjee was, when it suited him, healthily superstitious. He was ambivalent about the whole idea of trekking off into strange forests in search of Dealers in Demons or what-have-you all by himself.

Thus, he countered The Frog's perfectly valid assessment of their verbal contract with a totally fictitious version of his own: to whit, that The Frog had been engaged to help him, Snatteerjee, retailer of Minfadlek, find the Fabulous and Wonderful Frowla and seeing as how this end had not yet been successfully accomplished to the satisfaction of all parties subject to said agreement, he Snatterjee (see above) did not feel justified in releasing him (The Frog, rat worrier of Mud Wallow) from his contractual obligations. The contract could, however, be rendered null and void upon the payment of an undefined but large compensation payment in lieu.

The Frog was not at all happy about the bits of Snatterjee's rhetoric that he actually understood but his memory of what had *actually* been agreed was rather hazy after all these days of travel and excitement. As a compromise, he suggested that he might forgo any payment and just go home. Snatterjee countered this by saying his home was forfeit if he did not fulfil the terms of the contract. This terrified The Frog. His home in Mud Wallow was all he had ever known and had been handed down through the generations. The fact that it would take him all of ten minutes to build himself a new home escaped him.

Then Snatterjee tried his second tack – appealing to The Frog's cupidity.

'Think how wonderful it was in Dorien. Now think of all the marvels a fully-fledged wizard can produce. Stick with me and you will really see all that the world has to offer. You don't want to go back to Mud Wallow just when the whole world is opening up to you, do you?'

'Yerst,' said The Frog, 'I do. I likes it there.'

'No! This will be the making of you. Think what an important person you'll be when you *do* eventually get home, loaded with fame and fortune. Why, I bet they'll even give you Mr Bates' job.'

The Frog regarded him suspiciously, like a puppy that has puddled the floor and can remember doing it before and is being coaxed out from under the sofa by its master, who is holding a rolled-up newspaper (don't do this at home).

'Do you really think so?' he asked, his eyes wide and innocent.

'Would I lie to you?' demanded Snatterjee in shocked and

hurt tones at the very hint of such a suggestion, his fingers firmly crossed behind his back, 'My faithful guide, and, may I say it, *companion,* in this great adventure.'

'I'm not sure.' confessed The Frog, warily. He *wanted* to believe Snatterjee but experience told him otherwise.

'Think of the never-ending feasts wizards are always having. They make the food at Dorien seem plain and the portions novelle cuisine.'

The Frog had no idea what novelle cuisine was but he *did* know that wizards were well known to be the possessors of magic porridge pots and never-emptying bottles and tables that magically spread themselves with sumptuous arrays of delicacies served on golden dishes at the slightest word of command.

And it was then that Snatterjee played his trump card.

'And when we find the Fabulous and Wonderful Frowla, I will give you *one whole wish of your very own!* Anything you have ever wanted shall be yours. How about that for a deal-clincher?'

The Frog was sold. He agreed to accompany Snatterjee to the ends of the earth, if needs be.

'Grimgrisle Forest will probably do,' said Snatterjee, somewhat aghast at the prospect of having The Frog round his neck for a moment longer than necessary.

19

The road took them south. The muddy, boggy country slipped away with each passing mile and the terrain changed gradually to flat grassland dotted with trees which became taller and more prevalent. On the second night out of the Swamp they stayed in a pleasant little village of thatched houses and spent the night in a clean and airy inn that served both good food and good ale.

While The Frog was eating and drinking as if this were the first time he had ever tried it, Snatterjee engaged the landlord of the inn in conversation.

'We are travelling to the Forest of Grimgrisle,' he said, 'do you happen to know it?'

'Aye,' confirmed the landlord with a nod of his head. 'It's a weird and wonderful place. So I've heard tell.' His voice darkened. 'No-one who ever goes into Grimgrisle Forest ever comes out again quite the same as they were when they went in.' And although his voice was ladened with dire and dark foreboding, his words were said with some relish and a manic gleam in his eyes.

'Why's that? What happens?' asked Snatterjee with a quick glance over to The Frog to see if he had overheard and taken fright but he was too busy stuffing his face as if this were his last ever opportunity to eat and drink to take any interest.

'I don't rightly know,' the landlord confessed. 'You see, I've never been there myself. Never wanted to. I'm happy just as I am.'

'Aha!' Snatterjee thought, 'it's another story like the

Houmjars.' He felt a sense of relief – he knew the truth about the Houmjars, after all.

'But,' continued the landlord, popping Snatterjee's bubble, 'I've heard it reliably said that it's an easy place to get *into* but not quite so easy to get *out of* again. Just saying, like.'

'Yes,' remarked Snatterjee slowly, 'you said something like that before.'

The landlord casually looked around the taproom to see if they were being overheard. Satisfied that they were not, he leaned in closer to Snatterjee and whispered: 'What's more, it's full of Ne'rdowells.' He leaned back in triumph, watching Snatterjee closely to gauge his reaction to this revelation.

(*Ne'rdowells (n)* As the name implies, the generic term for all manner of anti-social elements that have no place among decent, law-abiding folk – as judged by themselves)

'Ne'rdowells?' Snatterjee shook his head. This was one myth he's never heard before. He supposed that every place had its bogeymen, used to frighten the children into obedience and impress strangers. Take the Houmjars, for instance. But then he remembered that the Houmjars were real!

'Yes! Ne'rdowells. Folk that have a good reason to hide away from other, honest, decent folk. Know what I mean?' He winked at Snatterjee, man to man of the world.

'No. Quite honestly, I've no idea what you are talking about.'

'Robbers. Crooks. Folks that have run away from home. Or worse! Cheats. Swindlers. Cardsharps and gamblers.'

'Oh,' said Snatterjee grinned in relief. '*Those* sort of Ne'rdowells!' He didn't understand what the landlord was making such a fuss about; he was talking about most of the citizens of Minfadlek and Snatterjee was perfectly comfortable in such company. But from the landlord's serious demeanour, it dawned on Snatterjee that he must have stumbled upon a seriously honest and upright part of the world. He saw the inn with fresh eyes. The customers sat and drank in moderation, their voices never raised. No-one spat on the floor – there wasn't even sawdust on the floor – or farted loudly to impress their drinking companions. No-one took a sly pull out of another's glass when the person got up to go to the toilet. And there was an *actual* toilet, rather than the alley outside.

'Yes,' Snatterjee mused, 'I can see how bandits and robbers and their ilk would not be welcome here. But a good grifter could clean up!'

'Aye, those sort,' the landlord was saying. 'If you're really planning to go into Grimgrisle Forest, young fellow-me-lad you'd best keep your wits about you and your hand on your money pouch. Me? I'd avoid Grimgrisle Forest like the plague. Terrible tricky folks, they are, them Ne'rdowells. So I've heard.'

Snatterjee looked suitable shocked, thanked the landlord profusely for his words of wisdom and shortly afterwards took himself of to bed, whistling a carefree air.

*

Three days later they passed a small, neat farmstead with a freshly whitewashed fence by the side of the road. They had passed many such, but what made this one remarkable was a large sign displayed by the front gate. It read:

The last honest house before Grimgisle Forest

You have been warned!!

'What do you think that means?' The Frog asked Snatterjee.

'Nothing. Someone's idea of a joke,' responded Snatterjee,

who had not bothered The Frog by repeating the innkeeper's words to him. The Frog was easily upset and Snatterjee did not want to set him off on one at this late stage. 'Ignore it.'

That night they stopped at a well-appointed campsite with all mod cons and a hand-written sign announcing that the campsite was called:

Grimgrisle View

Free Camping

And there, indeed, was the Forest, a dark, lowering and forbidding mass of trees stretching away as far as the eye could see in the sombre twilight.

Gratefully, they pitched their tent and enjoyed a reasonably-priced and reasonably cooked meal in the small restaurant on the site. Happily sated, they crept into their sleeping bags and slept an uninterrupted night's repose.

But hardly had they packed up to leave the next morning when they found themselves confronted by five very large men who demanded an equally large sum of money from them.

'What for? The sign says "free camping"' Snatterjee argued.

'Campin' *is* free,' growled the largest of the five, a man whose bulk would give a grizzly bear an inferiority complex.

'Then why do we have to pay? There must be some mistake.' Snatterjee was prepared to be sweet reasonableness in view of what obviously a misunderstanding of some sort.

'Ter *leave*,' snarled the giant. 'It's the toll, see. Fer usin' the gate. Wear an' tear. Now, pay up!' He clenched a fist the size of a firkin and glowered.

As he extracted some coins from his fast diminishing stock, Snatterjee reflected ruefully on the landlord's warning, mentally kicking himself for not recognising one of the oldest scams of all. Many establishments in Minfadlek that featured exotic dances as a part of their cabaret employed just such a ruse for extracting money from their punters.

He gave himself a mental pat on the back for having the foresight to secret a stash of cash in his boots.

*

A broad path led into the Forest. Massive trees intertwined their branches to form a great green tunnel into which the light of the sun filtered in, soft and diffused, dappling the mulch on the forest floor with spots of buttery sunshine. Dust motes danced in the sunbeams. Birds sang, high overhead in the canopy, lost in the dense foliage. Ferns, luxuriant and dense, provided shelter for the small scurrying creatures that dared to be out in the daytime, taking their chances with the predators that stalked the undergrowth. The foreboding and forbidding aspect that the Forest presented to the outside world was belied by the cool calm within. The greens of the trees were the gentle summer greens of deciduous trees rather than the dark green needles of the conifers. Judging by their height and girth, Snatterjee reckoned these trees to be very, very old.

The overall impression of the Forest, as they entered it, was one of warmth and shelter, like a womb.

Snatterjee was instantly on his guard.

*

They had not gone very far when they came upon a small house built out of split logs and roofed with bark, overlaid by soil. Grasses and meadow flowers grew on the roof, giving the impression that this was a natural feature of the Forest rather than a human artefact.

A man was sitting on a stump of wood by the doorway. He had a long, scrawny neck and a pointy sort of face that reminded Snatterjee of a lizard. His hands, too, were thin and horny and restless. When he spoke, his voice had a sibilance to it.

'Visiting or stopping?'

'I beg your pardon?'

'I said, visiting or stopping?'

Understanding dawned: 'We're just visiting.'

'Play cards?' asked the creature.

'No, we most definitely do not,' said Snatterjee firmly and hustled The Frog off along the path before he could say anything.

'What did you do that for?' The Frog asked when Snatterjee released his grip on his arm and they were out of sight of the cottage. 'He seemed a nice person. My sort of person.'

'Yes, I *could* see a certain resemblance.'

'You can be very nasty at times, you know that?'

'Listen,' said Snatterjee with what he thought was great patience and forebearing, 'he would have taken you for everything you possess, you poor booby. You'd have come out of there stark bollock naked and no doubt in debt.'

The Frog made a humphing sound and sulked for the next hour.

During which time they encountered an alarming assortment of odd folk who eyed them up with a mixture of suspicion and/or greed.

They hurried past a notice nailed to the trunk of a tree that advertised murders committed for very favourable terms, with discounts for bulk or repeat orders.

Men wearing long raincoats leapt into their path from the shelter of tree, flashing their coats open to reveal rows of watches, cheap jewellery, packets of razorblades and other dubious-looking knicknacks festooned about the inside of their coats and calling out:'Psst, guv, wanna buy…'

For The Frog it was like some surreal dream; for Snatterjee it was just like old times in Minfadlek when he was just starting out in retail.

Most peculiar of all was the strange being clad from head to toe in a skin-tight costume of black leather who erupted from the shelter of the tree to hurl an object very much like a custard pie at them.

Before Snatterjee could stop him, The Frog caught it in mid-trajectory, gave it an exploratory lick and then devoured it in two monstrous gulps.

The figure in black howled, whether in rage or frustration Snatterjee did not know, and vanished back from whence it had come in the depths of the Forest.

'There are some very weird people around here,' said The Frog. 'Nice pie, though.'

*

The path forked at an enormous old oak tree that wore a covering of moss like a snug-fitting fur coat. A part of the massive trunk had been hollowed out and a red and yellow stripped booth set up inside the tree itself.

An old crone sat inside the booth, looking bored. She was wearing a spangled scarf wrapped around her head. Her gnarled old fingers were covered in rings and huge bronze hoop earrings hung from her earlobes to her hunched shoulders.

'Cross my palm, dearie,' she cackled when she saw them. 'Cross my palm and I'll unlock all the mystic secrets of your future for you. I've read the palms of crowned heads, I have. Just have a look at these testimonials.'

Despite his better judgement, Snatterjee was drawn closer to the booth where the crone had a collection of dog-eared pictures of her much younger self taken with a number of people, none of whom Snatterjee recognised.

'All famous, from all walks of life. Crown heads, some of them. None of yer riff-raff.'

'What does she mean about crossing palms?' The Frog whispered in Snatterjee's ear, much impressed (and a little intimidated) by all this talk of the great and the famous.

'She's after our money. What do you think they all want?'

'That other man gave us a pie,' The Frog pointed out in all innocence.

'There are people that your mother should have warned you about,' Snatterjee snapped back, rolling his eyes in exasperation.

'Why's that then?'

'Never mind. Never mind.'

In the meantime, the Fortune Telling Lady had taken all her things inside to make room for a scrying glass and what appeared to be a mishmash of at least three different Tarot packs. Not only were the styles of the cards different but the actual cards themselves were of different sizes and vintages.

'Now then, now then, step up, step up,' she barked, 'who's going to be first? Don't be shy. Have your future foretold. By the world-famous Gypsy Princess Annabella!'

'Gypsy Princess Annabella?' pondered a sceptical Snatterjee.

'Yeah, right!'

'We can't all be called Rose or Lee, dearie,' she shot back at him, her eyes narrowing as if she was racking her brains for a suitable curse to hurl at Snatterjee for his impertinence.

'Look, could you just possibly tell us which fork to take to find a magician or wizard or whatever called M'Fang?'

Gypsy Princess Annabella's reaction took them totally by surprise.

'M'Fang! M'Fang is it? That...Huckster!' she screamed, going an apoplectic red in the face and knocking over her pile of old Tarot cards as she waved her fists at them.

The Frog sidled round behind Snatterjee and watched the spectacle round his elbow.

'Ah, so you *do* know him, then?' confirmed Snatterjee genially.

'Gerroutovit!' yelled the enraged woman, threatening them with her scrying glass.

They fled down the left hand fork (without realising the magical symbolism) and for a long time they were perused by the angry screams of the gypsy, gradually fading away as they ran.

'Mountbank!'

'Charletan!'

'Faker!'

'Crook!

*

Before they knew it, the day was ending and the light was fading and somehow the Forest did not look quite so benign.

They found a clearing and Snatterjee entrusted The Frog with the task of putting up the tent while he scouted the immediate vicinity for any signs of life – animal or human.

When he returned from his patrol, having satisfied himself that they were in no immediate danger, he found that The Frog had not, in fact, erected the tent but had spent the time setting snares in the hope of trapping some small furry creature for supper, their rations from Dorien being on the point of exhaustion.

Cursing loudly, Snatterjee set about the task himself while The Frog smashed down bits of foliage for firewood for a fire that Snatterjee would not let him light.

'Do you want to advertise our position to people who offer a wholesale murder deal? Are you out of your mind?'

They spent an uncomfortable night not speaking.

20

At first light the next morning The Frog crept back to the camp carrying the still warm bodies of a variety of small furry animals that had fallen foul of his snares. Snatterjee awoke to the aroma of roasting meat and was forced to admit (through gritted teeth) The Frog's prowess as a hunter. He also pointed out that the smell of cooking was drifting through the Forest and that any Ne'rdowell with a nose would be homing in on them like iron to a magnet. The Frog, in a rare moment of considered thought, decided it was best not to mention the scruffy little urchin, (who had been mooching around near their camp to see if there was anything worth nicking that wasn't nailed down) caught by the leg in one of the outer ring of traps. The child's wide and inventive range of expressions had taken The Frog completely by surprise when he set the child free but the description of what revenge his extended family might take had persuaded The Frog that it might be prudent to strike camp as soon as possible.

Snatterjee, unaware of any lurking retribution, was impressed by The Frog's helpfulness and, indeed, alacrity, in packing the tent and stowing their bits of kit. He was pleased that The Frog had heeded his warning and was trying to make amends.

They were back on their road before the sun had climbed very high in the sky, munching their breakfast as they strode along in search of M'Fang, Practitioner of the Arcane Arts.

Luckily for them, the feral child who had been caught up in one of The Frog's traps, was a part of a clan of robbers, thieves, footpads, rustlers and contract killers that did not believe in rising early. By the time they had been roused to wreak revenge on The Frog for ensnaring one of their own, their quarry was long gone.

*

Snatterjee and The Frog journeyed on as the sun climbed to its meridian without meeting a living soul.

Once they saw a human skull perched in the crook of a tree where the branches divided but it didn't do very much (or *anything*) for the ten minutes they spent watching it so they resolved to ignore it and continue on their way. The Frog was noisily sucking the marrow out of the last of the bones left from their breakfast. Snatterjee whistled a tuneless air through his teeth and swung his arms back and forth as he marched along. The day was a pleasant one, temperate, not too hot, not too cold and the Forest was at peace as it lay in its tranquil green light.

It reminded Snatterjee of the interior of the Library in Dorien. All in all, it was an idyllic day – if a warm, drowsy forest rent by birdsong and a full stomach can be said to be idyllic and there is no danger of Ne'rdowells plunging out of the undergrowth to ruin the day.

The smooth path was getting noticeably rockier and was picking up a distinct incline. Where yesterday there had only been the occasional boulder, there were now great slabs of rock to either side. Trees grew precariously out of crevices, spearing their way into the sky. They were coated in blue-green lichen and hung with strands of wispy moss which gave them a decidedly unhealthy appearance.

The great press of forest trees thinned out and the light here was stronger, unfiltered by the canopy.

Without warning they came to an open meadow carpeted with flowers – yellow, pink, red and blue. A blizzard of butterflies drifted over the meadow, sinking down for a moment onto the blooms and then drifting lazily back into the still air.

Bees buzzed.

A tiny waterfall tumbled from a rocky outcrop and flowed into a little rill that vanished away among the trees to their left.

Into this rocky outcrop a cave had been hollowed out, either by the hand of man or the hand of nature. Around the entrance to the cave, in dayglo letters of lime green, was written the following message:

Dr M'Fang

And underneath that

Master of the Mysterious
Practitioner of the Arcane Arts
B.A, B.Sc., M.A., D.Phil
(and a lot more)

Surrounding this information were drawn the signs of the Zodiac and other Magical symbols and sigils, as well as chemical formulae, the odd mathematical equation and one or two symbols that Snatterjee was pretty sure he recognised from weather forecasts.

Seated on a folding canvas deckchair outside the entrance was a tall, thin figure dressed in a tweed suit and wearing over it a ragged black academic gown that was turning green with age.

On his head he wore a mortarboard hat. Its tassel hung down in his face and he kept blowing at it to keep it out of his eyes.

'Dr M'Fang, I presume?' said Snatterjee, extending his hand.

'The same,' replied the figure, uncoiling itself from the deckchair and shaking Snatterjee's hand.

'Yes!' Snatterjee punched the air.

21

The world and his brother were not beating a path to M'Fang's door these days. He blamed his isolation on an Age of Scepticism that held Personkind in its Thrall and had subverted the Seekers After True Knowledge into fiddling about with test tubes and similar apparatus rather than Mystick Circles of Power.

Thus, he was pleased as punch to receive Snatterjee and The Frog and his happiness knew no bounds when he heard they had actually been referred to him by the Librarian of the Library of Dorien. Once, long ago, he too had made the journey into Solo Swamp and visited Dorien. He had been disgusted by the technological society he had encountered there but he still had a soft spot for the erudition of the Librarian even if he thought the Maston's abandonment of Magickal Studies at best, misguided and at worst, madness.

Within scant minutes of their arrival M'Fang had found two more deckchairs from the recesses of his cave and had brewed up a nice cup of tea using clear water from his little waterfall. He cut some slices of bread from a rather stale loaf, apologising that he had neither butter nor jam to spread on it. This caused The Frog to suffer a severe attack of pique to discover that the wizard was not the proud possessor of a magical table that spread itself with a vast array of delicacies at the word of command and the wave of a wand. He consoled himself by eating all the slices of bread while Snatterjee and the wizard chatted about this and that and the doings of the great and the good of the world (as far as Snatterjee's very limited knowledge of the subject would allow).

M'Fang proved to be an open-handed host and swiftly offered them the freedom of his cave home for as long as they wished to stay. He also intimated that what was his was also theirs for the duration of their stay. This offer inclined Snatterjee to believe that M'Fang, in fact, had very little in the way of goods and chattels; people of great possessions tended to guard them very closely – that's how they accumulated them – and were not inclined to give them away to every caller that happened by.

It was true. M'Fang's possessions were few: a few dog-eared books on Magick, a moth-eaten Magician's Mantel, a Wand of Power (second-hand, it transpired), a Magick Dagger that also did duty as the breadknife, a High Altar (or table) made from the cross section of an old tree trunk, a Magickal Chalice that had started life as a toothmug and now doubled up as M'Fang's tea cup and a brass incense burner in the shape of a calaphel drover seated in front of a campfire (the campfire was lifted up and a little cone of smoking incense placed inside) and stamped with the mystical inscription:

A Souvenir from Minfadlek

For a wizard a great repute and terrible potency, Snatterjee thought, he doesn't have many of the trappings of success that you might expect. On the other hand, he mused, M'Fang might be one of those eccentric aesthetics who spurned material possessions in their search for a Higher Spiritual Truth.

Or Nutters.

After M'Fang had cleared away the tea things and Snatterjee had had a bit of a wash and refresh by the waterfall, they sat down in their deckchairs in front of the cave to enjoy the afternoon sunshine. Bit by bit M'Fang related his history.

'I was not always as you see me now, A Master of the Arcane Arts, you know.'

'Oh, really,' Snatterjee said politely.

'No. Once I was…a Scholar!'

'And was that good?' asked The Frog in an uninterested-but-going-through-the-motions sort of way.

'Oh, yes. I was a great and famous Man of Letters,' M'Fang boasted. 'In fact, I had a whole collection of letters after my name,' and he waved his hand vaguely in the direction of the dayglo letters painted around the mouth of the cave.

'So, what brought you to Magick, then?' asked Snatterjee simply to keep the conversation going along.

'Ingratitude!'

'Ingratitude?'

'That and the of pettiness of small minds. Narrow-mindedness! Spite! Jealousy! Envy!'

'You were all of those things?' Snatterjee was amazed at M'Fang's frankness with complete strangers. For his own part, he would not have admitted to half his faults and foibles.

'Not *me*! The Others.' He spoke the name in a voice heavy with a sense of doom and menace.

'What "Others"?' Snatterjee asked fearfully, looking furtively around in case they were lurking nearby.

'The short-sighted, blighted bigots that hounded me!'

'Ah, them,' said Snatterjee, relieved that they did not appear to be in any imminent danger.

'Yes. Indeed. Them!'

M'Fang got up and went into the cave. They could hear him

rummaging about for a few moments and then he returned with a cobwebby old bottle and the Chalice. He poured some of the contents of the bottle into the Chalice, took a good swig and passed the Chalice over to Snatterjee.

Snatterjee took an exploratory sip.

The liquid burned its way down his gullet, making his eyes water. Whatever it was, it was neat and very pokey. He took a good gulp and passed the Chalice over to The Frog who, in turn, took a long swallow, gasped, choked, spluttered, shook his head and decided to go off and turn over a few stones to see if he could find a tasty snack.

'I founded an Academy, you see,' M'Fang explained, launching back into his tale and swigging from the Chalice. 'It was one of the finest private education establishments in the land. "For the Sons of the Best People Only", that was our motto. It was very exclusive, you see.'

He passed the Chalice over to Snatterjee.

'It's true my fees were high, but only to discourage the riff-raff. Oh no. None of your riff-raff.' He burped and held his hand out for the Chalice. 'Only the Very Best. I taught them myself, of course.'

'Of course,' Snatterjee agreed.

'Well, if we are being totally honest, I *might* have employed some underlings to relieve me of the heavy day-to-day burden of teaching but I used to spend…' He drank from the Chalice and seemed to have forgotten he was sharing the drink with his guests '…a good hour a day at the school. It's not as easy as you might think, being a headmaster.'

'No, I'm sure it isn't.' Snatterjee had only the foggiest notion what M'Fang was talking about. Education was not very big in Minfadlek.

The Frog had returned and was munching something Snatterjee would rather not know about. Education in Mud Wallow was an alien concept.

'It was money, money, money all the time,' sighed M'Fang, giving the bottle a shake to check it still held some liquid.

'Yes, it must have been awful for you, being so rich and all.' Snatterjee was still harbouring the notion that M'Fang had deliberately chosen to divest himself of worldly trappings for the sake of his spiritual wellbeing. Why else would he be living in a cave in the middle of a forest heaving with criminals.

'It wasn't me that was rich!' screamed M'Fang suddenly, springing out of his deckchair and pacing around in great agitation. Flecks of foam appeared at the corners of his mouth. 'I *told* those swines at the Inland Revenue that I wasn't rich. But do you think those, those *leeches*! those *bloodsuckers*! believed the word of an honest man? Never! "How can you afford such a big house, Dr Sprite"?' he mimicked.

'Who?' Snatterjee had been taking sly nips out of the Chalice and was now somewhat befuddled by the combination of the drink and the introduction of Dr Sprite to the narrative. The Frog had given up and fallen asleep in his chair.

'ME! Me! That was my name in those days. Dr Nathaniel Sprite. I became M'Fang, Magician Extraordinaire after all that unpleasantness.'

'Oh!'

'Those fiends from the Customs and Excise wanted Double Value Tax off me. Double Value! I ask you! How can you place a value on the education of the tender minds of the young? It is beyond vulgar lucre. Here, pass that bottle, this is the last of the batch. Thank you.'

He ceased his pacing to sample a refreshing glug.

And then he was off again.

'And then the tradespeople, always carping on about unpaid bills and credit! I tell you, the world is obsessed with money. How was I supposed to be paying out all the time? I *needed* those holidays. I was under a lot of stress.'

He thrust his face up close to Snatterjee, his eyes wild, his breath rank. Snatterjee could only shrug and make sympathetic noises. In his life as a retailer in Minfadlek, Snatterjee had often been dunned by creditors. Even The Frog had tried it on.

Apparently satisfied that Snatterjee was onside, M'Fang continued: 'And those thankless wretches I gave the opportunity to aid and assist me in my great endeavour. Always bleating on about unpaid wages.' He gave a heartfelt sigh. 'The world is a thankless place and I am well quit of it.'

'I'm sure you are,' Snatterjee agreed.

M'Fang slumped back into his seat, brooding over the injustice of it all.

'They chased me out,' he said after a period of silence broken only by The Frog's snores. 'Dispossessed me of everything I had and still wanted more. Swines! Thieves! Vipers!'

There was another period of silence. Snatterjee was nodding off, lulled by the warm sunshine of the late afternoon, the buzzing of the pollinators in the meadow and the effects of M'Fang's lethal booze. He was just on the point of fully committing himself to sleep when M'Fang launched back into his tirade.

'I was forced to flee in disguise. Me! In disguise! Forced to live cheek by jowl in this Forest with frauds and con persons like that phoney Gypsy Annabelle who used to be a seaside landlady, you know. That's where she got the whole cross-my-palm scam from. The end of the pier. Life has not been easy for me since they hounded me out of my Academy.'

A great tear of self-pity welled up in each eye and rolled majestically down his cheeks.

Snatterjee did not know where to look, averting his eyes from M'Fang in embarrassment. He was just in time to see that The Frog had woken up and was dangling a large green caterpillar into his mouth and suck it down like a strand of succulent spaghetti. He felt his stomach start to heave and switched his attention back to M'Fang. Better to see a grown man cry than to see The Frog devour a tasty morsel of insect life.

M'Fang was dabbing at his eyes with a none to clean sleeve that appeared to have done duty on more than one occasion as a handkerchief.

'Oh, this is charming,' Snatterjee thought, 'trapped in a cave with a failed Ponzi-artist and a semi-human eating machine. What *have* I done to deserve this?'

'So,' M'Fang went on, oblivious as to whether he had the attention of his audience or not, 'I turned my powerful intellect to the study of the Arcane Arts. To Necromancy, Hydromancy, Cartomancy, Augury, Demonology, Phrenology and a little practical Psychology on the side. I am an Adept at ESP, Telekinesis, Astral Projection, Telepathy, Table-Rapping and Finding Things That Are Lost. I even once practiced the mysteries of EFL and EAP. I have studied the Clavicles of Solomon as well as the Humour of Heironymous and the Fibia of Philodotus. I have sought the Talisman of Set…'

'Talking of Talismans,' Snatterjee interrupted what was threatening to become a lecture length monologue of gibberish, 'that just what we've come to ask you about.'

'Eh, what?' M'Fang was so caught up in his litany of achievements that he was unprepared to field questions from the floor.

'A Talisman,' Snatterjee repeated. 'The Fabulous and Wonderful Frowla.'

'What's that?'

'That's just what I hoped *you* would be able to tell *me*,' Snatterjee wailed, 'you're supposed to be the expert on all things magical and mystic.'

'Oh,' said M'Fang. 'Let me think about it.' He placed his right arm on his left leg with the forearm extended, positioned his chin on his closed fist and proceeded to wrinkle his brow in a simulation of Deep Thought.

Time passed. Insects buzzed. The warm air was still. Snatterjee finally fell asleep.

*

'I've never heard of it.' M'Fang's voice rolled and echoed like some great bell tolling out the End of Days.

Snatterjee jerked awake, rubbed at his eyes and tried to pretend he had been giving M'Fang his undivided attention the whole time.

M'Fang himself did not appear to have moved. He was still in Thinker mode with his chin resting on his hand and his gaze focused on the distance in a meaningful sort of way.

The Frog lay sprawled out on the grass where he had fallen out of his chair, fast asleep and snoring.

'Sorry! *What* did you say?' Snatterjee asked as brightly as he could.

'I said that I've never heard of it,' repeated M'Fang. 'I give up. What is it?'

'Some expert!' thought Snatterjee, but kept the thought to himself. He dutifully recounted the tale of his quest and made a point of emphasizing that he *had actually* found a reference to the Fabulous and Wonderful Frowla in a book in the Library of Dorien so therefore it *must* exist.

Throughout the telling M'Fang made noises like 'Erm,' 'I see,' 'Uh-huh,' which reminded Snatterjee uncomfortably of a visit to the doctor

'Did you also find a reference to a Mithmath?' M'Fang asked.

(*Mithmath* (n) a creature very like a Calaphel (*cf*) but with three horns growing out of its forehead. It is entirely mythical, featuring primarily in children's stories and seasonal stage plays)

'That's not the point,' Snatterjee insisted. 'The Fabulous and Wonderful Frowla is *real.* I know it is. And the book said so!'

'Well,' said M'Fang after he had given the matter some more serious thought, 'I think this is a case for…' He paused. If he could have managed a drum roll, this would have been the time for it, '…Astereth!'

'Who's Astereth and where can I find him. Or her?'

'I see you know little of the Arcane Arts,' said M'Fang, shaking his head at the ignorance of the common herd. 'Astereth is a mighty and powerful Spirit. A Denizen of the Dark. An Elemental of the Earth. It is He who finds such things that are lost or hidden from the sight of Man. Or Woman,' he added hastily.

'A Spirit?' asked Snatterjee in alarm. 'You mean some kind of ghostie, a demon, a hobgoblin, a fearsome creature from beyond?' Tales of nasty supernatural things had always made Snatterjee uneasy ever since his mother used to threaten him with the attentions of Phagus the Devourer of Naughty Children when he wouldn't go to bed in the evening.

(*Phagus* (n) a supernatural entity employed to traumatise children in the city of Minfadlek in order to make them more amenable to the will of their parents and often scarring them psychologically for life. Also reputed to bring seasonal gifts.)

The folklore of Minfadlek abounded with stories of Djinn and Ifrits and ghosties and ghoulies and things that went bump at any time of the day or night. Snatterjee had grown up with a healthy respect for all such supernatural beings. They were up there with the Houmjars as far as Snatterjee was concerned. Best kept away from, although he had never actually made the acquaintance of any of the above. Apart from the Houmjars. And they turned out all right. But despite his experiences with the Houmjars/Mastons he was not at all convinced that he wanted any truck with a Denizen of the Dark.

'It's all perfectly safe,' M'Fang reassured him. 'It's all just a science, really. There are certain principles involved that are inviable. If a Conjuration is performed according to the set Ritual laid down over hundreds of years of experimentation there is absolutely no danger.'

'And you know this Ritual?'

'Oh yes.'

'Are you sure?'

'Of course I'm sure,' M'Fang answered in a testy voice. 'Am I not a Master of Magick?'

Of this, Snatterjee was less than convinced. The words 'bankrupt con artist' sprang readily to his mind, but he desperately wanted to find the Fabulous and Wonderful Frowla. It had become an obsession that filled his every waking minute and haunted his dreams. He was prepared to give anything a try and as he had very little options he was ready to give M'Fang a go.

What could go wrong?

'OK,' he agreed, with scant enthusiasm,' let's do it!'

22

M'Fang, over the moon at the prospect of having an *actual* client (although no negotiations *vis a vis* the payment of fees for services rendered had, as yet, taken place) scurried off into the depths of his cave. He lit a candle or two and spent the next two hours boning up on his books and scratching notes on an old bit of parchment with a quill pen and muttering mysteriously to himself.

The Frog slept on and Snatterjee wisely decided against waking him. Instead he wandered around the cave, careful to keep out of M'Fang's way. His emotions were going up and down like a rollercoaster and he eventually had to go and sit down in his deckchair to stop himself from upchucking with nerves.

Sadly, the bottle with M'Fang's homebrew was empty.

After what seemed like forever, M'Fang came out of the cave, beaming all over his face.

'I'm ready!' he said.

Snatterjee sprang to his feet. 'Now?'

'No. Patience. Soon. The Conjuration must be performed at the Hour of Tanith – that's eleven o'clock to the uninitiated – so you'll just have to wait. There are certain things I must instruct you in if you are to play a part in the Conjuration, so listen carefully.'

No sooner had M'Fang started to instruct a still very dubious Snatterjee on his duties in the forthcoming Ritual than The Frog woke up and demanded to know what was going on. Snatterjee took a certain delight in telling him about Astereth and the proposed Conjuration on the grounds that your own fears are always much alleviated by sharing the fear around and instilling greater terror in someone else. The Frog qualified admirably in this respect. His antenna for all things Frightful was much more finely tuned than Snatterjee's. Consequently, he took himself off to the very back of the cave where the ceiling sloped down to meet the floor, squeezed himself into the deepest nook he could find and pulled a pile of drying ferns over himself. He made it very plain that HE WANTED NO PART OF IT.

With The Frog neatly stowed away from under their feet, M'Fang showed Snatterjee how to draw a Mystic Circle using fine sand from the banks of the little rill. Then they described another, larger circle around it. Inside the Inner Circle they constructed a pentangle. M'Fang carefully placed mismatched candlesticks at the five points of the star. Next, he circumnavigated the perimeter of the Outer Circle chanting words that were unintelligible to Snatterjee, pausing dramatically every now and then to sprinkle fresh water onto the ground and raise his hands in the air. Lastly, using a battered old can of dayglo paint and a threadbare paintbrush, he inscribed Words of Power in the space between the circumference of the two Circles.

When he was satisfied with these preliminary preparations, he hauled out his Calaphel Drover incense burner and popped a cone of sandalwood incense into the fake fire. This he then placed to the West portal. To the East he placed the Chalice/toothmug/teacup (freshly rinsed out) filled with fresh water, over which he had muttered some spell or other.

The physical arrangements being completed to his exacting standards, M'Fang shucked off his teachers' gown and shuffled into his Magicians' Robe – which, to Snatterjee, looking remarkably like an old dressing-gown with moons and planets and signs of the Zodiak badly embroidered onto it. Lacking a suitable Magicians' Pointy Hat, M'Fang kept his mortarboard on but as a further precaution he drew another pentangle on the flat top of the mortarboard with a piece of yellow chalk.

Thus attired and ready for action he took up his Wand and thrust the Magick Dagger into his belt for use later.

'Right, then,' he said to Snatterjee when they were both standing in the centre of the circles and pentacle, 'we're just about ready to start. I want you to hop out and light the candles and then jump back in here smartish. Once I get started with the Conjuration you are not to utter a single sound, no matter what you see and hear. And whatever you do, you MUST NOT step outside the Magick Circle. If you do,' he added ominously, 'I can't answer for your safety.'

With that he produced a printed disclaimer form for Snatterjee to sign, absolving Dr M'Fang, Master of the Arcane Arts etc from any and all liability for any untoward accidents or misfortunes that might befall as a result of any Magickal Expcriments or similar Workings. The writing got progressively smaller until by the end of the document it was impossible to read in the flickering light of the candles.

With little or no choice in the matter, Snatterjee signed with the quill pen that M'Fang 'just happened to have about my person', sparing only a fleeting thought for The Frog who lay quaking under his rustling mound of ferns *outside* the protection of the Magick Circle. 'If anything does go wrong,' he thought, uncharitably, 'better old Astereth gets The Frog than me.' This thought afforded him much comfort and steeled his resolution for whatever was to come.

M'Fang raised his arm over his head and took a deep breath, like an actor about to launch into his opening speech.

'Adonai, Tetragrammaton, Snickerty-snack,' M'Fang chanted in a sing-song voice, 'lizards and toads and fierce fruit bat.' The candlelight flickered, casting weird shapes onto the walls of the cave. Snatterjee swallowed nervously: no backing out now.

M'Fang pulled the Magickal Dagger out of his waistband and waved it to the Cardinal Points – north, south, east, west – whilst invoking:

'Guardians of the North, South, East and West

Do what you do and do it best'

He dodged and weaved about inside the Circle, his Dagger in his right hand made several passes dangerously close to Snatterjee's nose. In his left hand, M'Fang held an open grimoire, which he glanced at from time to time to refresh his memory.

Snatterjee stood in the centre of the Circle, trying to avoid the wild passes of M'Fang's Dagger and feeling slightly foolish. Fumes of sandalwood drifted into his eyes and made them sting and water.

'Astereth, Astereth, Spirit of the Earth

Make haste and rise

For all you're worth!'

M'Fang gave another little hop and a skip and then flung himself face down in the Circle. The rest of the Incantation came out rather muffled and that might have been the reason why everything went pear shaped.

'You are the Lord of all on the Ground

You reveal what cannot be found

Arise, I bid you now and speak
Reveal to us that which we seek!'

For a moment, nothing happened and then there was a muted flash and a *pop* like the sound of someone sticking their finger into their cheek and flicking it out.

Before them, on the grass outside the cave, there appeared a large man wearing a pin-stripped suit carrying in one hand a large black briefcase and in the other a tightly rolled umbrella. Almost immediately after there came a second *pop* and another man, identically clad to the first, appeared.

What followed sounded like a regiment of small boys armed with pop guns discharging them in a volley.

Within seconds, or so it seemed to Snatterjee, the area outside the mouth of the cave was filled with a jostling, confused shouting mob of people, some angrily waving papers. He recognised a butcher by his striped apron, a grocer by his white coat, teachers by their gowns and mortarboards, tailors by the tape measures hung around their necks.

M'Fang gave a strangled scream.

'The creditors! The Revenue! The Customs and Excise! They've found me!'

The Conjuration had backfired badly, either that or old Astereth had a skewed sense of humour. All those who had sought Dr Nathaniel Sprite for non-payment of his considerable debts had been conjured up to appear in this place where he was hiding in the middle of the Forest of Grimgrisle.

The shouting and confusion died down. As one, the creditors turned and fixed their eyes upon the cringing figure of their quarry. There was a moment of terrible silence. Then a collective howl of demonic glee broke from every throat.

M'Fang stared desperately around, like some trapped creature surrounded by baying hounds. He spotted a gap in the encircling mob of creditors outside the cave and bolted into the night.

The creditors, smelling blood and the chance to get the money they were owed, streamed after him in close pursuit.

And suddenly, Snatterjee was left all alone in the middle of the Magick Circle, listening as the crashing and plunging of the pursuit of M'Fang faded away into the depths of the Forest.

'Bugger!' said Snatterjee.

*

As peace returned to the night Snatterjee became aware of a thin, keening wail coming from the back of the cave. The mound of ferns was shaking violently, exposing The Frog's bottom sticking up out of the quaking pile.

'It's all right. You can come out. It's over,' Snatterjee told him with a sigh.

The heap of ferns heaved and shuddered as The Frog crept out and squinted fearfully around the cave. When he saw that Snatterjee was not caught up in the talons of some Foul Fiend from Hell, he straightened up and brushed the last few fronds of ferns off himself.

'Where's the wizard?' he asked.

'He left with some friends.' Snatterjee replied, laconically and then related the whole sorry saga of the failed Conjuration.

'Where does that leave us?' asked The Frog when Snatterjee had finished.

'I don't honestly know.' Snatterjee admitted. 'Still, at least we've got a dry bed for the night.'

'Anything to eat?'

'It's great to have you back to your old self,' commented Snatterjee with only the teeny-weeniest touch of sarcasm.

23

They waited a full week but M'Fang never returned. Snatterjee became increasingly depressed and The Frog increasingly truculent. They fell out and argued bitterly at the drop of a hat. The Frog kept demanding his release from his contract and his wages in full and Snatterjee, just as adamantly kept refusing. He knew that if he were to pay The Frog off it was tantamount to admitting that the search for the Fabulous and Wonderful Frowla was over and he was not yet prepared to concede defeat Most of the time they just ignored each other and maintained a hostile silence. As the sullen days crawled by and he waited for M'Fang to return and bickered with The Frog, Snatterjee sank into a mire of despondency and hopelessness.

By the end of the week Snatterjee accepted the bitter truth: it was the end of the search. The Houmjars had failed him; M'Fang had not had the answer. Sadly, he had to admit to himself that it was time to chuck it all in, throw away his crazy dream and go back to the Gyroscope, Salt Pork and Amber Curios Emporium in Minfadlek. He was older, wiser and much travelled. He would have his memories and a fund of traveller's tales he could tell at parties to impress girls and entertain his grandchildren with – should he ever have any.

When he did finally make the decision to cut his losses and return home the sensation was like that of a diver who has dived down deep after a pearl, dropped it, it sinks down, the diver chases it down and staying down too long, become disorientated. The relief of making the final decision to return to Minfadlek felt like the diver breaking the surface of the sea and sucking in great gulps of air into his lungs and knowing that he was going to live.

Whilst Snatterjee did not have the slightest qualm about abandoning The Frog to his own devices whilst he, Snatterjee, set off for home a small voice somewhere suggested that it was useful to have a travelling companion for any number of reasons and The Frog was handy. Little did Snatterjee know that The Frog had been harbouring similar thoughts but was still trying to find a way to get his promised wages from Snatterjee. The Frog had a stubborn streak when it came to being cheated of what was rightfully his.

Snatterjee broached the idea of going home to The Frog after The Frog had been out on one of his foraging forays out into the Forest and was in an approachable mood. Snatterjee used the very sound reasoning that they both had to find their way home and as their path led in the same general direction, why not travel it together?

Both pretended to mull the idea over for forms sake but then shook hands and slapped each other on the back and swore to be best buddies from henceforth.

Both had their fingers crossed behind their backs.

And so it was that they set off, well rested, at a pleasant and balmy hour of the morning on the following day, leaving M'Fang's cave behind and heading off through Grimgrisle Forest.

By mid-afternoon they were hopelessly lost.

Somehow the Forest had closed around them and swallowed them up. Try as they might, they could not find the track back to Gypsy Annabelle's. They followed paths and tracks that led nowhere and then petered out altogether. There was no sign of life in the Forest apart from the grim-looking black birds that perched in the tops of the trees and watched their confusion with interested eyes.

The whole character of the Forest had changed. The soft and gentle ferns and the dappled sunlight gave way to nasty bramble bushes that snatched at them and scratched at them as they tried to make their way through. The trees became dark and sombre, lowering over them in silent menace. Even the temperature plummeted until they shivered in the chill air.

'I don't like this,' complained The Frog, with an accusatory glare at Snatterjee as if, somehow it was all his fault.

'It's not my idea of a picnic, either,' said Snatterjee, fighting off a briar. He instantly regretted his choice of words.

The Frog launched off on a long tirade about the scanty state of their provisions.

While they had been waiting for M'Fang to return they had consumed every morsel of food in the cave, such as there was.

The small furry animals that lived in the immediate vicinity had soon learnt to avoid The Frog's traps and give the area around the cave a wide berth. While The Frog was more than happy to live on invertebrates, a bagful of creepy-crawlies did not travel well and Snaterjee was still a bit sniffy about what he put in his mouth.

A hungry Frog was an unhappy Frog and he had only Snatterjee to vent his displeasure on. And vent it he did until Snatterjee was forced to stumble along with his fingers stuffed into his ears to muffle the drone.

Night closed in on them without warning or a by-your-leave.

One moment they were trudging along in the semi-gloom

they had been walking through all day and the next it was pitch dark with not even the moon or stars visible overhead.

The Frog, who usually had excellent night vision, was leading the way and walked slap into a tree trunk. He fell onto his back, clutching his nose and howling as if he were being murdered slowly and painfully by savage Houmjars.

Snatterjee stumbled over his prostrate body and crashed face first into a clump of thorny bushes, lacerating his face and hands.

Together they lay where they had fallen, moaning and groaning in pain. After a while The Frog really got into his stride and his moans became racking sobs broken only by the odd imprecation aimed at Snatterjee for bringing them to this sorry pass, until his sobs eased into a whimper and then died away altogether. Moments later he was snoring blissfully.

Snatterjee lay in a cocoon of pain, feeling *really* sorry for himself and trying to justify blaming The Frog for his misfortune.

The night was bitterly cold. Where the Forest had been eerily silent during the day it was now filled with the shrieks and screams of the victims of nocturnal predators meeting an unpleasant fate. Nature being red in tooth and claw. 'Not for me,' Snatterjee decided.

Snatterjee gritted his teeth and crawled deeper into the thorn bushes for greater shelter and protection, reasoning that anything large enough to seriously contemplating eating him would be too big to force its way through the ring of thorns.

And anyway, any predator with murder and mayhem on its mind coming in this direction was bound to stumble over The Frog before it found Snatterjee.

Despite this comforting thought, Snatterjee slept very little that night.

*

The next day proved to be no better than the first. The going was harder as the ground became steep and rock-strewn. For hours they struggled onwards but for all their efforts they covered little distance.

In the middle of the afternoon they scrambled over an outcrop of rocks that Snatterjee, with a sinking feeling, thought he recognised. To confirm his worst fears be built a small cairn of stones as a marker. Sure enough, as daylight was fading, they arrived back at the same outcrop again.

Snatterjee realised that they were in seriously deep doodoo.

24

The light disappeared again, as if someone had flicked off a switch.

Snatterjee flung himself onto the ground and covered his head with his arms. He was very hungry and very thirsty and very tired. His feet felt hot and sticky. He was convinced that if he pulled his feet out of his wellies, the smell would stun any wildlife lurking in the immediate vicinity.

The Frog was in no better condition, olfactory-wise. Even at the best of times he saw no pressing need to unnecessarily bother water by rubbing it over his body and with the exertions of the march he smelled like a walking midden.

Snatterjee was too whacked-out to care if he lived or was eaten by ravening beasts. He felt utterly sorry for himself and the rank unfairness of the deal life had dealt him. He curled up where he lay and wept himself to sleep.

When he awoke it was daylight. His whole body was stiff and cramped from lying on the cold, unyielding rocks. A fall of dew had soaked his clothes, adding greatly to his discomfort and misery. He was cold and shivery and managed to convince himself that he was about to die from pneumonia. He could hear a persistent rumbling sound that he thought might be a landslide somewhere out in the Forest, or perhaps the pre-amble to an earthquake before realising that it was, in fact, his own stomach complaining that it had been unemployed for far too long. His tongue seemed to be several times its normal size and made of cotton wool.

A sudden flash of inspiration struck him. Quickly he stripped off his sodden clothes and frantically sucked the moisture from them. Slowly, his tongue shrank back to its accustomed dimensions and the layer of sandpaper in his throat vanished.

Sucking the dew out of his clothes helped to allay his raging thirst but did little to alleviate his general state of wretchedness but with one pressing need sorted, he had time to take stock of the situation.

The Frog lay on his back, eyes wide open, staring blankly at the trees rearing overhead. He had turned a sort of greyish-greenish colour, which gave Snatterjee some cause for alarm.

'Are you all right?' Snatterjee asked, giving him a violent shake for good measure to see if he was still in the land of the living.

'We're going to die,' explained The Frog in a perfectly calm and natural tone of voice, as if he were saying 'Oh, by the way, we need some milk and a sliced loaf if you are going to the shop.'

'Nonesense,' replied Snatterjee with a heartiness that he did not feel.

'No, we are. I should never have left Mud Wallow. All you talk of wealth turned my head and was my downfall. I was happy worrying rats. I didn't need to go out traipsing around the world.' He turned his head and smiled the most beatific smile Snatterjee had ever seen. 'I don't even blame you anymore.'

'That's very kind of you,' Snatterjee snarled back at him. A strange sensation almost, but not quite, like guilt flared like a match in Snatterjee's soul, but just as quickly burnt out.

'Don't upset yourself. I forgive me. It was my own weakness and greed that brought me here to die,' The Frog continued in the same conversational tone. Then he seemed to remember something. 'Promise me you won't bear *me* any hard feelings.'

'Hard feelings?' Snatterjee was puzzled. Obviously, The Frog was in the last throes of delirium. 'Whatever for?'

'Well, if you go and die first,' explained The Frog in the calm and rational voice, 'I'll eat you.'

Snatterjee was too stunned to reply.

'But if *I* die first, I don't mind at all if *you* eat *me*. That way at least one of us stands a chance of surviving.'

The very idea of being driven by hunger to eat The Frog was so repulsive that Snatterjee completely forgot that The Frog had licked his lips when he spoke of eating Snatterjee. He thought at that moment he would far rather die a slow, horrible and agonizing death rather than eat The Frog. He had seen what The Frog had considered edible foodstuff over the past few weeks of their acquaintance and the very thought of what The Frog must have eaten over his lifetime fairly turned Snatterjee's stomach. He remembered the old adage: "You are what you eat!" and shuddered.

All his pangs of hunger disappeared.

Even the rumbling stopped.

Summoning his very last reserves of energy, he dragged himself over to a huge tree whose top was lost somewhere in the canopy.

The Frog watched him curiously as Snatterjee began to climb the tree, pulling himself from branch to branch and panting with the effort.

'When he was about half the way up the massive trunk, The Frog felt compelled to call out to him.

'Look, I wouldn't eat you until you were pretty well dead.

Until I was sure you weren't going to recover. You don't have to go and hide up a tree.'

'Shut up, you food-obsessed dip-stick,' Snatterjee shouted back, 'I'm trying to get us both out of here alive.'

'He's gone doolally-tap.' The Frog muttered happily to himself. 'It's the hunger. Hunger can do that to you. It's addled his wits.' He watched Snatterjee's painful progress up the tree with a keen interest; Mud Wallow had a fine tradition of observing the more eccentric doings of folk with mental health issues as a harmless (and free) form of entertainment and The Frog certainly felt in need of a good laugh.

Furthermore, there was always the possibility that Snatterjee would fall and break his stupid neck, thus bringing the prospect of breakfast a lot nearer.

By the time he had reached as far as he could climb, Snatterjee was lost to The Frog's sight. He was perched high in the swaying top of the tree with the wind whistling around his ears. On his way to the top of the tree he had disturbed a colony of the malignant black birds who protested his intrusion into their domain by flying around his head, squawking and bombarding him with guano.

But it was all worth the effort.

He could see for miles over the roof of the Forest that stretched for miles in every direction in an unbroken sea of green. Here and there he could see faint columns of smoke rising from the dwellings of the various crooks and oddballs who had chosen to make the Forest their refuge but he judged that none were close enough to provide them with aid; in any case, they were just as likely to be murdered by the Ne'rdowells as to receive any kind of help. Grimgrisle Forest was that kind of place.

He could not even make out where M'Fang's cave was any more, so dense were the trees, so the idea of retracing their steps and starting out again was out of the question.

But wait a minute! Were his eyes playing tricks on him?

No. He saw it again – the flash of sunlight reflecting off moving water.

A river. If they could reach it they would be saved. They would not die of thirst and there might well be fish in it. And a river had to *go* somewhere. That is what they did.

Snatterjee reasoned that there was a very good chance that it might flow into Solo Swamp and even if it didn't it was bound, sooner or later, to flow out of the Forest. Also, a river attracted people and animals to its banks.

They were saved!

SAVED!

Carefully marking the direction of the river by taking a bearing on the sun, he slithered down the tree trunk, jumping the last few feet and nearly landing on a surprised Frog.

'Err, you're all covered in bird shit,' said The Frog, both unhelpfully and unnecessarily.

'Never mind that. We're saved. Saved, I tell you. SAVED!'

'Now, don't you be getting yourself all over excited,' said The Frog, humouring him to see what antics he might get up to next. He was firmly convinced that Snatterjee was missing a whole bag of marbles out of his toybox and could hardly wait to see what he might do next.

'But we are,' Snatterjee insisted. 'There's a river and a river means water, food, people, food, safety, food.'

All this talk of food brought The Frog to attention in a hurry, all thoughts of their impending deaths forgotten.

'Where? And why are we hanging around here?'

'Over there,' Snatterjee pointed. 'Look, if we keep the sun in front of us and keep checking our direction by climbing trees like I've just done, I reckon we'll get there without any trouble.

"Well come on then, come on. What are you waiting for?' urged The Frog, pulling on the lighter of the two packs and plunging off into the undergrowth.

Laughing, Snatterjee followed.

25

And, amazingly, the plan *actually* worked.

Now that they had a definitive direction to follow and had come up with the means to check their passage, they made real progress. That their luck was on the turn for the better was proved when they came across a wild peach tree laden down with low hanging fruit shortly after they set off from the rocky outcrop where they had spent the night.

The peach tree was covered with large golden globes of succulent fruit that just called out to be picked and eaten. Snatterjee and The Frog answered the call without a second's hesitation. They gorged themselves until their arms and faces were sticky with juice and their bellies were full to bursting and then they fell asleep where they lay while their stomachs got on with the job of digestion.

Given long enough fruit juice can ferment in a stomach. Or the pulp of the fruit can pass through and into the intestinal tract, which is what happened to the two travellers. With unfortunate consequences.

Snatterjee awoke to the sound of groaning and moaning.

'I'm not well,' The Frog informed him. A loud PARP erupted from The Frog's person. 'Ooohhhh,' said The Frog, leaping to his feet and heading into the bushes and then 'Ow, ow, ow,' as the brambles caught and pricked.

Moments later Snatterjee felt an earthquake rumbling in his bowels and he, too, headed for the shelter of the bushes.

Progress for the rest of the day was, at best, intermittent with frequent asides for calls of nature. Happiness it was when the tangle of thorn bushes gave way to banks of soft ferns growing in the spaces between the trees – ferns being a *much* better alternative as a personal hygiene and cleaning aid than brambles.

Life began to look up again.

*

Distances measured from the top of a swaying tree in the forest canopy can be deceptive and what with their frequent 'comfort stops', they did not reach the river that day. Nevertheless, they managed to spend a pleasant and mainly stress-free night curled up on a bed of soft ferns inside their battered tent. The Frog's skill as a trapper of unwary forest creatures provided them with a supper of sorts although neither of them had much in the way of an appetite after their ordeal by peach.

First light saw them break camp. Snatterjee shinned up the nearest tall tree that afforded him an unrestricted view over the canopy and reported back that he thought the river was very close.

He was right; they reached it by midday.

As rivers go, this one wasn't in the Premier Division – not one of the Great Rivers of the world but certainly in consideration as a runner-up in the Tributary Class. Its banks were grassy and pleasantly shaded by overhanging branches of the trees that grew close to the water. Swift brown fish flitted in its cool, clear waters amidst smooth stones.

To Snatterjee and The Frog this river represented the River of Life. It offered food and drink and a way out of the Forest if only they followed its downstream flow long enough.

Snatterjee and The Frog shucked off their backpacks and plunged their hot, sweaty faces into the river, rising with the cold water streaming off their hair and laughing with the pure joy of people snatched from the jaws of death. For a moment there was a serious possibility that they might hug each other but each immediately thought better off it. To be alive and safe was one thing, unbridled intimacy was quite another.

Besides, there was serious business to attend to.

It took The Frog only a matter of a few moments to tickle his first fish and flip it, arching and flapping onto the grass.

Snatterjee soon had a fire going as the pile of fish grew and then fell to gutting the fish as fast as The Frog caught them. The Frog was in full hunting mode and Snatterjee had to shout at him to make him stop. Already they had more fish than they could eat. Snatterjee impaled the fish on sticks and in next to no time had them grilling over the fire.

They gorged. The lesson of the peaches already forgotten.

Stuffed, they fell fast asleep in the drowsy heat of the afternoon.

When they woke up, they had an encore for supper.

*

Three lazy days of resting and re-cooperating after their trek through the Forest passed in a flash.

By the end of the third day of their sojourn by the river bank the message had sunk in to fishy-kind that there was not much of a future in the particular stretch of the river and they were giving it a wide berth.

'Time to go,' said Snatterjee.

'I think so, too,' The Frog agreed.

They journeyed slowly downstream, catching the odd fish that had not got the message on the piscatorial grapevine to steer well clear and trapping the occasional small animal that was desperate enough to risk coming down to the river at dusk to drink.

Now that things were going right for them and they had resolved on a firm plan of action – they were going home and The Frog was eating better than at any time in his life with the exception of their interlude at Dorien – all their former acrimony and squabbles were almost forgiven and forgotten. The spirit that had *almost* prompted them to embrace at the riverbank hovered over them and they were constantly on the brink of becoming friends. Indeed, there were moments when Snatterjee had to forcefully remind himself that, sadly, no-one with the slightest shred of self-respect could openly admit to counting The Frog amongst his circle of friends, even if that circle was restricted to those you could count on the thumb of one hand. At times it was almost hard to have any self-respect.

Sometimes they just sat by the bank of the river and talked.

Snatterjee regaled The Frog with exciting (if embellished) tales of his adventures in the retail trade in Minfadlek, the hustle and bustle of an exotic trading city on the caravan routes while The Frog elaborated on the finer points of rat worrying and all the different types of mud to be found in the vicinity of Mud Wallow.

It was mind-numbingly boring but Snatterjee was in an expansive frame of mind and simulated a deep and abiding interest. This proved to be a mistake, as it only encouraged The Frog to go on in ever more excruciating detail. Snatterjee allowed his mind to drift free during The Frog's recitation and almost missed it.

'What?'

'I said: my name is Wilberforce. In all the time we've been together, you've never asked me what my name is.' He said this with a quiet dignity that greatly impressed Snatterjee and for a fleeting moment *almost* made him feel ashamed of his treatment of The Frog.

But only for a fleeting moment!

26

One fine morning found them camped on a swathe of lawn on the bank of the river. The sun shone into the tent through the partially open flaps and onto Snatterjee's face, waking him up. He stretched, yawned, scratched his crotch and crawled towards the open flaps to stick his head out and see what was happening, if anything, in this immediate part of the world before he ventured out of the tent for a pee.

To his very great surprise, he found himself staring into a pair of bright blue eyes at a level with his own. They, in turn, peered out from a mass of shaggy yellow hair, reminding him of a very hirsute kind of dog or even, perhaps, a limbeck.

(*limbeck* (n) a small, rotund rodent native to the Great Flat Empty Nothing (cf). Its body is covered in curly fur up to several inches deep making the limbeck resemble a ball of tumbleweed(cf) It is blown across the GFEN by the wind and has mainly given up moving under its own steam, thus making its legs redundant and liable to atrophy over the process of evolution.)

Snatterjee immediately shut his eyes on the sound principle that when confronted with the strange, unexpected or inexplicable, denying its existence often makes it disappear. This is especially true if one has been drinking heavily or experimenting with recreational-type materials (where legal!).

When he opened his eyes again, the head was still there, scant inches from his own. He noticed that the head had a mouth and that the mouth was working away in a slow, steady rhythm, bits of masticated grass tumbling from its prominent lips.

"Greetings and grazing, Flock Friend,' announced the apparition in a peculiar bleating voice. More grass tumbled from its mouth.

'Meep!' said Snatterjee, otherwise lost for something to say in reply.

'May you never be anointed with the Cursed Herb!'

'What?'

'Chew of the Grass of Life, Ewe Brother,' continued the strange creature in what Snatterjee now realised was a long, drawn out and complicated ritual of salutation.

'You brother?' said Snatterjee weakly, still very confused as to just what exactly he had stumbled into. Situations like this had no business cropping up before breakfast or the first pee of the day.

'Meh, meeeh!'

"This cannot be happening to me!' Snatterjee spoke aloud, shaking his head. He seriously contemplated going back to bed and starting the day afresh and uncluttered with hairy freaks bleating at him outside the door of his home.

'What's going on?' came The Frog's sleepy voice from inside the tent. Snatterjee had already forgotten that The Frog did, indeed, have a name.

'I'm buggered if I know,' Snatterjee replied, unhelpfully. "Either we've got some sort of visitor or there was sometime seriously wrong with that fish we ate last night and I'm having an hallucination.'

'Amongst the Flock I am known as Sheepshank the Five-Toed,' Snatterjee's hallucination informed him.

Snatterjee had, on occasion, consumed some disturbing mind-altering substances (always *perfectly* legal in his own lounge) but he had never experienced anything like this – an hallucination that attempted to hold a conversation.

The chilling realization that this must be reality comforted him not one whit. He decided to play it cool.

'Yeah. Whatever. Pleased to meet you.'

Their visitor, Snatterejee could now see fully by drawing his head back into the tent like a tortoise retreating into its shell, was a youth of about fourteen. He was stark naked but as well as the mane of hair on his head, his body was covered all over with light, downy hair. He was down on his hands and knees and from the look of the calluses on his elbows and knees, this was his normal posture.

Snatterjee made a snap decision, deciding that, for the moment, Sheepshank was probably harmless. However, he reserved the right to change his mind at the first sign to the contrary.

He crawled out of the tent; Sheepshank moved back to make way for him.

'Hoo, boy,' thought Snatterjee, 'this is the weirdest one yet.'

As he went over to the nearest bush for his pee, he noticed that Sheepshank had fallen to cropping the grass with evident gusto, every now and then uttering a small bleat of ecstasy.

'He thinks he's a sheep,' Snatterjee thought in a moment of revelation. He watched Sheepshank (surely a clue in the name!) for a little while longer. 'He really does think he's a sheep.' He strolled down to the river for a wash, giving Sheepshank a friendly pat on the head in passing, just as one might pat a pet dog.

The Frog emerged from the tent feeling grumpy at being woken up. As soon as he saw Sheepshank all his professional instincts kicked into overdrive:

'Mint sauce! Mint sauce!'

Sheepshank bolted, bleating piteously and hid in the trees, quaking in terror.

The Frog burst into cruel laughter, slapping his thighs and dancing a little jig to celebrate a job well done.

Snatterjee felt a stab of an emotion that might well be pity for Sheepshank and anger at The Frog's cruelty. He scooped up a double handful of water and flung it at The Frog, drenching him. The Frog shrieked in horror as another scoop followed the first and fell on his back, arms and legs still pumping their jig.

Sheepshank crept out of the cover of the trees and butted Snatterjee gently on his leg.

'Hail to thee, Flock Hero, Guardian and Saviour of the Fleeces, Succour of the Spring Lamb.' Great tears welled up in Sheepshank's eyes and made a damp runnel through the hair on his face down to his chin.

Snatterjee experienced another unaccustomed emotion – embarrassment – and tried to hide it by turning away but Sheepshank followed close behind him, still gently butting his head against Snatterjee's leg and bleating.

'You've got a cruel and vicious streak, you have,' The Frog snarled, recovering from his dousing and glaring daggers at Snatterjee.

'Me? *I've* got a cruel streak? Why did you have to go an upset the poor thing for, like that? He wasn't doing any harm.'

Sheepshank gave Snatterjee's leg another adoring butt. 'I wish you'd stop doing that!'

Sheepshank managed to combine looking hurt, rejected *and* sheepish all at the same time.

The Frog saw an opportunity to twist the knife.

'Any of your friends about?' he asked, innocently, adding, with an evil grin. 'Very partial I am, to a bit of mutton.'

'Knock it off,' Snatterjee warned, 'or I'll pick you up and toss you into the river and give you a damned good washing!'

Sheepshank, realising that he was under the protection of a Mighty Shepherd, stuck out a long pink tongue (covered in bits of semi-masticated grass) at The Frog, from behind Snatterjee. The Frog relatiated when Snatterjee wasn't looking by mouthing the word 'chop' back at him. Sheepshank skittered around behind Snatterjee again for safety.

'Sheepshank, forgive my curiousity, but just *what* are you doing here?' Snatterjee asked him when all had calmed down and The Frog had gone off to inspect his traps to see if there was anything for breakfast.

'Meh. Baa. It is the Time of Sheepishness, when all the young tups go off to be alone. I have left the Flock for my annual holiday.'

'And what's with this whole sheep business, anyway?'

'It is a long and fat tail,' bleated Sheepshank. He cropped a mouthful or two of grass, giving himself time to compose his story.

'Many years ago, when I was but a little lamb I did not live with Flock Kind. I was born into a different Fold. The Old Ram, Flock Father Baa Cotchbaa, told of how I was found abandoned in the Forest and adopted into the Flock and afforded the Shelter of Sheepdom. I grew up as one of the Ewe Brothers, although I was different from the Lamb Kin. That was many Lambings ago. Now I am a Ram of the First Rank, Second Grade,' he concluded with pride.'

'Ewe Brothers, Lamb Kin, Flock Father! What a load of old bollocks,' The Frog muttered.

Snatterjee chose to ignore him.

'I have told of my tale,' Sheepshank said in his quavering voice, 'tell me now, Flock Hero, of thine own Herd and its Grazings.'

'We got lost in the Forest,' Snatterjee answered prosaically. 'We are trying to find our way out and get back to the city of Minfadlek.'

'And Mud Wallow!' added The Frog, making sly shearing gestures with his hands.

'And Mud Wallow,' Snatterjee conceded.

'Let me be your guide,' Sheepshank pleaded. 'I know the Forest and all its byways and paths. I know where the best grasses and fragrant herb banks are.'

'Know where I might find some mint?' The Frog asked.

'Shut it!' Snatterjee warned with a meaningful look at the river.

The Frog shut it.

'If you wish, Flock Hero, for whatever reasons of your own, to seek fresh Grazing, then I can take you to where the Two-Legs roam.'

'You're on!' Snatterjee did his own interpretation of a small, but intricate, jig of glee.

The Frog looked happy and made a mental reservation not to worry Sheepshank for the duration.

*

Four days later (Sheepshank did not travel very fast and kept stopping to munch the vegetation) and they came to the end of Grimgrisle Forest, having dodged the importunities of a man offering to sell them: a) encyclopaedias; b) brushes; and c) insurance against being bothered by tree to tree salesmen. They also met, and shook off, a man who offered, for only five glimps, to show them how to become fabulously rich. It was a scam Snatterjee knew well. Mug A (you) give the man five glimps. He then tells you to do the same with Mugs B, C, D, E and so on. It was a scam that worked *very* well for the first person to think of it, but not so well as it became common knowledge.

The Frog was all up for it but Snatterjee refused to give him any money so he sulked for hours, which both Snatterjee and Sheepshank thought was a bonus.

And then, through the last few trees on the riverbank, they spied open ground.

Snatterjee and The Frog ran those last few metres and burst out of the Forest - free at last, free at last!

About a mile away across the plain they could see a group of buildings that looked like giant bells carelessly dropped by a giant on his way to decorate his Christmas tree. Sheepshank assured them that the clump of buildings was a caravanserai where the calaphel caravans that crossed the Great Empty Nothing rested up before their final leg to Minfadlek.

Snatterjee wept tears of joy. He was going home after all his adventures out in the hostile world.

Bidding their ovine chum a fond farewell and good grazing, they struck out in the direction of the buildings.

Behind them, at the edge of the Forest, they could hear Sheepshank's plaintive bleating.

'I shall miss him,' said Snatterjee.

'MINT SAUCE!' shouted The Frog over his shoulder.

They heard one last, frantic bleat and then Sheepshank passed out of their lives.

27

As they approached nearer to the bell-shaped buildings they could see that they were constructed out of adobe bricks and had once been brightly painted to resemble the yurts that the caravan traders of old had lived in the year round. The paint had faded with the passing of years and the buildings projected a rumpled, comfortable, lived-in look.

There were six buildings in all and they were spaced like the points of a hexagram with tunnels or covered corridors connecting them along the sides of the hexagram that served as a defensive wall. An ornate gateway flanked by stubby towers faced with bright blue tiles gave access to the interior. The massive wooden gates, studded with large iron rivets, hung open.

Snatterjee and The Frog strode up to the towers and peered cautiously through the gates.

The interior of the caravanserai complex held a huge open courtyard which was packed with calaphels seated more or less peacefully, chewing the cud and spitting at each other for fun. Men were weaving to and fro between the seated animals on errands of evident importance and urgency.

The Frog sidled his way round the tower and through the gates until he stood under the archway and goggled, round-eyed, at the scene within. The great caravans that traversed the Great Empty Nothing gave Mud Wallow a miss.

For Snatterjee, on the other hand, being Minfadlek born and bred, this was the very stuff of life. He could tell at first glance that this was a caravan assembling and getting ready for the off. His blood tingled in his veins and his heart beat faster. This was the world he knew and loved, a *melieu* he was completely and comfortably at home in. The clamour and the bustle was like a homecoming.

He strode boldly through the gate as if he had every right to be there and made enquiries of the nearest traders as to the whereabouts of the Uzmuk.

(*Uzmuk* (n) The leader of a caravan. His is the responsibility of getting the caravan to its destination safely and in the shortest time without mishap or loss. He must know the swiftest routes across the *Great Empty Nothing* (cf) and where to find water and fodder for the *calaphels* (cf) in all seasons of the year. If the caravan is attacked by *N'erdowells* (cf) it is his task to act as general and lead his troops from the front. For all this, he is paid one hundredth part of the total value of the goods carried in the caravan. A successful *Uzmuk* is a man of enormous wealth.)

The facades of the buildings facing into the courtyard were very different to the faded painted faces they presented to the world outside. Here the blue tiles that adorned the gateway towers decorated every building, catching the sun and sparkling with reflected fire.

The Frog stood and gawped.

'Leave this to me,' Snatterjee said. 'Stay here and don't touch anything.'

The room that he had been directed to was dimly lit by light coming in the windows set in the ceiling. The floor was cool white marble and covered with rugs of a dazzling abstract intricacy and bright colours, made of silk and wool. A quick mental appraisal led Snatterjee that the value of any one of these would be sufficient to purchase Mud Wallow, lock, stock and water barrel three times over. Although why anyone might wish to make such an investment escaped him for the moment.

More of the blue-glazed tiles set with geometric patterns covered the walls from the floor to the ceiling dome. A bronze lamp of ancient craftmanship hung down low from the ceiling on a gilded chain, but was not lit. Cushions covered the floor and the low, folding traveling tables used by the caravans, inlaid with nacre and silver thread were scattered here and there.

On one of these tables stood a silver hookah pipe, aromatic smoke escaping from its bowl. Sitting next to it on a calaphel-hide pouffe a man with a long beard and an even longer robe was puffing away at the hookah's mouthpiece and letting dribbles of smoke escape from down his nose.

There were other people moving about in the chamber but he was the calm centre of the maelstrom of activity that ebbed and flowed around him. He answered questions and issued instructions in a low, self-confident voice, his minions speeding off to do his bidding, bowing respectfully as they backed out of his presence.

Snatterjee waited for a break in the stream around the Uzmuk, spotted a lull and slipped over to him.

'Your Greatness,' he said, bowing his head to the floor in the traditional manner.

'Do I know you?' inquired the Uzmuk, peering closely at Snatterjee through heavily. Lidded eyes.

'I think not, Sire, for I am insignificant, although I am well-known in my home town of Minfadlek.'

'Really? You're a bit out of your way, then, aren't you?'

'Alas, I am indeed and therefore crave the honour of being

allowed to serve in your esteemed caravan on the road to my home.' Snatterjee was not just taking a chance that this caravan being here assembled was going to Minfadlek; all caravans crossing the Great Empty Nothing sooner or later passed through Minfadlek.

'Oh yes,' said the Uzmuk, his eyes narrowing shrewdly. A supernumerary working his passage meant more profit for the Uzmuk.

'Whatever task your heart desires of me, O Mighty One.' Snatterjee *was* laying it on a bit thick but that was how you addressed Uzmuks if you wanted a favour done. There was a very strict pecking order in caravan society and at this moment, Snatterjee was at the bottom of it.

'What's that?' said the Uzmuk sharply. 'Is it anything to do with you?'

Snatterjee looked around to see if he could spot what the Uzmuk was referring to. His eyes clamped on The Frog, whose curiosity had got the better of him and was now peeping through the doorway.

'That? Oh. Nothing. A guide, a travelling companion. A worthless creature, Your Plentitude. He can stay here if the sight of him offends your Worship's eyes. I can't say that I would blame your Magnificence in the slightest if you have him cast out'

The Uzmuk gave Snatterjee a hard look, perhaps recognising a ruthless kindred spirit to himself. You didn't get to be a caravan Uzmuk by being a shrinking flower. He ran his fingers through his beard, tapping the fingers of his other hand against his thigh, weighing Snatterjee up. That he was prepared to abandon his companion was a plus; the fact that he was prepared to ditch his companion was a minus. He then asked the all-important and deciding question:

'Can you pay for your passage?'

'Woe is me, but alas, I cannot.' Snatterjee made a great show of wringing his hands and smacking his forehead. 'We have been on the road these many weeks now and my resources are at an end. However, once back in Minfadlek...' He let the sentence tail off.

'Ah, yes,' said the Uzmuk, a knowing smile twitching his beard, 'in Minfadlek you'll disappear down the first dark alleyway and I'll never see hair nor hide of you again.'

'Greatness!' Snatterjee ladled out the shock and hurt at this defamation of his good character like a master whilst thinking 'Bugger!' as that was *exactly* what he had planned to do.

'The silks go in the vanguard,' the Uzmuk instructed in reply to a question from a minion. Snatterjee shuffled his feet and fidgeted, seemingly forgotten or dismissed by the great man. 'And an armed guard for every four animals. By the way,' he said as the minion prepared to hurry off and put the Uzmuk's orders into operation, 'how many Shovellers have we got for this trip?'

'Pray forgive me, O Light of the World,' wailed the minion, banging his head on the floor at the Uzmuk's feet, 'there are none to be found. The Uzmuk Armand (Great be his Glory) took the last of them with him a month ago. I have scoured the caravanserai but not one is to be had for love or money.'

'And just when were you intending to inform me of this fact?' asked the Uzmuk, his voice dry and laden with menace.

The minion quaked and his knees actually knocked together. 'I had not yet given up hope, Your Magnanimity.'

'Hmm,' said the Uzmuk and dismissed the minion with a flick of his fingers. He turned his attention back to Snatterjee. 'You are in luck,' he said. 'You can work your passage. You *and* your funny friend. You're Shovellers.'

'Shovellers, Highest?'

Snatterjee had been around caravans all of his life and had a fair idea how they worked but only those who lived and travelled with the caravan knew all the ins and outs of what was, in effect, a society within a society. He had no idea what a Shoveller was, or did.

'Yes, Shovellers.' The Uzmuk was accustomed to his word being final and not questioned. His brow knitted in a frown. "Now go with Nizz here before I change my mind.' He waved a hand in the general direction of the cringing minion. 'He will kit you out. If you have packs you may load them onto one of the calaphels for a very reasonable cover charge. If you can't pay, you'll just have to carry them as well as the Bags. Now. Go.'

Snatterjee went, following Nizz and collecting The Frog who was hovering around the doorway.

He did not care what a Shoveller was or did. The main thing was that he was on his way home in the comparative safety of a large caravan. Despite not being successful in his Quest for the Fabulous and Wonderful Frowler, he *had* braved the dreaded Houmjars, *traversed* Sloo Swamp, *survived* M'Fang's disastrous magick and come out of Grimgrisle Forest both alive *and* uncheated by the Ne'redowells. Now he would be happy just to get home and put his feet up in the Gyroscope, Salt Pork and Amber Curios Emporium and let the world come to *him*.

He knew now that there were worse places than Minfadlek (Mud Wallow being a prime example) and harder lives than that of a retail entrepreneur. He was a wiser man; he had learnt a lesson. Nevermore would he stray far from home and hearth.

He gave a little sigh of contentment. Life was not so bad, after all.

28

'You're in luck,' Snatterjee announced to The Frog, 'I've got us both jobs with the caravan.'

'What sort of jobs?' The Frog asked, eying him suspiciously.

'Really good ones,' Snatterjee lied to him enthusiastically. 'Trust me. We're Shovellers.'

'And that is what? Exactly?' asked The Frog as they weaved their way between seated calaphels and across the courtyard behind Nizz.

'What's what?'

'A Shovellaghhh…' The word turned into a scream of alarm. A calaphel, its long neck towering over The Frog as it rose to its feet, had taken a dislike to him and had snapped at him, missing him by a mere inch. The Frog and the calaphels were a new phenomenon to each other and were not sure they liked what they saw. From The Frog's point of view, it wasn't so much their long, serpentine necks, their hump, their fine woolly fur or their long, threshing tails. It wasn't even the short, giraffe-like horns. It was their teeth. They were the size and shape of camels' teeth and as calaphels *never, ever* sought the ministrations of a dental hygienist, their breath was a further weapon in their arsenal. Calaphels can also spit, accurately, over a considerable distance. All things considered, they are not counted amongst the world's cute and cuddly animals.

The Frog had done little to endear himself to the creatures by giving this one an experimental poke with a stick to see what would happen.

The calaphel reared its head back to have another go at The

Frog. It made a horrid gargling noise as it hawked up another wad of gob to project at The Frog, who ducked aside just as something that looked disgustingly like an oyster slashed past his face and hit another calaphel square in the eye. In an instant, the struck beast reared up, ready for the challenge and nipped its immediate neighbour in a pre-emptive strike.

Within seconds chaos ruled.

In the ensuing nightmare of roaring, hawking, spitting beasts, waving necks, gnashing and biting teeth the calaphel handlers tried to restore some kind of order whilst trying to rescue bundles of trade goods from being trampled and flagons of liquids being overturned or smashed.

Nizz had disappeared. Snatterjee and The Frog crept into the lee of a wall for shelter.

'Whoops!' said The Frog.

'Please tell me that was nothing to do with you.'

'Nothing to do with me!' The Frog agreed, all wide-eyed innocence. 'What do we do now?'

'Make ourselves scares till the riot dies down,' Snatterjee shouted over the din, pulling The Frog in the direction of the gateway. 'We'll come back later.'

'Good thinking,' said The Frog.

*

Later that afternoon, as the shadows are lengthening, Snatterjee and The Frog stroll nonchalantly through the gates of the caravanserai from where they have been hiding behind the complex. Snatterjee whistled an innocent tune but stopped short as he surveyed the scene before him. Scattered over the courtyard was the debris left by a herd of squabbling calaphels who had been partially loaded in preparation for their journey.

'Oh dear, oh dear, oh dear,' he said, shaking his head sadly. 'Tsk, tsk, tsk. *Someone's* been a bit careless.'

The Frog, wisely for once, said nothing.

'Anyone seen Nizz?' Snatterjee asked the minions who were sweeping up the mess.

Hearing his name called, Nizz detached himself from the knot of calaphel drovers and came over to where Snatterjee and The Frog were standing.

'It was you, wasn't it?'

'What was?' Snatterjee could do injured innocence to perfection.

'You set them off!'

'Who?'

'You!'

'Set off who?'

'Never mind,' said Nizz, realising that he wasn't going to get anywhere. 'Follow me. And don't TOUCH anything, especially not the calaphels.'

He led them to one of the great chambers. If the Uzmuk's court could be described as opulent, this room could certainly not. Shabby *might* be a kind description. The walls were plain and had once been whitewashed but that would have been over a century ago. They were now decorated in an interesting and unusual motif of smoke stain and grease. One end of the chamber served as a kitchen for the duration of the caravan's stay in the caravanserai. A large open fire blazed in a large fireplace and clouds of steam rose from a great black cauldron suspended over the fire from a hook on the end of a chain. The heat at that end of the room was stifling. Sweating cooks chopped and diced food at work stations, getting ready for the evening meal. The raw food was liberally marinated in their sweat. Snatterjee made a note to give supper a miss.

On the floor of the chamber (packed earth, no marble or exquisite rugs here) was a carpeting of straw matted with grease and fat that made walking an adventure. Here and there were cloth bundles that held the portable possessions of the caravan's minions, all of whom were now frantically involved in the last-minute preparations for departure and the delay occasioned by the riots of the calaphels earlier.

The caravan was scheduled to move out at first light the next day and everyone was hoping to get done with their tasks and have an early night before the journey began.

Nizz pointed down at a patch of lumpy straw. 'You'll sleep here tonight,' he told them gruffly. 'Come with me, I'll get you're your kit. Leave your packs here.'

They dropped their packs where they stood and followed Nizz outside again, The Frog pressed against the wall and keeping a wary eye out for stroppy calaphels (difficult – *all* calaphels are stroppy, it's in their nature). However, the livestock seemed to have settled down to chewing their fodder after the pre-prandial excitement of earlier, but The Frog was taking no chances and kept well away.

Nizz led them into a third chamber which obviously did duty as a warehouse or storeroom. It was now nearly empty – all the more portable goods having been assembled for fast loading at first light in the morning. Leaning against the wall was a number of large wooden shovels and hanging above them on wooden pegs were an assortment of enormous leather bags.

'Those are yours,' Nizz told them. 'Take your pick.'

'Thanks very much,' said The Frog, always pleased at being given a present and these great leather bags looked *very* useful indeed.

'What, *exactly*, are they for?' asked Snatterjee with a sinking heart as a nasty suspicion wormed its way into his mind.

'You're Shovellers,' said Nizz slowly and precisely as if he were explaining the finer points of quantum physics to a rather dense plank. The Frog continued to look blank and Snatterjee looked away in dismay.

'You follow on behind the caravan and shovel up caraphel shit with your shovels. You then put said shit into your dung bags and then you do it all again until we get to wherever it is we are going to. Didn't the Uzmuk tell you?'

'Erck,' moaned Snatterjee, sinking wearily to his knees in abject surrender. 'I might have guessed. I thought my life was taking a turn for the better. Stupid of me, I know.'

'Why do you want to save calaphel crap?' asked The Frog with genuine interest. Jobs that occupied a particular niche on the edges of society held a professional fascination for him and he was eager to learn all about his new calling.

'Well,' replied Nizz, glad to see that at least *one* of his new Shovellers was taking a keen interest in his work, 'First of all, it makes a good fuel for our cooking fires at night. Saves having to carry other sources of combustibles. It's a recyclable resource. Very environmentally friendly. Secondly, any dung that is surplice to requirements at the end of the journey the Uzmuk flogs off to keen gardeners to put on their rose bushes. Very good for roses is calaphel dung. Highly sought after. Nothing gets wasted on a caravan.'

'Sell it, eh?' mused The Frog. Snatterjee could almost hear

the cogs grinding in The Frog's feeble excuse for a mind. 'Tell me,' The Frog whispered to Nizz conspiratorially, 'do you know if there is a market for rat pellets?'

'Shut up! Shut up! Shut up!' screamed Snatterjee, fearing his brain might spin out of control at any minute.

'Could just be the beginning of my future,' The Frog murmured, undaunted by Snatterjee's screams.

In desperation and in fear for his sanity, Snatterjee snatched one of the leather dung bags off the wall and thrust it over The Frog's head and upper body.

Muffled protests issued forth. Nizz took a step or two backwards and gnawed worriedly at his thumbnail, apprehensive at the prospect that these two madmen were to accompany the caravan across the Great Flat Nothing.

'That was uncalled for,' The Frog said, extricating himself from the dung bag. 'You've got to plan ahead if you want to get anywhere in this life, after all. Might be a future in rat pellets.'

'Watch out for that calaphel!' Snatterjee shouted.

The Frog whirled round, tripped over the dung bag and crashed to the floor. Snatterjee fell about laughing and even Nizz allowed himself a broad grin.

The Frog sulked. 'Not funny,' he said.

'Pick up your gear and let's go and have a drink,' Nizz suggested. 'It's traditional before a caravan sets off. You can meet some of the lads you'll be travelling with.'

Snatterjee agreed that it sounded like a good idea and he and Nizz set off together, leaving The Frog to follow on behind, sulking.

29

Life in the caravan for The Frog and Snatterjee could not, in all honesty, be described as a bundle of laughs. Their working day started at first light with a round of the tethered calaphels collecting the night's offerings. Then, from the time the caravan set off until the Uzmuk called a halt for the night, they trudged along behind it, coughing and choking in the dust kicked up by two hundred plodding animals and their human drovers, shovelling shit.

And then there was the heat.

And the flies attracted out of nowhere to buzz on the dung that Snatterjee and The Frog were trying to shovel into their dung bags – bags that grew heavier with each passing hour.

Now and then the Uzmuk would send a minion to check up on them and ensure that they weren't slacking. They found, very early on, that the slightest hint that they were not diligently working flat out meant a fine deducted from their water ration for the following day.

They swiftly learnt not to miss a single lump.

As well as the two hundred pack animals, there were seventy-six people in the caravan, including Snatterjee and The Frog. There was the Uzmuk, his deputy, sixteen merchants and assorted drovers, servants and guards. Caravans drew the attention of bandits and Ne'redowells as well as flies but there was little danger of one of this size being attacked. Nonetheless, the position of being at the very tail end (literally) of the caravan and thus in the most vulnerable spot, did little to brighten the Shovellers' days.

The evening and the nights, however, made up for the discomforts and miseries of the days.

The Uzmuk called a halt an hour and a half before sunset, wherever possible in an oasis or by a well and the animals were hobbled and allowed to graze, if there was anything to graze on. Otherwise, handfuls of hay from the hay wain were scattered onto the ground. The caravan servants set off to find any game drawn to the vicinity by the presence of water or collect anything that they might stumble upon that was, at a pinch, edible (The Frog, an acknowledged expert on these matters, soon built up a reputation for an ability to regard virtually *anything* as some form of foodstuff).

While The Frog was out on his expeditions, to Snatterjee fell the task of building the communal fire out of the dried harvestings of the day before – which was carried in an open pannier to air dry carried by one of the animals. Occasionally, he got some help, but not always.

With the evening meal cooked and eaten, the whole company, including the Uzmuk (displaying the common touch beloved of leaders who in no way regarded themselves as anything like common), would lounge about in the glow of the fire to talk, boast, tell tall tales or simply snooze until it was time to go to sleep in earnest under the star-spangled banner of the night sky of the Great Flat Nothing.

It was on one of these dreamy evening sessions that Snatterjee learnt a lot more about the Fabulous and Wonderful Frowla.

He had been relating the tale of his adventures (suitable censoring any favourable mention of the Houmjars – let them keep their fearsome reputation!) from the time he had first overheard that whispered conversation in John's Frothy Cocoa

Shop up to his escape from Grimgrisle Forest and joining the caravan to an engrossed circle of listeners when one of the merchants, a man called Irm, joined in the talk. This was a rare condescension – a merchant rarely had any truck with a Shoveller.

'So, in actual fact, you never did find out very much about the Fabulous and Wonderful Frowla, eh?'

'No, sir,' admitted Snatterjee politely and just a *touch* defensively. He half expected to be made the butt of some jibe or other and was preparing to, mentally, gnash his teeth.

'Then let *me* tell you the story as I heard it many years ago on my travels in the far world.' He settled himself down more comfortably and with the practiced eye of the storyteller looked around his audience to make sure he had their undivided attention. With the exception of The Frog, who was asleep, he had.

'There was once, long ago,' he began and then stopped for a nip from his hipflask and to heighten the dramatic narrative, 'a race skilled in the arts of Magick and Natural Lore.' Seeing a degree of scepticism on the faces of his listeners, he went on hurridly: 'They knew *lots* of other things as well. Anyway, they built great buildings and cities so marvellous that none have been able to copy them, even though they have crumbled away into ruins these thousands of years.

'Oh yeah?' thought Snatterjee to himself, 'tell that to the Mastons.'

'Among this race was one named Amhotep, the wisest and most cultured and cleverest of them all. He knew things most other people didn't realise they didn't know, he was *that* clever. He it was that recognised in a humble creeping insect the secret of Life and Power.' Irm paused again and checked out the rapt faces in the firelight. He had them now! He took another refreshing swig from the hip flask.

'Well, Amhotep studied these insects for many years – as well as doing a multitude of other really clever things and it was he who gave them the name Scabs by which they were known among the natural philosopher community for ever after. At least, by Amhotep and his mates. It is said that after many years of trial and error he finally managed to actually communicate with one of these creatures. No-one now knows *how* he did it but he did. Amhotep and the Scab taught each other many Fabulous and Wonderful things. Although what was so great about being a creepie-crawlie I'm not so sure. Is there any of that roast zingba left?'

'Here,' said Snatterjee, fully engrossed in the story, 'have mine.'

'Very kind of you,' said Irm, taking the slice of roast meat and nibbling on it with painful slowness while Snatterjee writhed with impatience and the rest of the audience fell to talking amongst themselves.

'They taught each other things,' Snatterjee prompted when he could stand the suspense no more.

'Did they? Oh, yes. Well,' Irm resumed his story, licking zingba fat off his fingers, 'because Amhotep was the only person ever to try and befriend this race of insects instead of stepping on them and squishing them or whacking them with a rolled up newspaper like everyone else did, this insect trusted Amhotep so much that he revealed his secret name to Amhotep. And that secret name was…Frowla! Now, as soon as old Amhotep knew that insect's secret name he had it in his power because that was a part of his Magickal skill. I should point out that Amhotep had always been at pains to impress upon the Frowla that he, himself, was called Jimmy, so as not to fall into the same trap.

Anyhow, as I was saying, Frowla was now in Amhotep's power and all of Frowla's great secrets and mysteries were now Amhotep's. So, what do you think he did?' Irm stopped speaking, well aware he was leaving his listeners on a cliff-hanger. He uncapped his flask again, took a sip, shook the flask next to his ear, tut-tutted, resealed it and popped it back into his pocket.

'Go on! Go on! What did he do?' Snatterjee pleaded, his tension level wound up to a dangerous notch. The other members of the caravan who were sitting around the fire, equally hooked by the story, joined Snatterjee with a chorus of encouragement for Irm to continue.

'He stuck a pin through its head and killed it, that's what he did!' Irm sat back on his haunches and surveyed his audience with a look of triumph, his story told.

'Why did he do that, then?' someone asked.

'Ah, well,' Irm explained. 'Now that he had the Fabulous and Wonderful Frowla's power, he didn't need the *actual* Frowla alive and kicking, so to speak. Alive there was a chance that the Frowla might be able to turn the tables on Amhotep; dead he was *very* useful.'

'What do you mean: useful?'

'Oh, yes, did I forget to mention it?' Irm asked, innocently, well aware that he had. 'The story goes that anyone who knew the secret name of a Scab and had its physical manifestation in his possession could invoke its power to have any wish he uttered using that name granted. Just like that. And that was exactly what Amhotep was after. He wished for many, many things. The usual: money, a palace, the hand of the king's daughter, half the kingdom and then the other half. When he was king he promptly exiled every other natural philosopher to Sloo Swamp and they are probably there to this day. I've heard it is a most unpleasant place.' He shuddered at the very thought.

'So, go on,' Snatterjee begged. 'What happened to the Frowla?'

'Anhotep had the Fabulous and Wonderful Frowla set in some kind of reliquary that he wore round his neck every day for the rest of his life. Apparently, it was kept in the family for many generations. They became rulers of a mighty empire, of course. Goes without saying.'

'Is that the end of the story?'

'No. It went missing, of course. That's why *you've* heard of it. These things have a habit of mysteriously disappearing. I imagine someone let the baby play with it or it fell down the back of a sofa or a maid chucked it out when she was cleaning up after a party. Anyway, it went missing. That's what makes the story interesting and,' his eyes twinkled, 'it *might even be true*! You are not the first person, young man, who has gone off on a perilous quest looking for legendary treasures.' He laughed. 'They are very seldom found. My advice to you is to go home and stay there. Make money. Be happy with what you've got and be thankful you survived your adventures.'

'But what does the Frowla look like?' Snatterjee insisted, unable to drop the subject; Frowla Fever had him in its grip again in the aftermath of Irm's tale.

'I've not got the faintest idea,' Irm said, shrugging his shoulders. 'Do you know just how *many* species of insects there are?

Quite a lot! I'm a rug merchant, not an entomologist.'

'Wossa Nentolomologist, then?' asked The Frog, waking up and deciding to take an interest.

'Someone who studies Ents,' a calaphel driver told him.

'Wossa Nent?'

'Go back to sleep.'

Snatterjee was working his way through the assembled members of the caravan, asking them if anyone had any idea what a Scab was.

'No idea.'

'Haven't the faintest.'

'Give over.'

'Don't go on.'

'Let's get some kip.'

'Bugger off.'

Snatterjee flung himself to the ground and pummelled at the ground with fists and feet, shrieking and foaming at the mouth in rage and frustration in the grip of extreme Frowla Frenzy. He bit clods of earth and wept bitter tears.

'Ants!' He sprang to his feet. 'Got to be. The Frowla was a Queen Ant. The intelligence. The organisation. The ability to communicate. Has to be!'

He went in search of Irm, who had retreated for the night in the exclusive Merchants' only compound.

A guard told him to get lost.

'Or maybe,' he mused,' a woodlouse. I've never really trusted them.'

But, somehow, he and Irm never managed to cross paths again.

30

Minfadlek had not changed in the slightest in the time Snatterjee had been away.

He and The Frog were discharged from the caravan at the caravanserai on the outskirts of town and Snatterjee duly handed over the last of his money to the Uzmuk in return for the carriage of their packs and sundry undisclosed expenses. They handed in their shovels and unslung their bags for the last time and then headed off into town like cowboys coming off the Chisholm trail in search of assorted whoopie.

Snatterjee took a proprietorial pride in pointing out the sights to The Frog, who was suitably impressed but, don't forget, he *had* seen Dorien and so was prepared to adopt a less then overawed stance to the place, although he *was* prepared to concede its superiority to Mud Wallow.

There was, for starters, the Great Square, fully fifty metres wide and packed with stalls and booths selling virtually any kind of junk and tat you could name. It was here, Snatterjee informed The Frog, that he had started his life in retail with his barrow with the wonky wheel.

Leading out of the north end of the Grand Square was Bazjann Road, lined with the imposing houses of the rich and famous and, indeed, paved for much of its length. Both sides of Bazjann Road boasted a drainage ditch which carried away the effluent of the affluent, whose front doors were reached by means of small bridges spanning the ditch. For years there had been proposals to cover the ditches but it was always pointed out by those concerned tax-payers (who did not, in fact, live on Bazjann Road, that when it rained (which it did on average twice a year) the water would have no run-off and would thus flood the road and spill into the Grand Square. So, nothing was done. The rich and famous had their little bridges and the *hoi pollio* made the best of it by wading through the sewage.

The other three sides of the Grand Square were bisected by the typical narrow alleys of Minfadlek, known familiarly as 'the narrow alleys', which were not paved and were either very dusty or soggy and slippery depending on what had been fly-tipped into them. All the thoroughfares were packed with people hurrying to be somewhere else or standing and talking, usually at the top of their voices or just lying down in the shade of the ramshackle houses and trying to get a bit of kip. Many of the humbler sort of Minfadlekian citizen had forgone the dubious security of living in the pest-infested fire-traps that passed for houses in the alleys and simply lived on the streets. It was far cheaper and the climate of Minfadlek was a clement one.

Commerce was the life-blood of the city. Everyone seemed to be trying to sell something to someone else. It was said that a man could sell something first thing in the morning and buy back the same item, thirty-ninth hand last thing at night.

Indeed, one of the very few humanitarian, socially conscious laws passed by the Oligarchy of Minfadlek (or a cynical attack on the Free Market, depending on your point of view) was the ban on the buying and selling of children within the city limits. Prior to the passing of this statute, whole families had changed their composition several times a day and in the resulting confusion everyone became related to everyone else and the probate of wills became a nightmare for all except probate lawyers, who quickly managed to acquire property on Bazjann

Road. A child could start their day with a mother and father, a brother and maybe a sister or two and by the time it was tucked up in bed have acquired two new parents and half a dozen new siblings, none of whom knew the others.

Moving through this tide of humanity, like an undertow in the ocean, was the animal life of the city. This ranged from assorted vermin through domestic pets such as cats and dogs to beasts of burden. All used the alleys as public conveniences.

The Miasma of Minfadlek was famous and completely ignored by all Minfadlekian citizens older than four days.

The contrast between Minfadlek and Dorien was total.

*

Snatterjee, although he had been overawed by the splendours of Dorien, was thrilled to be back on his own turf, albeit that his quest had ended in failure and disappointment.

The Frog, accustomed to a more settled and sedate life of solitude, hated it and couldn't wait to be off on the road home to Mud Wallow. His mood was not lightened after he tried shouting '*atouille!*' at the local rats, only to be completely ignored.

'All these people are making me ill,' he complained to Snatterjee.

'Nonsense! It's great to be back in civilization.'

'Well, I'm not stopping here a moment longer than I have to. You just pay me what you owe me and I'm off to Mud Wallow quicker than you can say 'atouille', though it doesn't seem to do much good here. I might even try to get back to Dorien one day. *They* knew how to look after a guest,' he added pointedly.

'Does that mean you're hungry?'

'Thought you'd never ask. Is that a restaurant over there? The place with the sign of a crossed knife and fork over the door?'

The establishment The Frog had spotted was the most expensive eating house in Minfadlek and prided itself on the exclusivity of its clientele. They prided themselves on serving all their dishes on plates and admission was strictly based on male customers wearing a tie, a cummerbund and a minimum of two rows of medals and sundry decoration and orders.

Safe in the knowledge that there was absolutely no way they would be granted entry, Snatterjee sauntered over to where a resplendently attired doorman stood guarding the entrance and was unceremoniously told to push off.

With an apologetic shrug Snatterjee automatically set off in the direction of John's Frothy Cocoa Shop where his credit was good.

*

'What am I thinking?' Snatterjee asked himself in horror as he was about to enter John's Frothy Cocoa Shop through the batwing doors. He slapped himself hard on the forehead to bring himself back to his senses. 'I'm known and respected in this place. If I'm seen in here in the company of The Frog I'll never live it down.'

He did a hasty U-turn, grabbed The Frog by the arm and set off quickly down the narrow alleys before anyone saw him.

'Come on,' he said to The Frog, 'you wouldn't like that place. Too common. I'll show you the Emporium instead. You like salt pork, don't you? I'll see what I've got left in stock. And then…' he paused, dangling a verbal carrot, '…I'll see about paying you what I owe you. How about that, eh?'

'Promise?' asked The Frog in disbelief.

'Yes,' said Snatterjee in a resigned tone. 'Really.'

And, for once, Snatterjee was as good as his word.

After letting The Frog loose on his (very stale) stock of salt pork Snatterjee duly handed over a gyroscope and the amber bead that The Frog had become enamoured with all that time long ago in Mud Wallow. And while he was in the grip of this mood of untrammelled generosity, he gave The Frog permission to hunker down in the shop doorway for the night. He drew the line at letting The Frog sleep *inside* the shop.

He had his standards.

'Well, bye bye,' said Snatterjee, shaking The Frog by the hand as he carefully locked and padlocked the door to the Emporium. 'It's been nice knowing you. I don't suppose you'll be round this way again but look me up if you are. I'll miss you.' *Just like you miss really bad toothache.*

The Frog squatted down in the doorway and examined his treasures, dreaming of the reputation as a fearless explorer he would establish for himself in Mud Wallow. The innkeeper would allow him to enter the inn and drink pints of Best if he promised to entertain the regulars with the tales of his adventures and travels out in the wide world. Mr Bates might even notice him and perhaps grunt at him, a singular honour in Mud Wallow.

The Frog's future lay ahead of him, gleaming with promise and hope. He soon fell asleep, his treasures tuck away safely in the depths of his clothing where not even the most desperate of thieves would venture.

He intended to make an early start on the road home in the morning.

*

Snatterjee, meanwhile, was in John's, the centre of an admiring group, a bevy of Beverage Beauties on each knee and on a promise with the pair of them. Free flagons of cocoa flowed in his direction all night. Earnold, Dog John and Banjackle Smeed were all there, hanging on his every word. Of his circle of intimates only Rollin' Robin Rawlins was missing: he was out on a tour of the Great Flat Nothing.

'Did you find it, then?' demanded Dog John (*not* the same John who had once owned the Frothy Cocoa Shop and given his name to the place. It was now owned by a man called Kevin, who was a front for a cabal of the Oligarchs who owned just about everything in Minfadlek).

'Not exactly,' replied Snatterjee, cagily.

'Well, did you or not?'

'Put like that: not.'

'But did you at least discover what it is? Does it really exist.' Earnold pressed him.

'Oh yes, that I did do,' and he proceeded to tell them the tale Irm the merchant had told him that night under the stars out in the Great Flat Nothing and employing artistic license to add to the interest.

'But,' said Banjackle Smeed at the end of Snatterjee's recitation, 'you still don't know what a Scab is.'

'Not fully. But I've got a pretty good idea that it's a Queen Ant.'

'You could always go back to the Great Library place in Houmjarland that you were on about,' Banjackle Smeed laughed, wiping cocoa froth from his mouth with the back of his hand. "I reckon they must have a book about it there.'

'You could even try the local lending library here in town,' suggested Dog John.

'I never thought of that,' admitted Snatterjee. 'Perhaps that's not such a bad idea.' He gave each of the Beverage Beauties an exploratory squeeze and was rewarded with compliant giggles.

It was good to be home.

*

The next morning he arose late in one of the beds kept upstairs over the bar for guests who wished to spend the night on the premises for whatever reason. He stretched, scratched and sent the two Beauties on their way with his heartfelt thanks and set off to find Minfadlek Lending Library which was tucked down a rarely visited alleyway in the Cultural Quarter of town and rarely, if ever, visited by the citizens of Minfadlek. One of the Oligarchs had set it up years ago as a tax loss and as such, it was wildly successful.

He found a dusty and cobweb encrusted volume (*Volume XIX – Rat Worrying to Shibboleth* of the *Encyclopaedia Totalis* in the Reference Section and with trembling fingers turned the pages.

And there it was:

Scab (n) Species of beetle (*creepus crawli*) related closely to the *cockroach* (cf). Known in myth for the legendary member of the genus known as the *Frowla*, reputed to have had long conversations with *Amhotep* (cf), the first human to learn the *Carapace Shuffle* (cf) dialect of *Scabbish*. Race now believed to be extinct. See illustration of *Frowla*.

Snatterjee looked at the illustration. His face, which had been becoming more and more flushed with excitement, drained of colour. Huge beads of sweat broke out on his forehead. Gasping chokes gargled out of his mouth. Ignoring the sign admonishing silence up all patrons of the library, he beat his head against the table and howled and howled until the Librarian, a large, muscular lady, threw him out onto the street.

*

On the road out of Minfadlek The Frog was making slow progress. He mused that ever since Snatterjje had intruded into his life he seemed to have been walking, walking, walking and he was getting heartily sick of it. He muttered to himself and fiddled with his treasures deep in his pocket.

'Frowla! Hah, if there really were such a thing as a Fabulous and Wonderful Frowla, which I doubt…' As he spoke he took out the amber bead he was playing with and held it in front of his eyes, letting the rays of the sun sparkle off the carapace of the beetle trapped inside, '…I'd say: "Frowla, take me to Dorien where they know how to treat a guest"'.

And quite suddenly, the road was empty.

And finally

This very short story was written in October 2022 and entered in the Hampshire Writers' Society competition for that month. The brief was:

Tell the tale of a historic event and add a terrifically haunting twist.

It didn't win First Place but it did get a Highly Commended.

Stag

Gaius Metelius is on stag. Again. He seems to be doing a lot more than his fair share of sentry duty but there again, he is a very junior recruit, with no money to bribe the Centurion. The night is misty and he has to concentrate hard on his watch. There doesn't appear to be another soldier either to the right or left of him and that is just not right. Still, there is a lot about this place that is not right. The weather, for a start. Gaius is from the south of Gaul, from the Province, a Romano-Celt who misses the warm sunshine. He and his fellow recruits had marched their way through Gaul and crossed the sea to join their Legion in Britannia. Their progress had been halted by rumours of revolt and they had been ordered to strengthen the garrison in Camulodunum. By his reckoning, tonight must be Samhain, which is celebrated by all Celts, even in this benighted land of savages. And savage they are. He was on stag when they erupted into the city, led by that red-haired she-devil screaming for revenge and Roman blood. He remembers standing with the veterans in the Temple of the Devine Claudius here in Camulodunum and being terrified. He is only seventeen and this was his first taste of action. Strangely, he cannot remember waking up in Sick Bay. He can only remember a huge brute of an Iceni throwing a rock that hit his helmet. After that his memory is kind of hazy but he seems to have been on stag ever since.

'I told you there was something odd about that mist!' Dan says excitedly, waving his mobile at the other University of Essex students who share the house.

'What?' asks Mary.

'Look closely.' Dan hands her the phone.

'That's really weird. It looks just like a Roman soldier.'

'Trick of the light. It was dark. Shadow from a car headlight, maybe,' says Ian.

'Or someone dressed up for a party,' says Jane.

'Yeah, you're probably right,' says Dan. 'Even so, creepy thing to happen on Hallowe'en.'

'That's what Hallowe'en is all about,' says Dan.

This last offering was also submitted for an HWS competition to write a gossipy letter. It, too, was Highly Commended!

Gossip

Dear Harriet,

Funny you should ask about George and Mary. I bumped into her the other day at the Food Bank where I volunteer two days a week. She was dropping off a great bundle of fresh sausages. You remember, her son gave her that sausage maker for Christmas. Alan, that is. Not Peter. He's moved to Kazakhstan. Something about a problem with the tax people.

I haven't seen him for ages. George, that is, not Peter. Mind you, he doesn't come out much. Just stays at home and lets her run around after him. Between you and me and the bedpost, I think he's usually three sheets to the wind by lunchtime. Never does a tap. Makes her run around after him, wait on him hand and foot.

She seems to be doing up the garden, digging up part of the lawn. I suppose shes laying down a patio. He won't help her, lazy bugger. My friend Joyce saw her in B&Q the other day, in the tool section. She was buying an axe. Funny thing is, there are no trees or bushes in her garden. Maybe she'll plant some to go with the new patio.

She gave me a couple of pounds (in old money!) of her sausages which I cooked for our tea. I must say, she made a really good job of them. Henry ate four of them straight off and you know what he's like with his food. She said she was off to drop some off at the care home, too. What is she like? An angel, that's what. Bless.

Will I be seeing you over Christmas? I might have some of her bangers left!

Love
Jenny.

Acknowledgements

Thanks to Liane for the author photograph, and everything as always.

Thanks to Charlotte Mouncey for the cover design.

Also by the same Author

Uther Pendragon

ISBN 978-1-913567-63-7

410 AD. The Roman Empire is in flames as the Barbarians break through the frontier and flood the land. Rome needs every soldier she has to protect the Empire and so the Legions are withdrawn from Britain, leaving the British to defend themselves as best they can.

Uther Pendragon is the last prince of the Belgae when Rome withdraws the Legions from Britain. Tutored by Merlin he is thrust into manhood by the tumultuous times into which he is born. Betrayed by his allies he is forced to flee to the Roman province of Brittany where he is recruited by the Roman warlord Aetius. He becomes a player in the drama of the Decline and Fall of Rome in the West: a lover of the Empress Dowager and the father of the Once and Future king: Arthur.

Appearance and Illusion

ISBN 978-1-911546-69-6

Dr. Wendy McPherson is a thirty-something academic English lecturer approaching a mid-life crisis. She has not been in a stable relationship for two years, drinks too much and is bored with her job. The offer of a teaching job tutoring the son of the dictator of the Central Asian country of Kesheva offers her a possible life-changing experience. But when she's caught up in a violent revolution she finds her life in great danger and makes new discoveries about love and trust that turn her life around and give a new meaning to everything.

A Place in the Country

ISBN 978-1-911546-33-7

When yuppies Mitchell and Jocasta Dever move into Yew Tree cottage in the Hampshire village of Itchen Prior they fondly imagine they'll be starting a new life of bucolic bliss in a rural idyll. In fact, things don't exactly turn out like that. What they find is a seething pit of incest, sexual jealousy, paganism, exploitation, sharp business practices, feudalism and murder.

A Place in the Country - whose galaxy of characters includes Sherborne St John, the lord of the manor and his scheming wife, Gwendolyn, who keeps her stable hand, Crux Easton, as a sex slave; Jed Smith, exploitative garden centre owner who uses the Bosnian student Jagoda Doboj and her friends as cheap illegal labour, and the deeply dubious Warren family - is a novel that takes a hilarious, jaunty, and also often moving and disturbing look at a rural idyll that is anything but.